Masquerade

An Allingham Regency Classic

Merryn Allingham

MASQUERADE

This novel is entirely a work of fiction. The names, characters and incidents portrayed in it are the work of the author's imagination. Any resemblance to actual persons, living or dead, events or localities is entirely coincidental.

First published in Great Britain 2018 by The Verrall Press

Cover art: Berni Stevens Book Cover Design
Copyright © Merryn Allingham

Merryn Allingham asserts the moral right to be identified as the author of this work.

Chapter One

London, 1816

Cassandra Latimer perched on the stiffly brocaded bench and wondered, not for the first time, why she had ever agreed to her mother's suggestion that they meet Hugo at the Palantine Gallery this morning. Lady Katherine had insisted they attend what was billed as the show of the Season, but for Cassie the delights of London had long ago palled. The salon was overheated and far too crowded, and her delicate skin was already flushed.

'Have you heard the latest?' The voice came out of nowhere.

She stopped fanning herself and glanced at the mirror which hung on the opposite wall. Two women were reflected there and she was not acquainted with either.

'About the Trelawny boy, you mean?' one of the women continued.

The name hovered in the air. The buzz of inconsequential chatter faded into the distance and every fibre of Cassandra's body became alert.

'He's hardly a boy now, of course.'

'Indeed no. How long has it been? Lady Trelawny must be overjoyed her son is coming home at last.'

Cassie felt her heart beating far too fast. Suddenly she longed to be far away from this conversation, away from this room. A shaft of sunlight streamed through the gallery's long windows, breaking through a lowering sky and burnishing her curls to a fiery cloud. The warming light was gone almost as soon as it appeared, but to her it seemed to beckon escape. Escape to where, though? To a country of grey slate and blue seas, a landscape of moor and rocks? To Cornwall, to home? But that could not be – her future lay elsewhere.

'We can only hope the man actually arrives.' The woman's voice was hushed.

Her companion shuddered theatrically. 'I understand the journey from Argentina is very long and most dangerous.'

'My dear, yes. You must remember *The Adventurer* – just a few years ago. It sailed from Buenos Aires...'

The women moved away and Cassie heard no more. It was sufficient. After all these years – five, six it would be – Luke was coming back. Her deep green eyes stared into the distance and saw only memory.

She was seated on a stone bench in the garden of the Trelawny's London mansion, the lush fragrance of rose blossoms tumbling in the air. Luke was standing straight and tall in front of her, his mouth compressed and his face white and set. She had just told him that she could not marry him and was offering his ring back. She could not marry him because she was in love with Joshua. And Joshua just happened to be Luke's closest friend.

What a wretched business that had been. The family estates bordered each other and she had known Luke all her life. They had drifted into an engagement, more to please their parents, it seemed, than from any passionate attachment. But her visit to London to buy bride clothes had introduced her to a different world: Cornwall and their shared childhood had vanished in a sea mist.

Instead, there was a thrilling round of parties, balls, picnics, assemblies and, at the end of it, Joshua. No, she couldn't marry Luke. She was too young and too passionate and friendship was not enough.

'Miss Latimer, please accept my sincerest apologies for arriving so late.'

A well-dressed man in a puce tailcoat and fawn pantaloons stood before her. He took her hand in his and kissed it with elaborate courtesy, bowing politely to Lady Latimer who had broken off her conversation with a chance-met acquaintance to smile benignly at the man she hoped would become her son-in-law.

Sir Hugo Thorne's pleasant face wore a rueful smile. 'I fear the committee took longer than expected. There is always such a deal to do for the Shoreditch Widows and Orphans. I hope you will forgive me.'

'Naturally, Sir Hugo, how could I not? You lead a truly benevolent life!' Cassie's musical voice held the suspicion of a laugh, but her face was lit with the gentlest of smiles.

'Now that I am here, may I get you some refreshment?'

'What a good idea. It is so very hot in this room. Lemonade, perhaps?'

'It will be my pleasure,' he said gallantly, 'and when we are once more comfortable, would you care to make a quick tour of the paintings with me? I am anxious to hear your views. You possess a most refined sensibility.'

Cassie sighed inwardly but nodded assent, while her mother beamed encouragement. She knew Lady Katherine was counting on Sir Hugo's proposal. At twenty-five Cassandra was already perilously close to being on the shelf and she could no longer delay the decision to marry. Sir Hugo might not be the most exciting of men, but he was solid and dependable and would make a restful husband. More than that, he would be an adoring one. And she could trust him. After the bruising experience of her girlhood, such a man was surely worth any amount of excitement.

If she made this marriage it might help repair some of the destruction she had wreaked all those years ago. Her parents had loved Luke as a son and his dismissal had hit them very hard. As for Luke, he had remained heart-whole, she was sure. He had never loved her with the passion she craved. Instead he'd been angry and humiliated. It was the gossip he had loathed, the being on everyone's tongue. Within a sennight he had escaped England and was on a boat to Argentina. Lord Thomas Trelawny had told the world it was needful that his son administer the family's growing estates in South America, but the *ton* knew differently. They knew the true reason for Luke's sudden departure.

He had escaped, but Cassie had paid the price for her indiscretion. Jilting a man three weeks before the wedding was the height of bad taste and scurrilous gossip had swirled around her head for months. It was difficult to recall six years later just how vulnerable she'd felt. Today she was an acknowledged leader of fashion, an ice-cold beauty who had remained impregnable despite countless suitors. But then she had been a raw, passionate girl, in the throes of a thrilling infatuation and unable to dissemble.

'I'm afraid the lemonade is as warm as the salon.' Sir Hugo had emerged from the crush and was at her elbow proffering the glass he'd fought hard to procure.

For a moment she looked blindly up at him. Past distress was crowding in on her and for the second time that morning, she looked for escape. She needed distraction, needed to be on the move.

'I think I would prefer to view the pictures after all, if you have no objection, Sir Hugo.'

She rose from her seat as she spoke and smoothing the creases from her amber walking dress, took her suitor's arm. They began to stroll slowly around the gallery. As always, her elegant figure drew glances of frank admiration from those she passed and Sir Hugo, feeling pride in his possession, held her arm even more tightly.

While they walked, he spoke sensibly about the paintings they inspected and Cassie tried hard to conjure interest in his carefully considered opinions. He was a good man, she told herself severely, and she must not hanker for more. That way lay disaster. She had learned that lesson well. It had taken her little time to discover that Luke was worth twenty times the man who had displaced him. The relationship with Joshua had petered out, destroyed by her guilt and his inevitable betrayal.

'I must say that I find these colours a little too forceful. They jangle the nerves rather than soothe.'

Sir Hugo was standing before a group of canvases whose landscapes pulsated with lurid crimsons and golds, an anarchic depiction of the natural world.

'What do you think, Miss Latimer – am I being old-fashioned?'

'Not old-fashioned precisely, but perhaps a little traditional? One needs to open one's mind to different possibilities,' she hazarded, thinking that just one of the pictures on her bedroom wall would be enough to keep her awake at night.

'As always you are right. I will try to look with your eyes and endeavour to see these canvases anew.'

Why did he always have to agree with her? Luke would have mocked her pretensions, laughed openly at her, and they would have ended sharing the joke together. But Luke's companionship was long gone.

How strange to think that he would soon be in England, but returning as the new Earl Trelawny. It was three months since Lord Thomas's life had been brutally cut short by a riding accident. Luke would have left for home the minute he'd received the dreadful news, but a long and treacherous journey meant his father had been buried while he was still on the high seas. At the funeral Lady Trelawny had been beyond grief; it would be the saddest homecoming for her son.

Sir Hugo continued to talk, but Cassandra's thoughts were elsewhere, straying inevitably towards a lone man adrift on a distant ocean. With a great effort she forced herself to return to her escort's enthusiastic recital of his morning's work. The small successes of Shoreditch's deserving poor had never seemed less riveting.

Chapter Two

A few hundred miles away, the new Earl Trelawny gazed blankly over an ocean threading itself swiftly past the ship. He was deep in thought, the last image of his father playing through his mind: the stocky figure waving from the dockside, a bright red handkerchief in his hand, growing smaller and smaller as the ship made its way to the open sea. Luke had been away from England for too long; he had not been there for his father when he needed him. Now at last he was returning home, but to an unfamiliar life. The Great Hall would no longer echo to Lord Trelawny's greeting, his dogs barking at his heels, his arms outstretched to enfold his son. This would be an empty homecoming.

And he must straightaway step into his father's shoes and assume the burden of a large estate. Luke knew himself to be well capable, but he was sorry to be leaving Argentina. The country had been good to him. The rugged outdoor life had taught him authority and decisiveness. Honed him physically and created an inner strength he'd not known he possessed.

It had been hard work, but eased by a social round that

was lively and largely free of the stifling conventions of London society, and the tall, handsome Englishman had been a popular guest. There had been music and laughter and plenty of beautiful women happy to engage in a light flirtation or more. He had enjoyed their favours freely and indifferently, determined to consign love to the vault of history and enjoy only the pleasures of the moment. It had become a way of life for him, demanding little emotion and no commitment.

The moon cut a path across the surface of the small waves so bright it made him blink. His eyes focussed on the expanse of water, at the different shades of silver and black stretching to the horizon, then to the lanterns which hung above him, swinging comfortingly to the rhythm of the ship.

The crew were engaged elsewhere and he had the deck to himself. He wondered if he dared smoke a cigar, a disastrous habit he had contracted in Argentina, but decided he had better keep that delight for later. Dinner would be served soon and he had no wish to escort Marianna to the table smelling of tobacco.

The boat gave a louder creak than usual with the sudden swell of the ocean, but the vessel soon recovered its peaceful passage. A sailor appeared from the deck below and waved a greeting.

'Fine weather, sir, and the forecast's good. Should be a quiet landfall, I'm thinking.'

It had not always been so calm. Since leaving Buenos Aires they had suffered tempests aplenty and there had been moments when he'd wondered if they would ever make it to land again. But it was tranquil now and he had time to think.

The meeting with his mother would be painful, but there would be joy, too. To be home again; to feel Cornish air on his skin once more and to awake to the sound of Cornish surf breaking on the rocky cove below Madron Abbey.

He saw in his mind's eye the winding path from the house, across the green headland and then, the sudden dramatic fall of cliffs tumbling into wild seas. He had walked that pathway so many times in memory. In just a few weeks he would be walking it in reality. Immediately the ship berthed, he would post up to London and ensure that Marianna was safely consigned to the care of her aunt. The sooner he could do this, the sooner he would be on his way to Madron.

'There you are, Luke. I've been looking for you everywhere.'

The speaker was a diminutive brunette who barely came up to his chest. A pair of soft brown eyes met eyes of hard grey, and she smiled sweetly. Luke smiled back.

'Not quite everywhere, it seems. I'm not exactly invisible.'

'I didn't expect you to be behind the lifeboats! Were you thinking of leaving the ship without telling me? Or, more like, you were just about to smoke one of those noxious cigars of yours.'

He looked guilty and she crowed with delight, clapping her hands together and doing a little dance around him. 'You see, I know you so well.'

He doubted that, but it would hardly be surprising if she thought so. They had been cooped up together in this small vessel for nigh on a month. When he'd first been asked to escort the Spanish ambassador's daughter to London, he'd been aghast. His mind was beset with worry for his mother and grief for his father, and he had no wish to assume the responsibility of a seventeen-year-old girl.

But Señor Marquez had been persuasive. Marianna had been invited by the English branch of her family to spend a Season in London and then to make the journey on to Spain and her paternal home in Madrid. Ernesto Marquez was insistent that his daughter should experience something of European society.

'Argentina is a pioneer country, you know, Luke, and not the place for a young girl,' he'd said.

'She seems to have thrived well enough in Buenos Aires,' Luke had protested, trying to escape the fate he saw coming.

But Señor Marquez was adamant. Marianna must be launched on society and not in a rough-and-ready place like Buenos Aires. As a considerable heiress, and charmingly pretty, his daughter could look to the highest for a husband.

'It's a very long journey for a young girl. There are dangers.' Luke made a last attempt to dissuade his friend, but to no avail.

'Yes, yes, I have considered well,' Señor Marquez reassured him. 'The time is right – Napoleon is captive and confined on St Helena. He can do no further harm. Marianna can travel in safety to England and then on to Spain.

And you will be with my darling to protect her on the long journey.'

And so he'd agreed with reluctance to chaperone the girl aboard ship. He would see her safely on land and delivered to an aunt in Curzon Street, but after that his duty would end.

Marianna was speaking again. 'When we get to London, Luke, will there be many parties and balls?'

'Almost certainly. Otherwise why would you leave behind all your admirers in Buenos Aires?' His dark straight brows had lost their furrow. This sprite of a girl made it impossible to stay serious for long.

'My father says I must make good use of my time in London. I can have fun, but I must make sure that I meet lots of gentlemen, too. Eligible gentlemen.' She rolled the syllables off her tongue and pulled a face.

'That will be for your aunt to decide. As your chaperone she will tell you who is eligible and who is not.'

'Are you eligible, Luke?'

'For you, no. I'm far too old and a deal too worn.'

'How old are you?'

'Twenty-eight.'

'That's not old. My father was ten years older than my mother when they married. And I love to see him in their wedding pictures. He looks worldly and experienced.'

She looked up at him trustfully, the melting brown eyes smiling a clear invitation. Luke was taken aback. This was one outcome he had not foreseen. He knew too well how painful young dreams could be and had no wish to be part of Marianna's.

The image of a pale-faced girl with a torrent of red curls and glinting green eyes swam suddenly into his vision. He was startled. It was a long time since he had thought of Cassandra, really thought of her. It must be that he was nearing England, coming home after so many years. She would be settled amid the London society he hated, no doubt married with several children to her name.

He didn't know for sure. His parents, mindful of his feelings, had never kept him informed of her whereabouts or her doings. And he had not wanted to know. It had been enough to know that she had betrayed him. And with a man he had considered his closest friend.

That moment when he'd realised, when he'd known for certain that he had been blind and a fool, came rushing back to him. The whispers that he'd ignored, the sympathetic looks he'd refused to see, and then the two of them – Cassie and Joshua – secret smiles on their faces, secret murmurs on their lips, emerging from the darkened terrace into the lighted ballroom, walking side by side, bound together as one.

The sharpness of that moment still cut at him. He'd looked around the room and realised that every pair of eyes was fixed on him, wondering what he would do, what he would say. He had left the ball abruptly, incensed and distraught in equal measure.

The next day she'd told him. A little late, he'd thought bitterly, just a little late. Three weeks to their wedding and she was sorry, she loved another. Sorry! Sorry for betraying him with a fly-by-night, a professional third-rater who had pretended friendship only to get closer to his prey. And she, she had been willing without a second thought to betray those she professed to love, and to expose him to the most shameful tittle-tattle.

Now standing on this weathered deck, her sensual beauty enveloped him once more and he felt himself grow warm and hard with longing. He cursed silently. To feel passion after all these years was ridiculous.

'Are you all right, Luke? You look quite angry.' Marianna's eyes held a troubled expression and he pulled himself back to the present. It was only memory that aroused such feelings, he told himself, memory that no longer had the power to hurt.

'I'm fine,' he replied easily. 'I'm not at all angry. But we mustn't stay on deck any longer – it's grown far too cold for you.'

But I love it here. The moonlight is so beautiful, isn't it?'

He had to agree and for a moment they stood motionless before the beauty of the ocean, caught up in their own thoughts.

But as if on cue, a voice behind them called out, 'Dinner is served, Lord Trelawny, when you're ready.'

Neither of them had heard the captain as he'd approached from the saloon. 'Thank you. We'll come now,' Luke replied swiftly and offered Marianna his arm.

'Lord Trelawny? That sounds so grand.'

'It's meant to. Take heed, and obey!'

She giggled and made haste to the table that had been prepared for them. The smell from the kitchen was not encouraging. She pulled another face and her eyes danced with mischief. Her aunt would have to stop her showing her feelings quite so evidently, Luke thought. It would not do to be too natural in London society. In his experience the Season involved nothing but sham. He heaved a sigh without realising he was doing so.

'Something troubles you, Luke? Are you not looking forward to going home?'

'Indeed I am. I'm returning to the most beautiful place on earth. How could I not be looking forward to it?'

'More beautiful than Argentina?'

'To my mind, but everyone thinks their homeland is the best in the world, don't they?'

'Tell me about Cornwall.'

'Let's see, what can I tell you? It is wild and free. Its colours are green and grey – granite cliffs and slate-roofed houses, but rolling green fields. Above all, the sea is blue within blue and never still. I can hear the sound of the surf breaking on the beach from my bedroom window and smell the salt on the air.'

'You make it sound a paradise. And what about your house?'

'The Abbey is very old and built of grey stone. It has mullioned windows and a massive oak front door studded with iron. Every room is panelled in the same dark oak.'

'That sounds a bit gloomy – but perhaps abbeys always are?' Marianna puckered her forehead in disappointment.

'It could be, but in the summer the garden is a cascade of colour – Cornwall is so warm that some of the flowers are as vivid as those in the tropics. And in the winter, the rooms are lit by the flicker of open fires, and the house is filled with the sweet smell of burning apple wood.'

'Ah, then it does sound wonderful after all.'

It had been wonderful, he thought. And against his will, the memories came flooding back, for it had been a night like this – a night when the world was bathed in silver – that he had gone swimming in the cove with Cassandra. Forbidden, thrilling, an intimation that Cassie was no longer the child she had once been. And he had gloried in it. The water contouring itself around her slim form. The long, shapely legs glimmering through a gently rippling surface. All he had wanted to do was wind himself around her and stay clasped, fast and forever.

Marianna was speaking again and he had to jerk himself back to the present.

'And do you have many friends in Cornwall?' she asked.

'A few.' His tone was indifferent.

'No one in particular?'

'No one,' he reiterated, this time with certainty. And the image of flying red hair and shining emerald eyes was banished from his mind.

Chapter Three

Cassandra returned early that night from a supper party and sat quietly in front of her mirror while her maid carefully untangled the knot of auburn curls. The evening had been insipid and she had been glad of the excuse of a headache to leave for home. Somehow she had managed to maintain an air of calm detachment throughout the day, but her mind had been troubled.

She'd not been able to put Luke out of her thoughts. There had always been a part of her, buried deep, that had kept his memory close, but the passage of the hours, of the years, had soothed the raw pain of his departure and the collapse of the world she had trusted. She had done all she could to forget him. Now a random conversation between two unknown women had brought his memory throbbing back to life.

She scolded herself. He would be so changed that she would hardly know him, nor he her. In all probability he would sail into Southampton with a new Lady Trelawny on his arm. Given the proximity of their homes – their two families had been friends for as long as she could remember – she was bound to meet Luke again. But not for many months, since he would be certain to post down to Cornwall immediately to be with his mother.

And where would she be, Cassie mused? No doubt by the end of the Season preparing to be Lady Thorne, and packing her valise for a protracted stay at Sir Hugo's Berkshire estate. She sighed involuntarily and Rosa stopped brushing her hair for a moment, thinking that she had hurt her mistress. Cassie was reassuring her when the bedroom door opened.

'I'm so glad I've found you still up. I wanted a quick word, my dear.'

She nodded a dismissal to her maid and looked warily at her mother. She could guess the nature of the quick word.

'I was so pleased today at the gallery to see you on such good terms with Sir Hugo. You do like him, don't you?'

'Yes of course, Mama, what is there not to like?'

'I mean,' her mother said doggedly, 'that you *positively* like him – it's not simply that you do not hold him in aversion.'

'I suppose so.'

Lady Katherine tried to restrain her irritation with this lovely but obdurate daughter. 'You don't sound very certain.'

'That's because I'm not. Sir Hugo is kind and charming and obviously a very good person perhaps just a little too good for me.'

'Stuff,' her mother exclaimed unexpectedly. 'How can you talk so, Cassandra! You deserve the very best.'

Her daughter remained silent, gazing gravely at her reflection in the mirror.

'Are you still thinking of that business with the Trelawnys?' Even her mother, she noted, dared not speak Luke's name.

Lady Katherine walked up to her and hugged her close. 'Cassie, my darling, that's over and has been for years. It's nonsense to let it determine the rest of your life. It was a bad affair at the time, but you must put it out of your mind and make a fresh start.'

Whether it was her mother's hug or simply because she'd had a jarring day, Cassie couldn't say, but she found herself dissolving into tears.

Lady Katherine soothed her lovingly and then spoke to her as if to a weary child. 'The time has come, Cassandra, to make a decision that will affect the rest of your life. You have received many offers of marriage and have refused them all. In a few months you will be twenty-five and in our society that is not a good age to be single still.

If you really dislike the idea of marriage to Sir Hugo, you know we will not try to persuade you otherwise. Your father and I have profited from painful experience. But if you feel you could live comfortably with him, then I would urge you not to wait too long. He is obviously deeply in love with you and you have only ''to throw the handkerchief'' – a vulgar saying, I know, but a perfectly true one nonetheless – and he will pick it up with alacrity.'

'I know, Mama.'

Her daughter's woebegone expression raised a smile on Lady Katherine's face. 'Try not to look so miserable about it. You will have a splendid life. You'll not want for a thing and will have by your side a man whose only wish is to make you happy.'

How to tell her mother how she felt? How to explain it even to herself? Cassie's head told her that a pleasant life with Sir Hugo was the best possible compromise she could make, but her heart murmured traitorously that pleasantness would not satisfy. What did she want then? Gaiety, exhilaration, adventure even?

But she knew her mother was right. She was a mature woman and she must behave like one, and that meant a sensible decision on her future.

Thinking that the homily had gone home, Lady Katherine decided to reinforce her message. 'Promise me, my love, that when the moment comes you will listen to whatever Sir Hugo has to say and consider his words favourably.'

'I promise, Mama.'

She made the undertaking in good faith. She must try not to disappoint Sir Hugo, nor let her family down again.

⁓

Her pledge was put to the test the following Saturday morning. She was quietly engaged with Rosa, selecting dresses from her wardrobe that needed attention and listing the new gloves and slippers she must purchase now that the Season was well advanced, when the second footman appeared at her bedroom door.

'Milady would like to see you in the drawing room, Miss Cassandra.'

She wondered what was toward and made haste downstairs. Her heart sank when she saw Sir Hugo perched unsafely on one of the decorative but spindly chairs her mother had recently hired for the drawing room.

He rose immediately. 'Miss Latimer, how good to see you. And how well you look in that ensemble.'

She looked down at the old dress she was wearing and wondered if her potential spouse needed glasses. 'But then,' he continued, 'you always contrive to look amazingly elegant.'

Her mother beamed appreciatively. 'Sir Hugo has been speaking of the new floral exhibition in Hyde Park. It sounds truly magnificent and has been especially designed as part of the celebrations arranged for the French Royal Family.'

'In fact,' Sir Hugo interjected eagerly, 'they are actually to celebrate the Prince Regent's assumption of power, but since his father is so very ill, it would be bad form for him to broadcast it, I daresay.'

Cassandra looked from one to the other in some puzzlement, wondering where she fitted into this conversation. Her mother was at hand to help.

'Sir Hugo has very kindly called to discover if you would care to see the display. I know you have no engagements this morning, my dear.'

Sir Hugo added his voice to the petition. 'I hope I do not importune, Miss Latimer, but I would welcome your company. And I am sure you will be charmed, knowing your highly developed sense of beauty. The southern tip of the park is a sheer blaze of colour.'

Cassie had no alternative but to agree, only stopping to change her gown and unpack the new bonnet which had just been delivered by Celeste, her favourite milliner. It was a charming confection, a light green cottager style tied beneath the chin with an enormous chiffon bow. It set off to perfection a gown of pale primrose silk. If she was to be wooed, and she had no doubt that was Sir Hugo's plan, she would at least look the part.

Hyde Park was unusually busy for a Saturday morning and for some time they had little leisure to converse, their attention distracted by the need to avoid a constant parade of slowly moving barouches and their elderly occupants, baby carriages with their nursemaids and schoolboys bowling their hoops. It seemed the whole world and his wife had come out to play this early April morning. And it wasn't hard to see why. The sun streamed down from an almost cloudless blue sky and spring was in the air.

⌒

Luke was also in the park that morning, carefully shepherding Marianna through its north gate towards Rotten Row, which was already busy with riders. It would be a good opportunity, he thought, for the young girl to experience one of the more popular pursuits of London life. Annoyingly, he had been forced to kick his heels in the capital for some days while legal documents were prepared for his signature. But he could at least enjoy this heaven-sent morning.

He glanced sideways at his companion, an amused expression on his face. She was in high gig now that he'd unexpectedly remained in town and her aunt had agreed to his chaperoneage. Lady Foyle's horror at the notion of a male escort the younger side of thirty had evaporated the moment Luke presented himself in Curzon Street. His manners were excellent and he showed an avuncular affection for Marianna that not even her worst nightmare could translate into any threat to her charge. She was only too pleased to accept his protection for her young niece whose company she was already finding exhausting.

They had hired hacks from the stables around the corner from Aunt Serena's house, but had instantly regretted it. Neither had any hesitation in characterising their respective mounts as out-and-out slugs. Marianna had already begun to feel irked by the restraints her aunt had found necessary to place on her and, after weeks of confinement on board ship, she was restless for the kind of unfettered gallop she had been accustomed to in Argentina. Her horse was unlikely to provide it.

Yet the morning shone with perfection and the greensward stretched invitingly in front of her. She could not resist the attempt, and before Luke could stop her, she had dug her spurs hard into the horse's flanks. Startled out of his wits, Firefly for once in his life was true to his name. He shot off across the park at breakneck speed to the shocked outrage of those sedately taking their morning promenade. Forced to ride sidesaddle, Marianna crouched low over the horse's neck in order to keep her seat, with her hair streaming inelegantly behind.

After a frozen instant of shock, Luke urged his mount into an unwilling gallop and rushed after her, fearful for her safety and intent on stopping her from creating the kind of scandal of which she had no notion.

Firefly hit the dust of Rotten Row, choking nearby strollers and scattering them to the winds as they leapt for safety, just as Sir Hugo had worked himself up to the point of a declaration.

'I shall be leaving for Thorne Park in the morning, Miss Latimer, and had hoped to depart with one very important question answered. It is a question dear to my heart and only you can settle it. If you would prefer, I am happy to wait, but I would be truly grateful if you would agree to think over what I have to say. You see, Miss Latimer, Cassandra –'

He was forced to break off mid-sentence and take drastic action as Firefly thundered towards him and his lovely companion. In a trice he had swept Cassandra up and literally jumped her out of harm's way. A second later another horse galloping headlong in pursuit caught up with the runaway and grabbed hold of Firefly's bridle.

'Never, ever do that again!' Luke's voice expressed cold fury.

Badly jolted by the headlong flight and realising she had committed a social sin, Marianna slipped from the saddle, her face white and frightened. She had never before seen Luke so angry and she was uncertain whether she should shout at him or burst into tears. He gave her no chance to decide.

Turning to the couple who had narrowly escaped Firefly's thundering hooves, he bowed in apology. Sir Hugo inclined his head at the irate stranger. He had no idea who the man might be, since he had been travelling on the Continent when Luke Trelawny had first come to town.

'Please forgive my companion,' Luke offered stiffly. 'She is a visitor to London and unaware of the rules governing riding in Hyde Park. I trust that you have received no harm.'

'I'm glad to say that we haven't,' stuttered Sir Hugo, now very shaken by the incident, 'but I feel your charge – I take it that she is your charge – needs a summary lesson.'

'She shall have it,' Luke said crisply, glaring at Sir Hugo with annoyance. Marianna had put him in the wrong and he did not like it.

He turned to apologise to the woman he had only glimpsed from the corner of his eye and for the first time in the encounter was struck dumb. For what seemed an infinity of time, he stood motionless and without expression, absorbing the picture before him, hardly believing what he saw.

He had not visualised the moment when he would meet Cassandra again. He'd made sure that his imagination never strayed into such dangerous territory. But if he had been tempted to speculate, it would not have felt like this.

He would have felt nothing – the meaningless liaisons of years would have done their work – and any images from the past he still carried would have shrivelled, should have shrivelled, in the cold light of reality. He *ought* to feel nothing. But that, it seemed, was not so. He stood and looked and his heart received a most painful jolt.

She was even more beautiful than he remembered. The misty green eyes and the tumble of red locks against translucent skin aroused every one of his senses. He looked searchingly at her ungloved hand. Astonishingly she was not married, at least not yet. That popinjay with her was no doubt the intended.

Cassie had known him immediately. He was still the

same tall, athletic man he had always been, but he seemed stronger now, more muscular, his face lean and tanned. There was an authority about him that had not been there before. His grey eyes, as they fixed her in an unwavering stare beneath black, straight brows, were lacking in all emotion. There was no warmth, no answering response to her tentative smile.

His voice was as cool as his expression. 'Miss Latimer? Your servant, ma'am.'

How hateful of him to speak to her thus, stiff and formal, as though they had met for the first time only yesterday. Sir Hugo looked questioningly from one to the other and Cassandra forced herself to perform the social niceties.

'Sir Hugo, may I introduce Earl Trelawny. Lord Trelawny, Sir Hugo Latimer.'

The two men eyed each other askance, instinctively hostile. Marianna, abandoned at a distance, walked her horse towards them and Luke was compelled to make her known to her erstwhile victims. She smiled sunnily at them.

'I'm so sorry, please forgive me for frightening you.' Her accent was marked as though she hoped this might produce a swifter forgiveness.

'I don't know the rules,' she continued, 'and Luke never told me, did you Luke?' And she smiled up at him, her eyes softly entreating.

But he was still looking at Cassandra and saw those extraordinary green eyes half-close. Was that perhaps unhappiness at Marianna's youthful adoration, an attempt to erase a discomfiting image? It seemed unlikely, given her ruthless rejection of him all those years ago. Yet undoubtedly she'd flinched at Marianna's display of fondness. The girl meant nothing to him, but Cassie was not to know that. Luke hoped she was suffering at least a little of the agonising jealousy he'd once known.

He was shocked by the vindictive thought, shocked that his emotions were out of control. That he should still be so susceptible, so easily disturbed, was dismaying. He schooled his face to remain expressionless as he bowed his formal farewell, but his mind was deep in thought. He walked swiftly away and Marianna had almost to skip to keep up with his long stride.

The unexpected meeting had unnerved him. He had felt his body conquered by desire and his mind battered by conflicting impulses. He was bewildered by his reactions for they made no sense. Of one thing, though, he was certain. He must overcome a weakness that had come out of nowhere; he could not allow himself to be drawn to Cassandra again. A vague sense grew upon him that if he could prove to himself, prove to the world, that her beauty was only skin deep, she would cease to bother him. The veriest shadow of an idea began to form in his mind.

Chapter Four

Cassie allowed herself to be escorted home, Sir Hugo steering her expertly along the pavement while remonstrating at length on the licence given the very young these days. She hardly heard him for her mind was in turmoil. The unexpected meeting with Luke would have been difficult enough under any circumstances, but his cold aloofness had at first amazed her and then upset her deeply.

Years had passed since she'd broken their engagement and she'd imagined that whatever anger he had felt towards her would have cooled long ago. But it was clear it was not so. Those steely grey eyes had expressed – what? Indifference, aversion, even enmity? Luke, of all people, the boy who had meant most to her for most of her life.

Sir Hugo continued his monologue as they made their way through the busy crowds that thronged Mayfair that morning. 'I am only glad that you sustained no lasting injury. How I could have reconciled myself to that, I do not know. It was I who invited you to view the floral display – if it had not been for me, you would never have been in danger.'

At this, she roused herself to reassure him. 'There can be no blame attached to you, Sir Hugo. The incident was not in any way your fault. How could you have foreseen such a thing happening?'

'That is true, but I feel a heavy responsibility still. And tomorrow I must go away. I cannot delay my visit to Thorne Park any longer. I have already put it off once and my bailiff remains most anxious to consult me.'

'Of course you must not delay. Why ever should you? As you see, I am perfectly unharmed. My nerves may be a little jangled, but they will soon recover.'

'You are a pearl among women, Miss Latimer. Others would have had hysterics in such a situation, but as always you are admirable.'

Sir Hugo's fussing was becoming an irritant. She might well have succumbed to hysterics, she thought, but not from the possibility of being crushed by a runaway horse. However she could hardly admit to her well-meaning companion the shock she'd sustained in encountering Luke's hostility, and she was desperate for him to drop the topic. Thank goodness he was to journey to his estates tomorrow and she would be free of his company for the next few days. But how dreadful she should feel this way about the man she was contemplating making her husband.

'I shall be back very shortly.' He had almost read her mind. 'And then, Miss Latimer, Cassandra, I hope to renew our conversation which was so violently terminated.'

They had reached the house in Mount Street that Lady Latimer rented every year and Sir Hugo bounded up the white stone steps and knocked sharply on the front door with his cane. Cassie wasn't sure if this was to impress since there was a perfectly good door knocker. But he was beaming down on her with a gentle kindliness and she tried to look suitably grateful for his concern. As soon as she could, she would send him on his way and seek refuge in her bedroom. She needed time to think, time to digest all that had happened that morning.

After a long delay, the bright blue door of Number Six finally swung open and the two of them made to enter, but were pulled up sharply on the threshold by a scene of rampant confusion. The hall was overflowing with trunks, cases, holdalls of all kinds and a decidedly sulky-looking parrot in a white ironwork cage. Cassie recognised the bird instantly.

'Annabel? Annabel is here?'

'Yes, Annabel *is* here.'

A strident voice emanated from behind the furthest stack of parcels. The young lady who emerged, smiling triumphantly at her sister, was not ill favoured but against Cassandra's pure beauty she appeared unexceptional.

'What on earth are you doing in Mount Street? Why have you left Cornwall?' Cassie exclaimed.

Before her sister could answer, a cheery male voice called out from the adjoining library, 'Hey, Bel, you could hang the bird in here.'

'Dominic? He's here, too?' She was dumbstruck at this sudden eruption into her life of a brother and sister she had supposed fixed at Boskenna Place for at least the next few months.

At that moment Lady Katherine floated into the hall

waving her hands ineffectually over the assorted baggage, as though by doing so it would miraculously order itself and march away.

'Cassandra, my darling, I'm so glad you're back. The servants are being amazingly slow at sorting this mountain and I need your help.'

'I'm not surprised they're slow – why on earth is there so much?'

Annabel drew herself up with an indignant puff and was just about to launch into an impassioned response when she spied Sir Hugo hovering just behind her sister. Cassie had been too surprised by the sudden appearance of her siblings to think of introducing him and he took the chance to excuse himself, saying in a rather nervous voice that he could see the family was extremely busy at this time and he would take his leave.

'May I call on my return, Miss Latimer?'

'Yes, of course, you may.' It was her mother who replied so readily.

Sir Hugo bowed himself elegantly out of the door and down the steps, but not before he heard Annabel's accusing voice. 'Why didn't you introduce us to your fiancé, Cassandra?'

The door shut behind him.

'He is not my fiancé.'

'That's very strange. We understood you were engaged. That's why we're here, isn't it, Dominic?'

Dominic smiled in a superior fashion. 'It may be why you're here, but I'm here to have fun.'

'Mama, may I speak privately with you for a moment?'

Cassie asked in a tight voice and gestured towards the library.

Lady Katherine looked flustered. 'Shouldn't we get the hall cleared first, my dear? The house is at sixes and sevens and the staff really do not like it.'

'In a minute, Mama. This is more important.'

Once in the library, she wasted no time. 'Why are Annabel and Dominic here?' she asked, fixing her mother with a minatory look.

'They are family. It is natural they should come to stay with us,' her mother responded defensively.

'But why now? You know as well as I that it was decided they would both remain in Cornwall for some while.'

'That was certainly the initial plan, but things have changed a little.'

'What things precisely?'

'Annabel is eighteen and should have the opportunity to partake of at least some of the Season.' Her mother appeared unwilling to answer her directly.

'She was eighteen when we left Boskenna for London, so I ask you again – what has changed?'

'Sir Hugo has changed.'

'What do you mean by that?'

'I mean that he is ready to make you an offer, Cassandra. You cannot deny it and if, as I hope, you will see fit to accept him, Annabel must be introduced to the *ton* at the earliest possible moment so that she, too, has the chance of contracting an eligible alliance.'

'But it was agreed that her come-out would be next year.'

'That was before we knew about Sir Hugo.'

'And what is it that we know about Sir Hugo? Annabel said that he was my fiancé. Why would she say that?'

'He is – almost,' her mother ventured.

'He has not asked me to marry him.'

'But he will. And I cannot think why he did not do so this morning. It was clearly what he intended.'

Cassandra ignored this and continued her relentless questioning. 'Have you told Annabel that I am engaged?'

'I may have written to your father that it was possible you were on the point of accepting a proposal.'

'And Papa has repeated this to Annabel?'

'He may have mentioned it.'

'May have? He obviously let it slip and, knowing Annabel, she will have plagued him to death until he agreed that she could come to London. Isn't that so?'

Her mother hung her head guiltily.

'I thought so. And I am to be coerced into agreeing to this marriage so that my sister can have her way?'

'No one is talking of coercion, Cassie. You know that you must be married, if not to Sir Hugo, then to someone else. We have had this conversation a hundred times before. And it is only fair to Annabel that she be allowed her place in the sun.'

'And is Dominic also to be allowed his place in the sun?'

'Don't be foolish. Dominic is still a stripling and only just down from Oxford. Your father thought it wise to let him gain some town bronze before he settles to learning the management of the estate.'

'What you mean is that he also plagued Papa until he was allowed to come.'

'He will be here only a month, my dear, and someone had to escort Annabel. I cannot understand why you are so cross.'

Cassandra took a deep breath and said with deliberation, 'I am cross because I feel my hand is being forced. I understood we would be on our own in London for this Season and expected to have time and peace to consider my future. Now I have virtually the whole of my family breathing down my neck and pushing me into a marriage I don't want.'

'You don't want to marry Sir Hugo!'

Her mother looked scandalised and Cassie felt stunned. She hadn't wanted to acknowledge such troublesome feelings even to herself, let alone express them aloud. She tried to recover her composure as best she could.

'I understand my position, Mama, and I will do what is expected of me. But don't demand that I am glad.'

And with that she turned on her heel and weaved her way swiftly through the still cluttered hall and up the stairs to her room without another word. Brother and sister, still standing amidst the clutter of baggage, looked after her in surprise.

Once in her room, Cassie flung herself down on the satin counterpane and closed her eyes. The morning had been full of shocks and she was not coping well. She needed to pull herself together. Annabel was an unfriendly presence that she could have done without, but nothing more. As for Dominic, he would be filling Mount Street with noise and disturbance, but maybe she should be glad of it. It might distract her from the reality of her life, which was what, exactly? Marriage to a man she did not love and hatred from the man she had once loved. The near-fatal accident, her siblings' unwelcome arrival, her mother's pretence, could all be forgotten. It was Luke's undisguised hostility that stayed with her.

⌒

Early the next morning she woke to a household already on the move. She had slept badly and wanted nothing more than to stay curled in bed. But she had hardly opened her eyes before Annabel bounced into her room, more than happy to explain the bustle.

'Mama has said that I am to go shopping and you are to accompany me,' she announced peremptorily.

Cassie blinked sleepily and reached for her cup of chocolate. 'Don't you have clothes already?'

'No, I don't. I shall need a completely new wardrobe to make a splash in London. **You** have a rail of exquisite gowns, so don't be selfish, Cass!' Her sister was at her most indignant.

She flounced out of the room only to be replaced by a second morning visitor.

'Cassie, I know you're not happy about accompanying Annabel, but I would count it a great favour if you would.'

'I will go, of course, but I'll not be able to stop her buying the most dreadful clothes.'

'My dear, Annabel listens to no one as you well know. But you have such good taste – I am hoping some of it will rub off on her.'

Cassie did not share that hope, but felt it only right she attempt to help. Her mother was looking unusually tired and harassed by the sudden appearance of two youthful and demanding offspring into her hitherto peaceful household.

Within the hour they were in the carriage and on their way to Lady Katherine's favourite modiste. The morning that followed was one Cassandra never wished to repeat. Again and again she sought to dissuade the younger girl from unwise purchases: heliotrope was not on the whole an immensely flattering colour; a bonnet sporting six ostrich plumes and a cluster of brightly coloured gemstones might be thought a trifle vulgar; a dress of gauze worn over a transparent petticoat was unlikely to ingratiate her with the most illustrious members of the *ton*. But she was helpless against the onslaught of Annabel in full cry and could only watch in despair as the carriage gradually filled with an array of packages containing the most unsuitable attire.

The clothes had been costly and eaten up most of the very generous allowance bestowed by Lord Latimer and still they had not purchased gloves, slippers, reticules – all the myriad of accessories necessary for a young lady about to embark on a social whirl. Cassandra's tentative suggestion that they go to the Pantheon Bazaar where she'd heard there were bargains to be had, was received with surprising enthusiasm and they drove immediately to Grafton House.

Very soon they found themselves immersed in stalls displaying an abundance of coloured muslins, ornate trimmings, silk stockings, fine cambric handkerchiefs, all at astonishing prices. The bazaar was not generally visited by ladies of high fashion, but within minutes of entering the emporium Annabel was exclaiming loudly over the bargains to be had.

The only drawback to the shop was its popularity since by noon it was completely full and shopping had become a tedious business of jostling elbows. Both young ladies were heartily relieved when the last piece of lace and the last pair of kid slippers had been chosen. Their relief was short-lived, however, for the increasing crowds made it necessary to wait a considerable time to pay at the final counter.

Annabel had at last reached the head of the queue when Cassie heard a voice that was faintly familiar. She turned her head and caught a glimpse of a stylishly gowned woman holding in her hand a collection of colourful loo masks.

'They will be just the thing, Aunt Serena, if we go to Vauxhall - and you did promise!' The woman's younger companion was almost jumping with enthusiasm.

'I think you may be stretching the word promise, Marianna. I said we *might* go.'

But Marianna had lost interest in the masks and was staring instead at Cassandra. She darted eagerly forward and offered her hand.

'Miss Latimer, isn't it? How are you feeling? I'm so sorry about the accident yesterday - I've been quite worried about you.'

Chapter Five

'Thank you, but as you see I am perfectly well.'

'Luke told me not to worry. He said you were were the coolest of women and most unlikely to suffer disordered feelings. You see, I've remembered his words exactly.'

'What accident, Marianna?' her aunt interjected.

'Only a small one, Aunt. It was a little frightening at the time, but it was over in a moment.'

Marianna looked from one to the other, a pleased expression on her face. 'I must introduce you. Aunt Serena this is Miss Cassandra Latimer – I have it right? Such a difficult name for my tongue! Miss Latimer, this is my aunt, Lady Foyle.'

'How do you do,' Cassie responded as warmly as she could. 'I'm very happy to meet you.'

Lady Foyle smiled anxiously as she shook hands. 'Marianna said nothing to me of an accident.'

'Please don't be concerned. I have taken no harm from yesterday's adventure.' Cassie smiled reassuringly at aunt and niece. She had no wish to get this vivacious young girl into further trouble.

'Is not this shop the most wonderful you've ever seen?' Marianna's eyes were lit with pleasure.

She glanced rapturously around her and Cassandra glimpsed a uniformed footman standing a few paces away, already loaded with packages. Lady Foyle saw the direction of her glance and said wryly, 'As you see, we have had a busy morning.'

'You know you've enjoyed it as much as I,' Marianna protested. 'And I did need to add to my wardrobe, didn't I? I have been invited to so many parties.'

Her aunt smiled indulgently as her niece prattled happily on. 'I've been in London such a short time, Miss Latimer, but I have already been to a dozen entertainments. It's been splendid. And Luke has been a wonderful escort. He has been wonderful, hasn't he, Aunt Serena?' She turned impulsively to the older woman, her cheeks glowing.

'Lord Trelawny has certainly been a good friend to us,' her aunt agreed.

The girl's soft brown eyes were smiling and she looked the picture of happiness. It was obvious to Cassie that she revered Luke and just as obvious that she knew nothing of his past. It was as though he had wiped the slate clean, obliterated that part of his life. The Cassie he'd known in his youth had ceased to exist for him. Instead a callous and unfeeling woman, a woman whose emotions were never disordered, had taken her place.

She was saved from making any further conversation by Annabel, who had finished at last paying for her goods. Before Cassandra knew what was happening, her sister had seized her hand and was dragging her towards the entrance of the shop without a glance at the couple standing nearby.

'Come on, Cass, or we'll be late for luncheon.' Cassandra had time only to execute a hasty bow before she was bundled outside.

'Really, Annabel, there is little point in buying smart dresses and clever fripperies if you lack manners to match,' she remonstrated, as they emerged into the fresh air and once more climbed into the waiting carriage.

'I had to get out of that shop. It was so hot I thought I'd cook. And we must go home this minute – I need to try on my new outfits.'

Cassie demurred. 'Before we return to Mount Street, I have an errand of my own. I'd like to call in at Hatchards and collect a book I've ordered. *Mansfield Park* is being spoken of everywhere and I'm most anxious to read it.'

'You can pick the book up tomorrow,' her sister complained. 'At this hour of the day Piccadilly will be blocked with traffic and it will take an age to get home.'

Cassandra remained unmoved. 'I would like to begin Miss Austen's novel today and we'll be in the shop a few minutes only. After this morning, you owe me a little time, don't you think?'

Annabel looked sulky, but did not dispute further. The traffic was lighter than expected and very soon they were standing outside Hatchards' impressive bow windows. The smell of leather greeted them as Cassandra trod briskly across polished wood to a large counter where a stack of volumes of different shapes and sizes was awaiting collection.

Already bored with the errand, Annabel began an immediate prowl around the lines of high-sided bookshelves in the hope of seeking out a possible acquaintance. Soon she had disappeared from view so completely that when Cassandra went to look for her, she was nowhere to be seen, even in the furthest recesses of the shop.

A carriage full of new dresses had been too much of a temptation, Cassie thought, and Annabel must have ordered the coachman to drive her home and left her sister to make her own way back. It was a nuisance, but not a disaster. Mount Street was a ten-minute walk away and she had no fear of undertaking the journey alone.

She began to make her way to the shop entrance, zigzagging around the rows of tall shelves, and was turning the corner of one particularly high stack of books, when she looked up to find Luke Trelawny barring her way. For a moment she froze. He was the last person she had expected to see. He wore a drab riding cape over a tightly fitting coat of blue superfine and what looked to be a recent purchase, a cut Venetian waistcoat. The palest of fawn pantaloons were subtly enhanced by a body long hardened by physical activity.

He smiled sardonically as he swept her a bow. 'Good morning, Miss Latimer. I trust I find you well. I hope you have not suffered unduly from yesterday's misfortune.'

For a moment she was mesmerised, unable to speak, unable to take her eyes from the figure who stood in her path. It was as though she were seeing him for the very first time. Yesterday his sudden appearance, when she'd imagined him still on the high seas, had sent her mind into disarray. She had been conscious only of those crystal-hard eyes raking her down. Now the full force of his masculinity hit her and she struggled to find words.

'I'm well, Lord Trelawny, thank you, and have suffered no lasting effects,' she managed to say at last.

'I'm happy to hear that. I would not have anyone injured from my lack of foresight, but I could not have anticipated Miss Marquez's actions. It was sheer recklessness, I fear, on the part of my young companion.'

'This is her first visit to London, I believe, and she can surely be excused,' Cassandra returned gently. 'She would not know the regulations governing riding in Hyde Park.'

'She does now, however, and in future she will follow them to the letter. Then we should go on well enough. Rules are a necessary part of civilised society, do you not agree? For myself, I've always placed a good deal of trust in observing them, but I imagine you must know that.'

Cassie said nothing. He was clearly intent on upsetting her.

'You are silent. Perhaps you are unwilling to criticise the young lady in question? Rest assured I have already done so. She has received a trimming she will not forget. But she has youth on her side and youth has one great advantage, I find – it can learn from its mistakes.'

'I'm sure Miss Marquez will. No doubt you are a proficient teacher, sir.'

'I trust so. I certainly should be. In my own youth I was lucky to have an equally proficient teacher, who taught me to learn from my biggest mistake.'

His face was grim and Cassie had an overpowering desire to flee, but he was barring her way and escape was impossible. She steadied her nerves and refused to be intimidated.

'I hardly know the young lady, but she seemed well able to manage her own affairs.'

'That is certainly the impression she gives to the uninitiated, but to those who know her well,' he said meaningfully, 'the case is otherwise. Her spontaneity is entrancing, but is like to run away with her. She needs a firm hand.'

'I hope she sees the situation as you do.'

'And if she does not?'

'Then she will reject your firm hand and simply be herself.'

'Exactly what I would expect you to say, Miss Latimer. I must not forget that you are an advocate of self-expression, no matter what the cost.'

His smile was belied by the frost of cold, grey eyes and she felt her stomach twist. It seemed he had deliberately accosted her in order to bait her. But she could not let him ride roughshod.

'You misunderstand me, sir. I was not encouraging Miss Marquez to break rules, simply proposing that everyone must have the freedom to make their mistakes.'

'You know a deal about such freedom, do you not? Dare I suggest that restraint is a more admirable quality?'

'Restraint and youth do not sit easily together,' she retorted.

'Yet for most they can be negotiated. Dishonour is a powerful deterrent.'

She was weary of the cat and mouse game he seemed to relish and made to walk forward. 'If you will excuse me,

I am meeting my sister and would not wish to keep her waiting.'

He made no move to allow her to pass, but instead looked around him mockingly. 'I don't see her. She is certainly nowhere in the shop. Are you sure you were supposed to meet her here?'

'Yes, indeed. She will be outside.'

'But if she is not, you must walk alone. May I offer you my escort home?'

'I thank you, but no,' she said hastily. 'I have my carriage.'

'I saw nothing of a carriage either. Your sister must have left without you. But perhaps you can call on Sir Hugo Thorne to take you home? He must live close by.'

Cassandra shook her head.

'I am surprised. From our meeting yesterday, he seemed a most attentive gentleman. I fear our untimely descent on you interrupted an important conversation. I do apologise if that was so – I would not wish to frighten him away. Where is he now?'

She was angered by his insinuations and also bewildered. How had he known that Sir Hugo was about to propose?

'He is visiting his country estate,' she replied. 'If you wish to see him, I suggest you call at his town house in a few days' time. It is in Brook Street, I believe.' She strove for a measured tone, trying hard not to betray her vexation.

'There you are, Cassie! I've been looking for you everywhere.'

Annabel bounced suddenly into view, almost running around the adjacent bookcase and only just preventing herself from cannoning into Luke. He turned round with annoyance; the interview had just been getting interesting. He had followed Cassandra into the shop on impulse, feeling an overpowering need to confront her with the words he had kept suppressed for so long. Even more compelling had been the need to protect himself from her, to keep her at a safe distance, by wielding ugly recriminations.

'Good gracious, are you who I think you are?' Annabel asked. She had been just twelve years old when Luke had left for Argentina and had only a vague memory of her sister's former lover. 'Whatever are you doing *here?*' she continued, a trifle too bluntly.

Cassandra intervened. 'Lord Trelawny is newly arrived in town. We met yesterday in Hyde Park when there was a slight accident. He has been kind enough to enquire how I go on.'

Luke glanced at Annabel with disfavour. She had never been an appealing child with her insistence on frills and furbelows and the constant preening in every mirror she could find. To his jaundiced eye, she looked very little improved. Cassie as a child had been so different – a skinny, reckless tomboy of a girl with a tangle of red hair and freckles to match. She had always been ready for adventure and just as always ready to drag him into whatever trouble she had been brewing.

Looking at her now, a slender vision in eau-de-nil silk, a matching ribbon threaded through those wonderfully fiery curls, he smiled inwardly, forgetting for the moment his purpose in accosting her. No greater contrast between past and present could there be. He remembered the day he'd returned from Oxford to find his one-time playmate transformed, a butterfly fluttering the hearts of all the local beaux. He had gazed at her spellbound, drinking in her beauty.

His reverie came to an abrupt end when he became aware of Annabel still scowling at him a few feet away. With a brief bow, he moved aside for the sisters to make their exit.

'Where were you? I've been an age looking for you,' Annabel scolded and marched forcefully towards the glass-paned doors. 'The carriage was causing an obstruction and Stebbings has had to move. Now we'll have to walk the whole of Picadilly to find him.'

Cassandra made no reply but walked swiftly along the flagged thoroughfare, thinking deeply. Luke had appeared in Hatchards at the very time that she had chosen to call at the shop. It was as though he'd been shadowing her, waiting for an opportunity to confront her. And it had been a confrontation. She recalled the ice in his eyes and the anger in his voice, as he sought to remind her of her crime.

And he'd been at pains to emphasise his new-found intimacy with Marianna Marquez, while a few hours earlier the young girl had made clear that she admired Luke greatly. Cassie did not blame her for that idolisation.

Luke was the perfect hero for an adolescent dream – a honed body, a handsome face alight with intelligence, and an air of innate strength that more than matched his elegance. If she were honest, he was a hero for more than adolescent girls. When he had appeared so suddenly before her, polished and powerful, she had felt a charge of pure sexual magnetism.

But it was momentary, and had quickly evaporated as it became plain he intended only to distress her. She must not dwell on his beautiful form and face, nor on his seeming desire to exact some kind of retribution. Her life would soon resume its normal peaceful rhythm. Sir Hugo would be returning and she looked forward to that, she told herself severely. By dint of repetition she was sure she would come to believe it.

Chapter Six

'You've not forgotten that Lady Russell is to collect you at eleven o' clock?' her mother prompted the next morning, whisking through the hall on her way to consult with the housekeeper.

'Lady Russell?' Cassie grappled with the name for a moment.

'Sir Hugo has arranged it, has he not? The tickets for Montagu House?'

'Ah, yes, I remember now,' she said heavily. 'He was keen that we view the Marbles that Lord Elgin has brought back from Greece.'

'A stuffy museum *and* Lady Russell all in the same morning,' interjected Annabel, as she emerged from the breakfast room in one of the eye-opening ensembles she had purchased yesterday. 'Rather you than me!'

Her mother rounded on her sharply. 'You are becoming far too pert for your own good, Annabel. You must learn to keep a check on your tongue or you will fare badly in society.'

This was an important consideration for an aspiring belle and Annabel looked suitably contrite. 'I'm sorry,

Mama, but Lady Russell is a gorgon. I can't imagine how she ever came to have such a charming brother as Sir Hugo.'

'That's as may be, but you had much better keep your opinions to yourself. And, Cassandra, you must hurry. You will need to dress in something a little more demure.'

Cassie glanced down at the low neckline and French trimmings of the apricot sarcenet and sighed. Her mother was right. Lady Russell was a stickler for correctness and only a simple day dress of sprigged muslin with a high neck and a matching spencer would satisfy that matriarch.

It was weeks ago that she had agreed to the visit. At the time she had been feeling more guilty than usual at her lack of enthusiasm for Sir Hugo's company and he'd been so touchingly anxious that she become better acquainted with what small family he possessed that she had felt forced to consent. Since then she'd acquired a genuine interest in the marble wonders that had travelled all the way from Athens and, were it not for Lady Russell, she would be looking forward to the morning's expedition with pleasure.

⤳

Sir Hugo's sister was punctual to the minute, an erect figure in a heavy but serviceable barouche, awaiting Cassie outside the Mount Street house with scarcely concealed impatience. The severe grey kerseymere gown and dreary poke bonnet she wore did nothing to lighten the atmosphere. Her greeting was perfunctory. She was not at all sure that this young woman was a suitable wife for her brother. She was altogether too beautiful, and beautiful women usually meant trouble.

And there was that unfortunate business years ago when

her name had been bandied around the town as a tease and a jilt by every wicked rattlejaw. Her modest behaviour since had done much to redeem this unsatisfactory reputation, but still one never knew when old habits would surface. One only had to look at that hair – wild to a fault. But Hugo was evidently head over heels in love with her and she could hardly blame him. Men could be very stupid, never seeing further than what was in front of their eyes.

'Are you looking forward to viewing the Marbles, Miss Latimer?' she asked her companion, as the barouche rolled smoothly forward. Her smile was one of gracious condescension.

'Indeed, ma'am, I am. I have been reading a good deal about them and my interest has been greatly stirred.'

Lady Russell unbent slightly. At least the girl had some intelligence, which was all to the good. It was necessary that Hugo marry a woman who was serious enough to understand and tolerate his charity work. As far as Lady Russell was concerned, her brother's projects for the labouring poor remained wholly inexplicable.

'I have learned,' she remarked magisterially, 'that a special gallery has been built for these statues at a vast cost. We must hope that they warrant such expenditure.' The faltering conversation was effectively closed down.

Once the carriage left Mayfair and was bowling towards Bloomsbury, the roads became a great deal clearer and they reached the entrance of the British Museum only a few minutes later than expected. It did not stop her ladyship tutting loudly at her coachman, who had made the journey to Montagu House in record time and was even now negotiating a difficult manoeuvre to bring the carriage exactly to the bottom of the flight of steps which led up to the impressive panelled entrance.

A steep staircase, a spacious entrance hall, and they were upon the Marbles almost before they realised. Two long white-washed galleries had been constructed to house the extraordinary exhibits brought back from Greece by Lord Elgin. The monumental size of many of the statues was staggering and both ladies paused on the threshold to adjust their perspective. Then they began a slow inspection of the initial gallery, first down one side and then the other, with Lady Russell insisting on reading aloud every handwritten label the curators had provided.

During this prolonged examination, the room had been gradually filling up and by the time Cassie was ready to tackle the second gallery, a considerable crowd had gathered. She looked across at Lady Russell, who appeared weary and a trifle disenchanted, and was not surprised to hear the lady excuse herself, saying that she would await Cassandra in the spacious hall beyond. The carriage, she reminded her severely, would leave promptly at one o'clock.

Cassie nodded assent, happy to be rid of the older woman's irksome presence. With a new sense of purpose, she crossed into the adjoining room. Almost immediately her attention was caught by the statue of a woman, a large sculpture of Iris which had once decorated the west pediment of the Parthenon. She stood enthralled, marvelling at the precision with which the intricate folds of the goddess's dress had been carved – the marble seemed to sing out life.

The harmony of its lines and the sheer exuberance of the goddess was a joy. Lost in thought as she was, the voice at her elbow startled her.

'It's so sad, isn't it, that she has lost her legs *and* her arms?'

She turned to her questioner. It was Marianna, looking freshly minted in primrose figured muslin and carrying a matching frilled parasol.

'She may not be complete,' Cassandra agreed, 'but it doesn't seem to matter. She possesses such enormous vitality, don't you think?'

Marianna gave a small laugh. 'What must she have been like as a whole woman, Miss Latimer!'

'Very powerful, I imagine, particularly as she enjoyed such a prominent position on the top of the Parthenon.'

'Poor thing, she must find it very cold in London.'

'No doubt.' Cassie gave an answering smile. 'But if she had been left to bask in her native sun, we wouldn't be seeing her today in all her glory.'

'I don't think I would have minded too much,' the girl divulged. 'There are so many statues to see and some of them are just fragments. To be honest, I haven't found them very inspiring.'

'You didn't wish to come to the exhibition?'

'Not really, but Aunt Serena said I should, as all of London is talking about it. She said that if I'd seen the statues I would be able to join in conversations and not sound too silly.'

'Aunt Serena has a point.'

'I know, but I would much rather have gone to Astley's,'

she confided. 'I've heard they keep troops of horses there who can re-enact scenes of war and that there are daring equestriennes who perform the most amazing acrobatics on horseback!'

'I believe so.' Cassandra answered her seriously, though she was amused by the young girl's enthusiasm for the less-than-refined pleasure. 'The equestrian ballet of Astley's is famous.'

'A ballet on horseback?' Marianna's eyes grew round with amazement. 'I *must* see that.'

'What must you see?'

A man's voice broke through the female weavings of their conversation. It was Luke. He bowed unsmilingly at Cassandra. He was again looking exceedingly handsome, this time in a claret-coloured waistcoat and light grey pantaloons, which fitted to perfection. The folds of his cravat were precisely arranged and held in place by a single small diamond stud.

'Miss Latimer says there's an equestrian ballet performed at Astley's. Can we go, Luke?' In her eagerness Marianna tugged hard at her companion's immaculate coat sleeve.

'You must ask your aunt to take you. In the meantime, where is your taste for higher culture?' He waved his hand carelessly towards the statues on either side of them.

'Aunt Serena will never agree to go to Astley's. It will be much too vulgar for her. Now she is even saying that she doubts we will go to the fireworks at Vauxhall.'

'Then you must be content with more refined pastimes, child.'

Cassie was disconcerted by his tone. He seemed almost

like a parent. The surprise she felt must have shown on her face and almost immediately he adopted a softer, even caressing note.

'By all means put Astley's on your list, Marianna, and we will make every endeavour to get there.'

She clapped her hands in pleasure. Luke watched her, an indulgent expression on his face, but his words were for Cassandra.

'Books yesterday, statues today, Miss Latimer. You are an avid partaker of culture.'

'Only as much as any rational woman, Lord Trelawny.'

'But then how many women are as rational as you?' She made no answer, but his eyes remained fixed on her. 'Very few, I make sure,' he continued.

'I bow to your vast experience, my lord.'

'Hardly vast, but enough – sufficient to suggest that logic and reasoning are not always becoming to a woman.'

Cassie felt herself being forced into another confrontation and was determined to meet the challenge. When she spoke, her tone was cold. 'I cannot imagine why you should find fault with rationality. My sex is usually criticised for precisely the opposite.'

'In general it is an excellent quality for a female to possess, I agree, but taken to extremes rationality can destroy a woman's natural affections.'

'I think that unlikely,' she retorted.

'Do you? Then consider the case of a woman who decides "rationally" to prefer one man to another on the grounds that he is likely to be the better matrimonial prize. When logic leads, a woman's heart is prone to wither.'

Fire began to simmer deep in the green eyes and her whole body tensed for combat. 'By that reasoning, sir, only women who are witless can know affection.'

'That is a trifle crude, but the sentiment is not without merit. I think it likely that many men would agree with me – Sir Hugo Latimer for one. By the way, does he accompany you this morning?'

'Sir Hugo is still out of town.'

'Dear me, he appears to spend a great deal of time in the country.'

Cassie took a deep breath and replied as levelly as she could, 'Thorne Park is a large estate and takes a good deal of his time.'

'Of course, he *would* have a large estate.' The trace of a sneer marred an unyielding mouth.

Marianna looked from one to the other, aware of the tension which crackled between them, but bewildered as to its cause.

'As you appear interested in the trivialities of my life, Lord Trelawny, you may wish to know that I am accompanied this morning by Sir Hugo's sister.' Cassandra's perfectly sculpted cheeks were flushed an angry pink. 'She is waiting close by so I must beg you to excuse me.'

And with a hasty bow to them both, Cassie turned towards the entrance hall, her mind seething, her figure stiff with unexpressed anger. She walked briskly, the frills on her muslin gown tossing as though caught in a tempest and the wayward auburn curls beginning a tumble from the satin bandeau that restrained them.

It seemed she was to be followed at every opportunity

and forced to submit to any taunt or goad Luke wished to aim at her. It was insufferable. She was truly reaping the whirlwind she had sowed all those years ago.

Chapter Seven

Marianna wore a puzzled look and remained standing beside the figure of Iris.

'Do you not like Miss Latimer, Luke?' Her tone was one of concern.

'I neither like nor dislike her.'

'I think you made her angry.'

'I would be sorry to give offence, but if she was angry, it was unmerited.'

Marianna frowned at this. 'She felt offended and I think she had good reason. You seemed to want to upset her. But why?'

Luke contemplated pretending ignorance, but then said, 'It's an old story and not for your ears.'

'Then you knew her before you came to Argentina? You knew her when you were last in England?'

'I have known her all my life.'

'How is that possible?'

'Her family's estate in Cornwall runs alongside mine.'

And that's why they had drifted into an engagement, he thought. It had been easy to fulfil their parents' dream, to imagine a life lived with each other in the Cornish homeland they shared. But in the end it hadn't felt that way. He had begun the affair in nonchalance and ended in love.

He had wanted to marry. He had wanted her: her russet curls tickling his chin as they walked together in the gardens, the sensation of her body moulding to his as they dared to learn the waltz together, the softness of her skin to his touch, the softness of her mouth to his lips when he'd first ventured to kiss her. It had been a revelation.

'We played together as children,' he said, and added drily, 'like brother and sister.'

'Then you should be friends.'

'Oh, we were, very good friends.'

Marianna was about to respond, but he pre-empted her. 'Shall we go – if you've seen enough?'

His young companion nodded and he gently shepherded her towards the entrance, but once outside, she began her questions again.

'So what happened? If you and Miss Latimer were such good friends, why are you so unhappy with each other now?'

'A betrothal. Come, let's walk on.'

'A betrothal? Whose?'

'My betrothal to Miss Latimer. We were to be married.'

'You were betrothed to Cassandra Latimer!' Marianna stopped in her tracks, gaping with surprise. 'You never said.' There was a pause. 'What happened?' she asked in a quiet voice.

'We decided that after all we did not suit each other.'

She considered this for a moment. 'But if you were both agreed, why are you still so unhappy with her?'

'It's complicated.' Luke gave a sigh. 'And we should

hurry, Marianna. Otherwise Gunter's will be closed and you'll lose the ice I promised you.'

She picked up her pace – an elderflower ice was a favourite – but it didn't stop her from pursuing the subject. 'It doesn't seem that complicated to me,' she said with decision.

He saw that he would have to tell her the full story or at least enough of it to satisfy her.

'I was away at Oxford for three years,' he began, 'either at the university studying or staying with friends in the vacations, so I didn't see her for a long time. When I finally returned home to Cornwall, I found her very changed. She had always been a tomboy, a thin, gawky girl with her dresses torn and her hair in a tangle. But now she was this amazingly beautiful young woman. I could hardly believe my eyes the first night I saw her again. She was the toast of the county, worshipped by every man from Penzance to Plymouth – and that's a long way, Marianna.'

He paused, remembering the evening when he'd walked into the drawing room at Boskenna and found her waiting, a slender vision of cream lace and gold roses. When she'd glided forward and laughingly put her arms around him in welcome, she had taken his breath away.

'I suppose I was irritated,' he went on. 'Whenever I visited Boskenna Place, I tripped over some lovesick swain clutching a posy of flowers or reading her the latest bad poem he'd written in her praise. It was comical, but also annoying. She had always been my particular friend and now I was supposed to share her company with all the fops and dandies from miles around. So I decided to woo her myself, win the prize and delight my parents – it was what they had been hoping for since we were children.'

'And Miss Latimer?'

'I think she was flattered by my interest. I was a welcome diversion from all the cloying attention, but only a diversion – until her come-out at the next London Season. But she never did come out that year. Her mother couldn't leave the younger children to travel to London, so she deputed the task of presenting Cassandra to a distant cousin. Then the cousin became ill quite suddenly and the plans were cancelled. Cassie had to resign herself to staying in Cornwall and it was then she agreed to marry me.'

'So when did you find out that you had both made a mistake?'

'When she made love with another man.' Luke had not been able to stop his bitter denunciation.

Marianna glanced across at him, thoroughly shocked. 'Is that really true?'

'His name was Joshua,' he said acridly, discarding any hope now of keeping the full story from his young admirer. 'My mother had accompanied Cassandra and myself to London to buy bride clothes. Instead Cassie purchased a very different item – the attention, for I cannot call it love, of a man I'd thought a friend. She confessed she had fallen in love with him. Perhaps she had. He was clever and handsome and the sole heir of a very wealthy uncle. She said she could no longer marry me and I left for Argentina shortly afterwards. The rest you know.'

Marianna thought about the story for some time. Cassandra Latimer had not seemed the kind of woman who would treat a man so shockingly, but there was no doubt that Luke had suffered hurt.

She turned to him impulsively. 'It happened such a very long time ago, can you not forgive her?'

'There is nothing to forgive,' he said in a breezy voice, as he opened the door of Gunters. 'It's over.'

But it wasn't, he knew. It was far from over. Cassandra had come back into his life, and the world he had built so carefully for himself had begun to shatter.

He remembered how in those early months in Buenos Aires he'd walked around a stunned man. He had lost so much, not just the girl he loved, but his entire life. Early one blistering hot morning, he'd walked on the beach when the world was still asleep. He was quite alone, and looking out over the limitless ocean, he'd willed himself back to his beloved homeland.

But friends and family had gradually faded from view and he'd been helpless to recall them. He had borne the rupture calmly, stoically, never allowing a hint of trouble to show, and he had grown to love Argentina. He had put down new roots, made new friends, taken new lovers.

So why was he allowing such furious resentment to seep into his life and destroy the pleasure of his homecoming? After the scourging he'd received, he had become adept at sidestepping deep feeling, but for the first time in years strong emotions were crowding in on him. Ever since he'd seen Cassie.

His constant need to provoke her, to disturb her, was a signal that he had never truly overcome her betrayal. He had simply shut it away. Seeing her afresh had reawakened feelings he'd thought dead.

He was angry with himself, as much as with her, and if he were to know any peace, he must exorcise that demon and do so quickly. But how to free himself of these unwanted feelings from the past?

In the heat of their first unexpected meeting, he had entertained some wild thoughts. But were they that wild? If he could prove Cassandra unchanged, prove that she was the same inconstant woman, surely that would get her from under his skin.

Instinctively, he knew she was not wholly indifferent to him. Her face might remain immobile, but her eyes gave her away. He had the power to rouse this newly cold woman to strong feeling – anger and love were bedfellows, after all. There was a lingering tie between them, he was sure, and he would take every chance to play on whatever jealousy Cassie might feel towards the young girl who sat beside him.

But there had to be more. He must entice her into his arms, tease her, goad her, until she was ready to say she loved him. Ready to betray Sir Hugo Thorne as she had betrayed him. The man who had taken her arm so proudly that day in the park would be forced to recognise her for the jilt she was. And if he could learn the same lesson himself, Luke thought, her power to perturb would be over. He would be free of her – forever.

༄

The Latimer family ate an early supper since Cassandra and Lady Katherine were engaged to attend Almack's. Cassie felt no joy at the prospect. This morning her pleasure in viewing the Marbles had been spoiled by Luke's antagonism and an evening spent at the exclusive club was no compensation. It would be a tedious few hours. Several glasses of lemonade, a series of country dances, a nod or two at acquaintances, and then they would be free to return home.

She had never understood what made the place exceptional, but her mother always held it to be good *ton* to attend regularly and made a point of escorting her elder daughter every week. Sir Hugo, too, was a frequent visitor, and Cassie derived some comfort at least in knowing that tonight he was safely lodged at Thorne Park many miles away and she would escape any renewed marriage proposal.

She had dressed with some care for the evening. After the unsettling events of the last few days she had felt the need to look her best. The emerald silk gown over an underdress of the palest green gauze was a stunning creation, her hair flaming in contrast and the green of her eyes reflected in its deepest tones. A low bodice revealed shapely breasts and shoulders as smooth as alabaster.

Without immodesty, she knew from experience that she would attract the attention of nearly every man there. Not Luke's, though. He would certainly not be at Almack's. Even in his youth it had been a place he had always refused to attend, though she had often begged him to be her escort.

Cassie looked across the table at her sister who was drinking soup with exaggerated caution, intent on preserving her gown. With a start, she realised that Annabel was dressed rather too elaborately for dinner at home and wondered why. The conundrum was soon solved.

'Annabel will be coming with us,' her mother announced with studied carelessness.

'To Almack's?' Cassandra asked blankly.

'Yes, of course, to Almack's.'

'But what about vouchers?'

'I have managed to obtain some. Lady Jersey was kind enough to bestow them on me at short notice. She understood the position and wanted very much to make Annabel's acquaintance.'

'Nobody gets tickets for Almack's that quickly, Mama, so you must have known for some time that Annabel was coming to London.'

Her mother made no reply, but Cassie's interrogation continued. 'You told me that you and Papa had decided only recently that my sister should visit, but in fact you must have been plotting it for weeks.'

She hated being at odds with her family, but the net seemed to be closing around her ever more tightly. Her mother's telltale blush revealed her unhappiness at the deception, while Annabel's face was one of untroubled victory.

'Hardly plotting, Cassie. Annabel's coming to stay was certainly not part of any grand plan. But when Sir Hugo began to grow ever more particular in his attentions, it seemed sensible to introduce your sister to *ton* society a little earlier than we had expected. I heard only last week that she and Dominic were on their way, but I said nothing because I knew you had much on your mind and I thought it would be a delightful surprise.'

'Delightful,' Cassie offered tartly. 'But if Annabel is to

come with us tonight, do you not feel she should change her gown? Her dress is not suitable for a first visit.'

'And what, pray, is wrong with my dress?' Annabel asked combatively.

Lady Latimer, who had unsuccessfully tried to direct her younger daughter to one of the more modest creations hanging in her wardrobe, interjected gently, 'Cassandra has such refined taste, my dear, and she is familiar with what is most fitting for Almack's. Why not reconsider the magenta? The rose chiffon would become you so well.'

'The rose is boring and I have no intention of being boring.'

'You won't be that,' Dominic put in unhelpfully, 'the whole world will see you coming at fifty paces.'

'You have no notion of female dress, so hold your tongue.'

'I have no notion of going to Almack's either, so I won't be the one who has to hand out the sunshades.' Her unrepentant brother grinned.

'What is this Dominic? Of course you are to come with us,' his mother chided. 'You will need to put on evening dress. I assume you have brought it with you.'

'But not to do the pretty at Almack's,' he grumbled.

There was a good deal more in this vein before he reluctantly agreed to squire his mother and sisters. Almack's, he stigmatised, was the waste of a good evening. When he took his seat in the carriage, it was with a bad grace, issuing a cryptic warning that he wouldn't be around for too long as he had far more interesting prospects in view.

Chapter Eight

Almack's was always crowded even at nine o' clock in the evening. The doors shut promptly at eleven and anyone arriving after that time, no matter how important, was barred. The patronesses controlled every aspect of the club with iron fists and Lady Jersey's vouchers had been hard won.

In the entrance hall Annabel stopped to preen herself in the Venetian mirror, which hung at the bottom of the red-carpeted stairs, but not for long. Her mother was soon ushering both girls upwards into the main salon, ablaze with a thousand candles hanging from crystal chandeliers and tucked into wall sconces. People looked curiously at the small party, finding it difficult to believe that this new young woman was Cassandra's sister. There could be no greater contrast, one tall, willowy, an ice maiden with flaming hair, the other shorter, rounded and an undistinguished brunette. No wonder the gown had to be magenta. It was Annabel's way of seizing some of the attention that always fell so unfairly to her sister.

In the event neither girl lacked for partners. For some Annabel's was a new face and a likely diversion, while for others she promised to be the means of an introduction to the peerless Cassandra. Happily she had no notion of this and smiled benignly on the world as she passed down the rows of the country dance on the arm of one partner after another. Dominic had discovered a few choice spirits who, like him, had been coerced into escorting family members and was content for the moment to bide his time. The evening was young and he felt sure it could only get better.

Only Cassie felt depressed. This night was one like so many others. She smiled gracefully at her partners and diligently performed each dance. Between cotillions and quadrilles she sipped lemonade and made kind conversation with those young damsels sheltering by the wall and too shy to talk to anyone else. But there was emptiness in her heart. Soon it would be time to call the carriage and return home, but for what? In two days' time Sir Hugo would return and her future be decided forever. If she accepted him, this was one engagement that would have to stick.

A sudden flurry at the top of the stairs made her look up. A small brunette, her dark curls glistening in the candlelight, had just made it through the doors before they were locked. The girl looked around her with animation and then turned to her companion, grasping his arm and pointing out the glittering chandeliers and frescoed ceilings. Cassandra drew a sharp intake of breath. It was Luke, of course. Luke, who had never before set foot in this hallowed place, now dancing attendance on the little Spaniard.

She watched as though in a dream as he presented Marianna first to Lady Sefton, one of the patronesses present that night, and then on to Mr Davenant, Lord and Lady Wivenhoe and the Misses Newcombe. The girl had an entrancing smile, Cassie thought, and though she beamed happily on everyone she met, it was clear that she smiled for Luke alone.

She loves him – the thought struck with an explosive force. Cassie's stomach began to churn sickeningly, but why she could not understand. Luke had been dead to her for six years. Why should it matter who his fancy now alighted on?

At that moment she was claimed for a country dance. Somehow she managed mechanically to perform the steps without making a mistake. Out of the corner of her eye she saw Luke and Marianna take the floor. In the years since he'd left England, he had become a graceful dancer, she noticed, and throughout kept up a lively conversation with his partner. It was evident he was delighted to be with Marianna. Social rules dictated that they could not stand up together for more than two dances, but when they were not on the floor, Luke talked to her; when she partnered other men, his gaze was never far away.

And so it went on, dance after dance, while Cassandra watched the clock and prayed for the carriage to arrive. She felt she could not bear to look at them a minute longer and yet her eyes were constantly drawn in their direction. They made a handsome couple and it was clear that others thought so, too. There were many admiring glances and much chatter behind opened fans.

When the orchestra struck up for a waltz, she was relieved to be sitting out the dance. For some years she had been permitted by the patronesses to waltz at Almack's, but Annabel was not in that fortunate position and she had no desire to annoy her sister. She had deliberately kept her dance card free in order to keep Annabel company.

'Miss Latimer, I believe you waltz?'

Luke Trelawny stood before her, immaculate in white ruffled shirt and black long-tailed coat. The crisp white folds of his silk neckcloth were tied in a perfect *trône d'amour*. Well-fitting black satin knee breeches did nothing to disguise the muscular thighs beneath. His attire was that of the most fashionable of London gentlemen, but the lean, tanned face hinted at another story.

Cassie once again found herself struggling to maintain her composure. His eyes, grey as flint, were fixed penetratingly on her and, without speaking, he held out a hand and with the other gestured to the dance floor.

'Thank you, sir,' she said, recovering her wits a little, 'but I do not care to waltz while my sister does not dance.'

Luke glanced indifferently at Annabel, who stared haughtily back at him.

'I'm sure Miss Annabel would not wish to keep you from enjoying a dance she must know you love.'

It was true. Ever since Cassie had learned to waltz, she'd treasured the joy of floating light as thistledown across the ballroom, her feet skimming the floor and her whole body responding to the music. Her sister pursed her lips angrily, but said nothing. Luke was still holding out his hand, his cold eyes seeming now to blaze with something akin to fire. She could not understand his persistence, but found herself mesmerised into accepting his invitation.

A slight pressure on her waist and he had led her into the dance. His arms encircled her body lightly at first, as twisting and pirouetting they became familiar with each other's paces. Soon they were in tune, step by step, movement by movement. The music's lush strains trembled through Cassie's limbs and she lost herself to its rhythms.

Gradually his arms tightened around her and she was acutely aware of the warmth of his body pressing her close. The heady smell of his scent enveloped her as she was held ever more nearly, his face almost bruising her cheek. Carelessly his mouth brushed the top of her hair and, without thinking, she melted more closely into his embrace. They were dancing now as one, their bodies a rhythmical caress which shocked those who witnessed it. Yet the power of Cassandra's beauty held them spellbound. She looked magnificent, almost otherworldly, the green silk of her dress sweeping the floor, little emerald slippers on her feet and that haze of red curls cascading downwards to meet wonderful white skin.

Her mother, seated on one of the small gilded chairs reserved for chaperones, looked up and caught her breath in distress. That was surely Luke Trelawny! She had no idea he had returned to England. And Cassandra was dancing with him and in a fashion that could only be described as provocative! Luke's hand was curved around her waist and his face so close to hers that he could, if he had wished, caress the soft skin almost touching his.

And he did wish. He felt his body hard against this woman he had loved so well. He felt her soft pliable form fusing with his and rejoiced in the sheer physical exultation of the moment. He could have danced with her all night and then – no, he could not think like that. It was his mission to entice her, and the dance must be a part of it. His delight in her proximity was something he must not admit.

The music stopped and for a moment they stood, still touching, and dazed. Then he led her back to the row of chairs, every eye in the room upon them.

'Thank you, Miss Latimer, for a most enjoyable dance,' he said formally.

'It was a pleasure, my lord,' she replied, equally formal.

'We must waltz more – I hope to see you at Almack's again very soon.'

'I fear that is unlikely. I shall not be in London long and I imagine you will soon be leaving yourself.'

'Why so sure?' He looked over to where Marianna was standing, wide-eyed and apprehensive.

'I beg your pardon, but I thought you would be returning to Cornwall to see your mother, to be with Lady Emma.'

'I can return. And return again – if it is worth my coming back,' he replied smoothly.

Once more he looked meaningfully across the room at the young girl waiting patiently for him. Cassandra was bewildered. Seemingly he wished her to understand that Marianna Marquez was the woman who held his heart, yet seconds ago he had been dancing with *her* in so intimate a manner that together they had shocked the assembled company. They had danced as one body, every one of their senses merged. She had felt his warm breath so close she could have reached out and tasted it. And now this.

'I do believe that finally I have found something to keep me in London,' he continued, making it impossible to mistake his meaning.

Cassie gathered up all her reserves of dignity and faced him with a studied calm. 'You are indeed fortunate.'

'I think so. And I trust that in time you will know the same good fortune.'

'You are all kindness, sir.'

His answering bow mocked her. With a kiss of her hand, he turned around and walked across the room to Marianna, who greeted him with a shy smile and outstretched hands.

'Well!' Annabel was at her elbow. 'You're a sly one. You seem to make a habit of meeting Luke Trelawny. You must have known he would be here, but you never said a word. And to see you dancing with him! It was shameless! What would Sir Hugo say?'

'It really is none of your business,' Cassandra snapped.

'It will be if you disgrace the family again by breaking a second engagement.'

'There is no second engagement,' she muttered though clenched teeth, 'and rest assured you are the last person I would ask for advice on my conduct.'

'You could do worse. At least I haven't made myself an object of scandal.'

Cassie had an insane desire to scream at her sister's spitefulness, but constrained by the hallowed portals of Almack's, she kept silent, biting her lip so hard that she drew blood.

'What *were* you thinking of, Cassandra?' Her mother was at her side, throwing more coals on a fire which was already burning brightly. 'To dance in that fashion with a man, and with Luke Trelawny of all people. What would Sir Hugo have said?'

Her mother's echo of the earlier taunt breeched Cassie's iron control. She broke free from Lady Katherine's clasp and said in a stifled voice, 'I'll not wait for the carriage. I will walk home.'

'But you cannot... ' Her mother's words were lost in the distance as she turned swiftly and made for the door.

Luke watched her go. He had been badly disturbed by their dance. It had thrilled him to take Cassandra's glacial beauty in his arms and mould it to his desire. The feeling of her body against his still resonated. While they had danced, the ardent girl of yesterday had broken through that frozen surface – and he had been the one to melt her. She was a magnificent creature and he had gloried in the moment. What was she doing contemplating a mediocre marriage with a milk-and-water nonentity?

But he must think objectively, he told himself, and objectively his plan was working. He should be pleased. He had stirred the embers of passion and soon he would awake such a frenzy of feeling in her that she would be desperate to know his love. He would have proved her inconstancy and be free to walk away. That moment was a little way off, but he should be satisfied with what he'd achieved tonight. He wasn't sure then why the victory felt forlorn.

Chapter Nine

'It's time I took you home, Marianna.'

Luke's tone was decisive. Once Cassandra had left, he'd no inclination to remain at Almack's and was anxious to return the girl to her aunt's care. Serena Foyle had been suffering from a chill for some days and this evening had finally succumbed to a fever and taken to her bed. It was inconvenient. He had hoped to dispense with his escort duties before now, not least because Marianna showed no sign of tiring of his company. He'd expected that once fully launched into the delights of London society, she would cease to have an interest in him. Instead, the wider she spread her acquaintance, the more she seemed to cling.

At the Curzon Street house, Lady Foyle's butler opened the door to them. Luke stepped into the hallway ready to wish Marianna goodnight, but instead of taking the hand he held out, she raised herself on tiptoe to reach his cheek and planted a gentle kiss. Seriously disconcerted, he remonstrated with her.

'You must not do that, Marianna. Remember that I stand in your aunt's place. You must think of me as a friend – an elder brother, if you will.'

'I don't see why,' she exclaimed rebelliously. 'You're by far the most attractive man I know.'

'I thank you for the compliment, but I am not a suitable partner for you.'

She shook her head as if to block out his words. 'I won't believe that. You think me too young to love truly, but you're wrong.'

'I am ten years older than you and my situation is not a happy one.'

'Because you're still in love with Cassandra Latimer?'

Surprise rendered him silent.

'You see, I have her name at my fingertips. How could I not? She is a truly beautiful woman and I cannot blame you for caring for her.'

There were tears in Marianna's eyes and her voice was that of a chastened child. He felt a deep sympathy for her.

'My relationship with Miss Latimer should not concern you,' he rebuked her gently. 'I was not talking of her but of my father's passing. In a very short while I must return to Cornwall. My mother needs my support and I have the management of the estate to consider. It has been allowed to drift since Lord Thomas's death and that cannot continue.'

'I understand,' she breathed eagerly. 'Of course you must go to your mother. But I can wait until you're settled. Then perhaps you'll invite me to Madron Abbey. I would love to see your home.'

'It will be a great pleasure to show both you and your aunt around. But you will come as a guest, Marianna, not as a future bride.'

The girl lowered her head, a mulish expression on her face. Baffled by her obstinacy, Luke spoke more bluntly than he intended. 'I am truly sorry you have feelings I cannot reciprocate, but you must be sensible. You are no longer a child. You have built a fantasy and started to believe in it. For your own sake, you must dismiss it from your mind. In time you will find a man that is right for you.'

'I have found him,' she said, gulping down unshed tears, 'but he is too stupid to see.'

Luke was tired and could argue no longer. He gave a brief nod of farewell and strode to the front door, but before he could open it, she called out to him from the marble stairway, 'Will I see you at Richmond Park tomorrow?'

'Richmond? Ah, yes, the Wivenhoe's alfresco lunch, otherwise known as a picnic.'

'I believe the Park is charming – so much countryside and so near the city. You *are* coming?'

He didn't answer directly. 'I am sure you'll find your aunt a great deal better in the morning and she will be looking forward to accompanying you to Richmond.'

〜

He felt too unsettled by their conversation to return immediately to his hotel. He had decided from the outset that he would put up at Browns rather than opening the house in Grosvenor Square. A solitary stay amid its lonely expanse did not appeal and the few days he planned to be in London would have meant unnecessary disruption for its skeleton staff. But tonight the hotel looked just as uninviting and he needed to clear his head. He would walk a while in the evening air and then look in on one of the gentlemen's clubs that lined St James's Street. A few brandies and a convivial chat or two might help to dispel his gloom.

He had been scrupulous never to suggest to Marianna that he could be more than a friend, but he still felt guilty for causing her unhappiness. It hadn't helped that he had been her constant escort since they'd arrived in London. If he had not spent so much time with her, what had been an incipient affection on board ship would have been nipped in the bud, he was sure. But Lady Foyle had shown herself only too willing to delegate her duties whenever possible and now the wretched woman had taken to her bed. Surely she would be better in the morning.

☙

Luke's resolve that he would no longer be Marianna's escort was broken almost as soon as it was made. A loud banging at his door early the next morning woke him from a deep sleep. It seemed as though he'd hardly been to bed and his head ached from too much brandy the night before. But the hotel porter, breathing heavily in the doorway from his climb up the stairs, was waving a badly folded sheet of paper under his nose and clearly expected an answer.

'Who brought this?' Luke asked blearily.

'A groom, my lord.' The porter was disapproving.

'Whose groom?'

'That I couldn't say, my lord.' The porter held his face aloof, expressing in no uncertain manner that Browns Hotel thought poorly of such early morning intrusions.

Luke pulled back the curtain better to read the note and groaned as the morning light flooded the room.

'Get me some coffee, for heaven's sake.'

'Certainly my lord. Shall I tell the groom to wait?'

'If he wants an answer. But get me that drink.'

He spread the crumpled note out and saw at once that it was from Marianna. He knew almost without reading that it would be a plea to accompany her that morning to the Wivenhoes' picnic. It seemed that her aunt was still not feeling well enough to undertake a long drive. And Marianna wanted so much to see Richmond Park. Could Luke please come and this would be the very last time she would ask, she promised. Aunt Serena had signalled her willingness for Luke to be her escort.

'I've no doubt she has,' he thought savagely. He hardly knew Marianna's aunt, but from his few meetings with her she seemed a woman for whom ill health, as long as it was not too severe, was entirely beneficial.

In an hour he had washed, shaved and dressed, and presented himself in Curzon Street complete with hired curricle. Marianna had evidently been watching at the window for she appeared almost immediately, tripping lightly down the front steps, her face glowing with pleasure. Her patent delight in going on the expedition almost reconciled him to the prospect of attending an event he had hoped to escape.

⌒

For Cassandra there was no escape: she would have to join the family party. She sat at the breakfast table, listlessly toying with a piece of toast and looking tired and pale in the harsh morning light. Her mother had accepted the Wivenhoes' invitation on her behalf weeks ago and at the last moment her siblings had been hurriedly included.

Her heart felt leaden. She was certain that Luke would be there, squiring his new love and flaunting his happiness. She would have to endure their close proximity for hours without giving the slightest hint of discomfort. It would be necessary to put on a guise, not only for her fellows, but for her family, too.

Her mother was worried, she knew. Late last night after Annabel had danced her fill at Almack's and the two had returned home to Mount Street, Lady Katherine had tiptoed into the bedroom. Cassie had pretended sleep and not answered her mother's anxious query. Instead she had lain silent and still, the tears pricking at her eyes and her heart a confusion of pain. She didn't understand what Luke was doing, nor even why she felt so deeply upset by his conduct.

It was evident now that he had not forgiven the broken engagement. But surely his humiliation could not still be so raw that he needed to wage a war. Yet that was exactly what he was doing. One minute he was haranguing her for past crimes, the next he was caressing her – with his smile, his voice, even his body. When last night she had danced with him so freely, she had been careless of gossip, careless of her reputation. She had given no thought to guarding her feelings; she had allowed herself to desire. Allowed him to stir emotions within her that she'd schooled herself never to feel again and now, today, she would have to face him once more. She would have to put on the performance of her life.

'Where's the ham?' Dominic demanded, as he breezed into the breakfast room and busily searched the side table.

He looked fresh and full of energy, despite having slept little.

'Cassie, where's the ham? Bel, you've eaten it all,' he accused, as his younger sister appeared in the doorway, elaborately dressed in a bright green velvet spencer over daffoldil-yellow silk.

'I've had a great many things to do other than eating breakfast, you stupid boy. If you want ham, ring the bell for more.'

'Who's stupid? At least I don't look like a parrot.' He gestured to Annabel's preferred apparel for driving in Richmond Park.

'Someone should tell you that making personal remarks is offensive.'

'Someone should tell you that dressing like a pantomime dame is even more offensive.'

'Do stop both of you.' Cassandra's quiet voice intervened, the steely tone surprising them into silence.

'Hoity toity,' Dominic said, half under his breath. 'By the way,' he offered as he sat down at the table, his plate groaning with devilled kidneys and a couple of eggs he'd unearthed, 'd'you know what they're saying in the clubs?'

'The rubbish that men bandy amongst themselves is of no interest to us,' Annabel said haughtily.

'It might be since it concerns a very close neighbour of ours.'

Both sisters looked at him, Cassandra's face devoid of expression, but even paler than before.

'Luke Trelawny. You saw him last night at Almack's?'

'Of course we saw him.' Annabel was impatient.

'He was with that pretty, dark-haired girl. She's from Argentina.'

'We know.' Annabel's tone was getting dangerous.

'Bet you didn't know the odds are mounting on his marrying the girl within the year. Can't be any earlier – he's in mourning – bad *ton*.'

'What do you know of bad *ton*?'

'It might surprise you, Miss Superior, just how much I do know. Anyway a lot of money was changing hands last night, betting on the marriage. Lucky old Luke, eh? Comes back from some outlandish place and walks straight into a title and now a fortune.'

His sisters looked blankly at him.

'Loaded,' he said succinctly. 'That's the word. Full of juice and a good looker too. What more could a man ask? I talked to her myself last night. Introduced by the *grande dame* herself, Countess Lieven. I think she thought Marianna Marquez – what a name! – was in need of younger company.'

'She certainly got it with you.' Annabel's tone was derisive.

'And she enjoyed it, may I say.' He ruminated for a while, chewing thoughtfully on the last kidney. 'Taking little thing, I thought, though she never quite mastered the steps of the cotillion.'

'And naturally you are the supreme exponent of the dance.'

Cassandra got up swiftly, unable to bear her siblings' bickering a minute longer. Dominic's words had washed away her earlier resolve. How could she possibly keep an impassive countenance when she knew for sure that Luke was planning to marry? She would make her excuses. The family must go without her.

'What's the matter, Cassie?' It was Annabel stopping her at the door. 'Can't face seeing your old beau getting wed? Why should it matter to you? After all, aren't you marrying Sir Hugo?'

Dominic gaped. He knew little of the events of six years ago, having been away at school, and had not realised the effect his news might have. But it was Annabel's words that cut Cassandra most deeply. In her pique, her sister had arrowed straight to the question that was causing Cassie such agitation. Why *did* it matter to her that Luke was to marry? She must prove that it did not. She must prove Annabel wrong. There would be no evasions – she would go to the picnic.

Chapter Ten

It seemed that the Wivenhoes could not have chosen a better day for their alfresco party. An almost cloudless sky and an unusually warm April sun enabled their guests to view the beauty of the park from open carriages. Herds of red and fallow deer grazed undisturbed in a pastoral landscape of rolling hills, grassy slopes and woodland gardens. The park's ancient trees were already clad in the fresh, untouched green of spring, and beneath their shade, the light shimmered a daffodil gold. The company drove leisurely through this sylvan setting before arriving at a central pagoda, where they were to be served refreshments.

Cassie, with her mother and sister, were soon ensconced on its terrace, sitting comfortably on a padded *chaise* and sipping a soft drink. Servants bustled to and fro, some bringing additional cushions and blankets for the older members of the group, and others plates of dainty sandwiches and small iced cakes. Annabel made ready to plunder the dish of madeleines left temptingly on their table.

'What a beautiful place,' Lady Katherine murmured to her hostess. 'And such a wonderful day!'

'Indeed – it seems that summer is already with us.' Lady

Wivenhoe's face wore a wide smile as she mingled among her guests gathered on the terrace.

Cassandra hardly heard them. The cream muslin gown she wore, trimmed with delicate chartreuse lace, might pay homage to the season, but her spirits remained locked in winter. She felt frozen in time, yet her mind was never still, never at peace. She felt she might be going mad.

For the hundredth time she tried to understand why in that faraway summer she had acted as she had. Luke had meant so much to her and yet, with hardly a thought, it seemed, she had returned his ring and thrown herself at a man who even then she'd suspected was not to be trusted. Why, oh why, had she done such a thing? Only the intoxication of her first sexual awakening could explain the wilful breaking into pieces of the jigsaw of her life.

But it was not quite the first awakening, was it? There was that evening in Cornwall when she and Luke had thrown themselves into the sea together. They had been just a little crazy and the swim had sparked something deep and elemental between them, or so she had thought. But almost immediately he'd turned away. He had not wanted that intimate bond and she'd been left bewildered, ashamed of the physical ache that had taken hold of her.

And then the trip to London with all its glamour, all its glories, had pushed everything else out of her mind. Joshua had swam into her presence, a man who was more than willing to set her body alight. She had loved him dreadfully. No, she corrected herself, she had lusted for him dreadfully. And lust had its own shameful penance. She'd thought she had paid the price, but it seemed she must continue to pay.

In the distance she could see Marianna laughing and prattling with Luke. On occasions he responded in similar vein, but there was a serious expression on his face which seemed at odds with the frolicking of his younger companion. At length the girl seemed to grow tired of entertaining him and turned to Dominic, who had just then emerged at her side and was making ready to reintroduce himself. When the two young people began to stroll together across the greensward towards King Henry's mound, the highest point of the park, Cassie thought that Luke looked almost relieved. How strange. But she had probably imagined it.

Annabel, meanwhile, was maintaining a critical commentary on her fellow guests as they strolled along the intersecting pathways which met at the pagoda. As each new costume passed beneath the terrace, it duly received the full force of her disapproval. Her own ensemble had attracted a mixed response and she was still smarting from some of the remarks she'd overheard.

Her mother, anxious to restore her to good spirits, extended a comforting arm, but in doing so caught her hand in the intricate pattern of the lace tablecloth and spilled the contents of her glass on to the disputed outfit.

'Mama, just look what you've done – how clumsy!'

He mother looked at her reprovingly. 'It was an accident, Annabel, and I am sorry for it. But your rudeness does you no credit.'

For once Annabel looked abashed. Her nerves were on end. She had dreamed of making her mark in *ton* society, but so far society had shown an entire lack of interest. This morning she had tried particularly hard with her *toilette*, but it appeared her efforts were still not enough. To add to her misery her elder sister sat next to her, seemingly serene and unruffled, but looking effortlessly lovely and attracting frequent glances of open admiration from the other guests.

'Come with me,' Lady Latimer urged, making for the small cloakroom at the rear of the pagoda, 'we must sponge your dress immediately.'

Annabel trailed miserably behind her and Cassandra was left alone with her thoughts. But not for long. The sound of firm footsteps on the stairway leading to the terrace made her look up.

'I trust I see you well, Miss Latimer.'

'Thank you, Lord Trelawny, I am most well,' she answered, her tone curt.

'And how are you enjoying Richmond Park?' he pursued.

'It is very beautiful.'

'You have seen it only from a carriage? It is even better viewed at close quarters.'

She nodded briefly but said nothing and averted her gaze. His shapely legs encased in well-fitting breeches and riding boots of dazzling gloss were an unnecessary distraction.

'If you would you care to take a stroll, I would be happy to escort you.' He was smiling and for once the grey eyes smiled with him.

'Thank you, but I have already walked a distance around the park,' she lied.

'Then you are before me.' A slight flush crept into his

lean cheek as he recognised the snub.

'It would appear so.'

He had been studying her from a distance, seen the sadness in her face, and felt his determination waver. But her flagrant rejection of his courtesies hardened his heart and spurred him once more into attack.

'Your energy surprises me, Miss Latimer. I would have thought you had little left after last night's magnificent dancing.'

'I am not such a poor creature.' And the flash in her emerald eyes was unmistakeable. He remembered well that indomitable spirit and once more his heart softened.

'You were never a poor creature,' he said quietly. 'Far from it, as I recall. I still have the scars as testimony.'

She looked at him in surprise.

'I spent my childhood following you,' he offered. 'Jumping rocks, climbing trees, hacking my way through woods. It was a tough training.'

Her face broke into the shadow of a smile, the troubles of the present for the moment cast aside.

'And were you always the follower?'

'Always. I rarely saw more than a tangle of red curls in the distance.'

Her smile broadened. 'Was I that far ahead?'

He smiled wryly. 'There were times when I got to see the back of two skinny brown legs, but never much more.'

'Why did you carry on if it meant so many scars?'

'Why wouldn't I? Life was a daily adventure with you and the scars I suffered simple ones. Childhood was the easy part. It was growing up that was difficult.'

'How sad it is that we cannot stay children,' she blurted out. Her smile had vanished.

'Sadly we cannot. Nor undo the life we have chosen.'

'But we can start again? Surely?' His reminiscences had emboldened her.

His face, though, had lost its earlier warmth and his response was stern. 'I fear not. We are prisoners of the life we make and must live with that knowledge.'

'I cannot agree,' she said vehemently. 'That would be to hold cheap the human spirit and its capacity for change.'

'I have never held your spirit cheap, Miss Latimer.'

His words were oblique, but she knew their meaning well enough. She felt sick to her stomach. He was still her enemy.

'Nor I yours, Lord Trelawny,' she managed at last.

'It seems that we are agreed on one thing at least.'

'It is immaterial whether we agree or disagree. If you will excuse me...'

And with that she rose in one fluid movement, pushed back her chair and was tripping down the steps before he realised her intention. The breeze caught her mane of red curls and ravelled them wildly into a fiery haze. He felt a momentary madness to rush after her and take hold of that hair, smooth it, caress it, cover it in kisses. It deserved to be worshipped.

'Luke? I thought it must be you. How good to see you again. You were at Almack's last night, I think, but I had no opportunity of speaking to you.'

Lady Latimer had appeared from the rear of the pagoda and was now standing close to him, looking, despite her words, not at all pleased. She had glimpsed the figure of Cassandra in the distance walking rapidly away towards the lake and drawn her own conclusions.

'Lady Katherine! How good to see such an old friend.' Luke felt genuine pleasure at meeting the woman who, for much of his life, had been a second mother to him.

'I have to admit some surprise at seeing you in London,' Lady Latimer returned. 'I had no idea you were in the country.' Her tone verged on reproof. 'But naturally I am delighted that you have returned safely. I make no doubt the voyage was a testing one. Your mother must be overjoyed to have you home again.'

He looked a little self-conscious, but felt there was no point in dissembling. 'She has only just learned that I am in England.'

Lady Latimer raised her eyebrows. 'Forgive me, but should you not have apprised her of your safety immediately.'

'I have been a little delayed in London, but intend to leave for Cornwall within the week. By now she will have had my letter telling her when to expect me.'

'I see,' she said thoughtfully, though in truth she did not. Whatever could have kept him in London? She had heard gossip about a young woman from Buenos Aires, someone he had supposedly escorted to England, but surely that would not have prevented him making for home as soon as he was able.

'Emma is sure to be in some anxiety waiting for you.'

Katherine fixed him with a severe expression. She felt strongly that he should be with his mother in Cornwall and almost as strongly that he should not be in London upsetting Cassandra. Particularly not at this delicate moment when her daughter was poised to accept Sir Hugo.

In the short time they had been talking she had noticed the sky begin to cloud alarmingly. A sudden clap of thunder shook the pagoda roof and in seconds shattered the gentleness of the April morning. A moment later shards of rain were beating on the woodwork and bouncing off the grass. The party on the terrace hastily decamped to the back of the pagoda for shelter, but Lady Latimer bethought herself of Cassie, under the open skies and without protection.

Luke was before her. He grabbed one of the umbrellas presciently provided by Lady Wivenhoe for her guests and ran down the steps, striding rapidly in the direction he had last seen Cassandra heading. On the way he passed a furious Dominic and a joyful Marianna. The rain had obliterated Dominic's carefully crafted hair style *à la Brutus* to the huge amusement of his companion. Despite being severely buffeted by the sudden tempest, her peals of laughter rang out across the park.

Luke ignored the noisy pair and hurried on. He found Cassandra in minutes, standing motionless by the waters of the storm-tossed lake. She was drenched, her skin translucent and gleaming beneath the downpour, and the curves of her lithe figure apparent through the sodden muslin of the once-beautiful dress.

Cassie turned at that moment and her face wore such a look of unhappiness that he wanted to take her into his arms there and then and put a stop to the nonsense he had started. But he knew that beyond the fragility lay pure steel. The deep-green eyes flashed anger at him and bade him keep his distance, just as surely as if she had spoken.

Mutely, he offered her the shelter of an umbrella. She was forced into a smile at this ineffectual gesture since there was no chance she could become any wetter.

'Thank you for the thought, Lord Trelawny, but I fear your rescue comes too late.' Her words, mere social courtesy on the surface, resonated with a deeper meaning.

He looked at the rain-soaked figure before him, his gaze lingering unwillingly on her form. The long shapely legs and the soft swell of her breasts were clearly visible through the transparent muslin and he knew desperate desire. He moved towards her as though in a dream.

Chapter Eleven

She remained where she stood, unflinching. She saw his arms slowly reach out to her and then her long, cold fingers were held tightly within his, sending a warmth coursing through her body until she was tingling from head to toe, from her saturated slippers to the riot of wet curls framing her face.

They stood, body to body, for what seemed an age. She felt her pulse beat tumultuously and her limbs tremble as wave after wave of heat flamed through every small part of her, melting resistance, dissolving protest. His hands were on her waist, pulling her urgently towards him, his body hard against hers. Now his hands were sliding upwards and over her breasts, cradling them, brushing at their fullness and sending swirls of shocked pleasure spiralling through her. Onwards and his hands were cupping her cheeks, tipping her face to meet his. She looked into his eyes and slowly drowned.

'Cassie,' he began, the soft whisper of his voice flowing through her and reaching to her heart. 'Cassie, I – '

'Cassandra! Come quickly.' It was her mother's urgent tones. 'We must get you home immediately or you will be ill.'

Lady Latimer was hurrying towards them, waving yet another umbrella. The moment of intimacy was at an end, faded into the misty rain.

Cassie's hands slipped from his and she walked away, leaving him to curse her power and his weakness. This was not what he'd intended, to be caught in the web of his own spinning. He must subdue this wretched, uncontrollable passion that once more threatened to tear him apart. He must stay aloof, even while he continued to lure her into betraying herself. There were only a few days left to accomplish his plan and every one of them must count.

By now Lady Latimer had reached his side and was observing him with disapproval.

'Miss Marquez is ready to leave, Luke. I understand that you are her escort?'

'Thank you for recalling me to my duties, Lady Katherine,' he replied stiffly, and began to make his way back to the pagoda.

Cassandra caught his words on the air and was deeply puzzled. Could he really be speaking of his future wife when he talked of "duties"? And if he were promised to Marianna Marquez, why had he allowed himself to hold her so long, to touch her so intimately? During their scandalous dance at Almack's she'd imagined for a moment that he felt the same attraction as she. But only for a moment. His hurtful rejection had soon disabused her.

This time, though, she could not be mistaken. There had been a charge so powerful between them that she was left dazed. Naked desire – that's what she had felt. Not even the errant Joshua, in her days as a green girl, had aroused such fervour in her.

And it was Luke, a man she had once dismissed as fitting only to be a friend, who had provoked it. Nothing made sense. Luke today must be a very different man to the one she'd once known – or maybe she had never really known him. Perhaps she had been too young, too inexperienced, to recognise what might have been. The irony of the situation hit her hard. It seemed that she could feel passion for this man, a passion that shook her to the very core, but only now that he was promised to another woman.

She thought back to the moment when she'd first seen Luke on his return from the university. He had grown into a dashing young man, a figure far superior to any of her local suitors and she was no longer the skinny, freckled tomboy he had known from the past. She had watched with amusement his stupefied expression when he'd first caught sight of her and knew instantly that she had captivated him. His jealousy of the gaggle of admirers who daily haunted Boskenna was evident and she thought guiltily of how she'd enjoyed playing one man off against another.

In her defence she was hardly more than a child and the game was a heady one. The distant cousin who was to present her at Court had fallen seriously ill and her planned come-out had not materialised. The excitement of having young men vie for her favours was a pleasing compensation.

Luke's courtship had been swift. He had capitalised on their long childhood friendship to infiltrate her life with ease, and in no time he'd succeeded in banishing his rivals and filling the centre of her world. Suddenly she was engaged and unsure of quite how it had happened. It seemed natural to be promising to spend the rest of her life with him, but also something of an anticlimax. She had been exhilarated by the excitements of the chase and revelled in the handsome and vigorous man Luke had become, yet she knew him almost too well. There were no secrets, or so it seemed, no concealed feelings, no hidden fire.

Until, that is, that one evening in the cove. In her memory she retraced their steps that night. They had walked out together after an early dinner, escaping the last frenetic preparations for the morrow when they would travel to London in company with Lady Trelawny. Cassie was to stay at the Trelawny's town house and Luke's mother was to supervise her purchase of bride clothes, her own mother being unable to leave her younger siblings for any protracted period.

It had been a beautiful evening in early summer and they'd sauntered at dusk towards the sea along a lane already heavy with hawthorn. Very soon the granite rocks and soft white sand of their beloved cove came into view. The sea was flat calm and Luke had begun to skim stones along the surface of the water. She had joined in, trying to make her stones bounce farther. It was an old game of their childhood. The competition between them grew fierce and he shouted with delight when he made a final, unbeatable shot. Beneath the newly polished surface, he was still not much more than a boy.

With mischief in her eyes, she had challenged him to another contest from their childhood: who could swim out the farthest without pausing for breath? He'd demurred; they were not dressed for the water and in any case it hardly seemed proper. In answer, she had stripped off her clothes down to her chemise, leaving Luke staring in wonderment at the lithe, willowy figure standing so close to him.

Then he had been seized by the same madness and was stripped and plunging into the cool water before she had time to reach the sea's edge. They had swum out until they were both exhausted, then drifted lazily back towards the shore, the waters around them silvered by the moon newly risen in a clear sky. She was floating beside him and on impulse, it seemed, he'd caught hold of her, encircling her waist with his arms and tangling his face in her salt-soaked curls. The feel of his hard, male body against hers took her breath away and she knew a frantic desire to hold him close, to meld her body to his. Her legs looped around him and their flesh met in a mutual caress. Even now she grew hot thinking of it.

But the moment was over almost as soon as it arrived, the spark extinguished, and they were scrambling up the beach and into their clothes as though pursued by the Furies, ashamed of that instant of burning connection.

The next day they had left for London and a round of parties, routs, ridottos, balls, such as she had never before encountered: a kaleidoscope of pleasure which took over her life. As an affianced woman she had enjoyed the freedom it conferred, freedom to talk unchaperoned with other men, freedom to dance and even to flirt with them, and freedom to meet a Joshua.

A magnificent rout party was to be held that evening at the Seftons' London mansion, a short distance from Mount Street. Annabel, insatiable as always for *ton* society, was greatly excited at attending such a prestigious event. It was sure to afford her a splendid hunting ground for potential partners. The torrential rain had done Cassandra little harm other than a ruined dress, but she was grateful that it served as an excuse for staying home that night. She was more than happy to spend a quiet evening by herself when the alternative was the painful spectacle of Luke and Marianna together.

She was lying curled on her bed, flicking through back numbers of *Lady's Magazine,* when her mother slid quietly into the room. 'Have you seen these extraordinary models, Mama? They must be at least ten feet tall,' she said, with an attempt at gaiety. The emaciated females depicted were so long and thin as almost to disappear off the page.

Her mother smiled slightly. 'Extraordinary indeed! They would be quite terrifying to meet in the flesh.'

She sat down on the bed and took her daughter's hand. 'I came to say that I'm not attending the Seftons' rout tonight. There is little need for my presence: their house is within easy walking distance and Dominic can act as escort to his sister for the evening. It will do him no harm to take on a little responsibility while he is enjoying his vacation. And it will give us the chance to have a comfortable coze.'

Cassie's heart sank; an evening spent alone with her mother was the last thing she wanted. Pressing her hand to her forehead in a gesture of pain, she hoped that she looked convincing.

'I'm so glad you're staying home, Mama. I'm not feeling at all the thing. I must have caught a chill in that downpour.'

Her mother glanced pointedly at the magazines her daughter had been devouring and Cassandra redoubled her efforts.

'I've been trying to distract myself with these,' she murmured, leafing through the periodicals with a weary motion, 'but without much success. I feel so hot – I think I may be developing a fever. It's probably best if I retire early and try to sleep it off.'

It was unlikely that Lady Katherine would believe in her illness, but Cassie was beyond caring. After this day's events, her mother's gentle enquiries would be the last straw. Until Luke arrived in London, her future path had been clear, if uninviting. The time had come for her to step out of her sister's way and there had been a simple choice: wed a good man who loved her or remain a spinster without consequence or respect.

For years she had kept at bay even the most determined of suitors. A glacial reserve had served her well, but now it had been ruptured. She had begun to feel again. The dance at Almack's, the encounter by the lake, had begun an unstoppable thaw which threatened to trigger an avalanche of feelings she must not entertain. Today by the lakeside she had known no reserve. She had responded ardently to her body's impulse, wanting desperately that Luke possess her. How truly shocking!

But *his* conduct was even more shocking. He was not hers to be possessed and yet he had sought her out, danced with her as though he could have danced her into bed – she blushed deeply at the thought – embraced her, caressed her, imprinted her with his passion. And at the very same time he had used every possible opportunity to taunt her with his new-found love, the girl it appeared he was ready to make his wife.

It had to be part of his plan to pay her back for betraying him – there was no other explanation. No matter how softly he spoke or how enamoured he appeared, he was intent on exacting a penance from her. The thought overwhelmed her. She felt as though a giant hand had descended out of nowhere and squeezed every vestige of life from her heart and her body. She was no longer the woman who had bid Sir Hugo farewell just a few days ago and she dreaded meeting him again.

Chapter Twelve

Sir Hugo, meanwhile, was looking in vain for his beloved at the Seftons' rout. He had despatched his affairs at Thorne Park as swiftly as he could and returned to London in time to attend the evening event. He knew that Cassandra had been invited and was hoping he would have the chance to talk privately with her.

He had unfinished business and was anxious to conclude it as soon as possible. He had no doubt of her answer – she had made it plain that he was her preferred suitor – and had not her sister called him Cassandra's fiancé, making it clear that the Latimer family expected an imminent betrothal? But he wanted their relationship settled, and the world to know. He was a man who liked an ordered life and was looking forward to planning their future together.

'How good to see you back so soon, Sir Hugo!' It was Annabel, looking a little less exotic this evening in rose-pink lustring.

Sir Hugo searched his memory, for he was sure he should know this young woman.

'Annabel Latimer, Cassandra's sister.' She helped him out.

'Why, of course. I am very pleased to make your acquaintance again, Miss Annabel.' Sir Hugo sounded genuinely glad to see her. If she were here, then Cassandra would not be far away.

'And how was your visit to Thorne Park?'

'Busy, very busy,' Sir Hugo mused, 'but restful, too. I find the house possesses great tranquillity.'

'So I believe,' she said encouragingly. 'Its aura is said to be most mellow. I read in *Ackerman's Repository* that it is one of the oldest houses in England.'

Sir Hugo's interest increased. 'I knew that certainly, but I had not realised that Thorne Park had been featured in such a well-known journal.'

'You are too modest, Sir Hugo. You must know that you own a most famous property,' Annabel cooed.

Feeling that the subject had now been exhausted, Sir Hugo was eager to discover his beloved's whereabouts.

'Cassandra?' Annabel responded carelessly. 'She's not here this evening.'

'How is this? Surely she was invited?'

'Naturally she was invited, but she didn't care to come.'

Sir Hugo's well-bred eyebrows rose slightly and Annabel saw her chance. 'Cassie is invited everywhere, Sir Hugo. She is the toast of the *ton*, I believe. She picks and chooses as she wishes.'

'I must admit I am a little disappointed. I returned from Thorne Park today on purpose to see her and was sure she would be here.' He breathed a small sigh and looked slightly wounded.

'She probably didn't give a thought to your being here

tonight. I fear she isn't the most reliable of people.'

'Miss Latimer has always been most scrupulous about keeping appointments,' Sir Hugo said a trifle sharply.

Sensing that she might have gone a little too far, Annabel carefully backtracked. 'Ah, now I recall – she was not feeling too well earlier this evening. She must have thought it best to stay at home.'

'Not well? But she was perfectly well when I last saw her.'

'Don't be concerned, Sir Hugo. There is nothing to worry over, I assure you. My family attended a picnic in Richmond Park today and all of us were caught in the rain. It meant nothing to me, of course, I am built of stronger stuff, but Cassandra is a little fragile.'

'Yes, indeed, almost ethereal, I sometimes think.'

This was not the effect that Annabel had hoped for, but she recovered quickly. 'I'm sure her decision to stay home was right. She would not have wanted to attend with blotched cheeks and a red nose.'

Sir Hugo looked aghast at this unimaginable picture of his loved one and sought reassurance. 'I trust that Miss Latimer is not seriously unwell.'

'She will be greatly improved in the morning, I'm sure. She is some years older than me, you know, and needs a little time to recover her spirits. And if she had come tonight, I doubt she would have had the energy to dance,' Annabel finished pointedly, as the orchestra struck up for a country dance.

The Seftons had decided that although refreshments and conversation were normally deemed sufficient for a rout, their guests would be treated to a little informal dancing if they so wished. Sir Hugo, mindful of his duties as a gentleman, immediately begged Annabel to grant him the favour of a dance. She accepted primly and only spoilt the effect by scowling at her brother who was leading Marianna Marquez down the opposite line of country dancers.

'Is that not your brother I see, Miss Annabel?'

'Yes', she admitted in a bored voice, 'he is supposed to be my escort, though he chooses rather to dance attendance on some foreigner.'

The foreigner was putting on a good show of enjoying herself despite an aching heart. Ever since the evening at Almack's, when Luke's lack of interest had been made so brutally clear, her happy spirits had been slowly and surely evaporating. The dance came to an end and Dominic, tired of having his feet crushed by an inattentive partner, said hopefully, 'You don't want to dance any more, do you?'

She shook her head and looked around the room in search of her aunt. Even her chaperone appeared to have deserted her.

Sensing her dejection, Dominic tried a diversion. 'Have you ever gambled?'

She opened her eyes wide. 'My father sometimes used to gamble in Buenos Aires, but he said that the clubs were not fit for young girls.'

'There are clubs like that in London, too.' Dominic grinned. 'But you don't have to go to them to gamble. There's usually the chance at most parties.'

'Really? You can gamble here?' She was genuinely taken aback. To be offered gambling in what seemed the wealthiest and noblest of settings was curious.

'Let's find out. I think they've set up a hazard table or maybe faro in the next room. Would you like to watch the game?'

It was a distraction. She would go and watch until her aunt found her. They strolled into the adjoining card room and saw that a game of faro was in full swing. The bank had already amassed what looked like a fortune in rouleaus and the expressions on the players' faces ranged from boredom through irritation to downright vexation.

With Dominic as her willing tutor, it took little time for Marianna to understand the simple rules. As she watched card after card emerging from the spring-loaded faro box, heard the click of tokens changing hands and felt the building tension as losses and wins followed in quick succession, she began to forget about the interview with Luke. Gambling, it seemed, was the perfect antidote for a broken heart.

'I want to play, too,' she whispered.

Looking into her glowing face, Dominic stifled any misgivings and deftly inserted her into the circle. Very soon she was in the thick of the play. Her flushed face and sparkling eyes spoke of pleasure, but Dominic began to feel uncomfortable. She had taken to the game rather too enthusiastically, he thought, and now, looking around the table at their fellow gamblers, he didn't like what he saw.

To Marianna they appeared unexceptional. The women perhaps were showing too much *décolletée*, but they were sumptuously and fashionably dressed and hardly differed from their sisters dancing a few yards away. And the gentlemen were very correctly attired in evening dress and treated each other with a jokey politeness that spoke of long-term intimacy. But from Dominic's limited knowledge some of those gathered around the table were hardened gamesters and whispers of compromised virtue swirled around a number of the women. There was at least one wholly disreputable rake in the room.

Lord Amesbury lazed at the head of the table in charge of the faro bank. It was customary for the wealthiest of patrons to take turns in running the bank and Robert Amesbury enjoyed riches enough to run a hundred faro banks and still have plenty left to indulge his every whim. At that moment his whim was turning to Marianna.

His weary eyes rested gratefully on her, savouring her youthful beauty and unsophisticated delight in this novel entertainment. As his eyes ran over her assessingly, she looked up from the table and caught his glance. She wasn't sure what to think of him. He certainly made a splendid figure, looking as though he could have stepped straight out of one of Byron's poems, but there was something in his glittering gaze that disconcerted her and she looked quickly away.

Dominic had seen that gaze, too. 'Let's go back to the salon and find a cold drink,' he suggested.

'Not yet, Dominic. Just one more wager. Next time I'm bound to win.'

'That's what everyone thinks, and you won't.'

'How do you know that? Just because you always lose.'

'I don't always lose – well, not all of the time,' he finished lamely.

'There you are, then. It's my turn to win.'

'I should take you back to the salon. Your aunt will murder me if she knows I've brought you in here.'

'If you're afraid of my aunt, you'd better go.

He was getting heartily bored with this recalcitrant girl. Perhaps if he upped and left she would follow. 'I'm going then, and if you're wise you'll come too,' he whispered rather too loudly.

Lord Amesbury raised a quizzical eyebrow, causing Dominic to flush with annoyance and make haste to leave. Once out of the room, he shrugged off any qualms at deserting Marianna. The girl wasn't his responsibility and he wanted to enjoy the rest of his evening.

Chapter Thirteen

Cassie came down to breakfast the next morning still looking pale. She had spent a difficult night, unable to sleep with any ease. For hours her mind had refused to stop its constant churning and it was dawn before she found any rest. She had made a decision.

From now on she must ignore Luke's behaviour. She had allowed herself to be manipulated, to be too easily swayed by feelings she should never have entertained. With great severity she reminded herself that she was the only person responsible for her actions. If she could hold to that determination, she would cope with what lay ahead. Annabel's chatter had alerted her to Sir Hugo's return to town and she knew that it would not be long before he renewed his proposal. She must be ready.

She saw that her mother must have taken note of her pallor and was looking at her with gentle concern. 'Cassie, are you well enough to pay that morning call on Lady Foyle?'

'I feel a good deal better, thank you, Mama. I'm happy to go.'

It was a lie for Marianna was likely to be present, and

the thought of meeting the girl so soon after the disaster of the picnic troubled her. But she needed to appear unconcerned in the face of any suspicions her mother might harbour.

Lady Katherine looked relieved. Her daughter seemed not to have been so badly affected by yesterday's events as she had feared. And she had a mountainous collection of letters awaiting her attention. Cassandra's offer to attend on Serena Foyle was most welcome.

'Perhaps Annabel would care to accompany you?' her mother suggested tentatively. But Annabel instantly forestalled that notion; she was far too busy this morning organising her steadily increasing wardrobe.

Cassie was more than willing to go attended only by her maid; a walk to Curzon Street would be a pleasant escape from the house. The rain clouds, which yesterday had appeared out of nowhere, had vanished entirely, and in their place was the deepest blue covering and a spring sun already climbing the sky and warming the world.

She sauntered along the tree-lined pavements with Rosa by her side. The slightest of breezes caught at the primrose ribbons in her hair and twisted them in and out of the auburn curls that framed her face. With each step on this glorious day she felt herself walking away from discord and entering a place of deep calm.

The night had brought counsel, if not rest. Whatever the truth of Luke's relationship with Marianna, it was their affair, not hers. It was immaterial, too, whether the passion he had poured on her was genuine or simply feigned as part of his plan to punish. Certainly those moments by the lakeside, moments scorched into her consciousness, had not appeared feigned. He had seemed as fevered, as impassioned, as she.

'Curzon Street is the third turning on the right, Miss Cassandra,' the maid reminded her. 'What number is Lady Foyle's?'

'Number Twelve, I believe,' she answered absently, her thoughts scurrying on.

No, it wasn't important whether or not Luke had meant the caresses he'd lavished on her– what was important was how she reacted to them. And so far her reactions had been far from laudable. Twice in the last few days she had been overcome by desire for a man who should mean nothing to her. The old Cassandra, rebellious and passionate, had risen again, and exploded into the ardour of yesterday's embrace.

But she was no longer the girl she had been and instead must be true to her new life. How could she have allowed herself to behave in that fashion when she was as good as promised to another man? And such an upright man, who would never give her cause for concern. Sir Hugo would never find himself locked in a fervent embrace with a lover from his past! The unlikely image made her smile.

'This day is meant for smiling, is it not?'

A male voice cleaved through her thoughts. Luke was there, directly in her path, doffing his curly brimmed beaver, his grey eyes smiling and flecked by the sun's rays. He wore hessians, polished to a blinding finish, and a pair of close-fitting cream pantaloons that displayed his legs to advantage. She forced herself to remember the vows of only a few minutes ago.

'It is a most beautiful morning,' she agreed, trying to keep her voice steady and her gaze neutral. Trying very hard not to think of their last encounter, their last few minutes together. A difficult silence began to develop.

'At least we can be certain we won't suffer a soaking today,' he said mildly, in an attempt to diffuse the tension. 'I trust you suffered no ill effects from yesterday's downpour.'

'Indeed, no, she responded, relieved at this unexceptional topic of conversation, 'though I felt very sorry for the Wivenhoes. They had taken so much trouble over the arrangements only to see their plans ruined.'

'Forces of nature cannot be gainsaid.'

He had meant the remark lightly, but it was not the most felicitous he could have made. A force of nature had destroyed the icy reserve which for years had defended Cassandra, and he was responsible. He was not proud of that. In the night watches he had argued himself into never-ending circles. It was essential that he prove her base, yet she was the woman who excited him, entranced him. His plan was a clever strategy, he told himself, yet he felt shame at its tawdriness.

The image of Cassie's abject unhappiness haunted him, knowing that he was its architect. It turned out that her unhappiness was his also. Yesterday by the lakeside he had wanted to take her into his arms and kiss the tears away one by one. And he *had* taken her in his arms. More than that, he'd felt every beautiful curve of her and his heart had sung. When he'd caressed her beneath that sheeting rain, she had responded as ardently as he could ever wish. What was that but inconstancy! He had surely proved what he'd set out to, proved that she was incapable of being true. By rights he should feel free, released from her spell, so why did he not?

In truth, in the deepest recesses of his heart, he could not believe her a false woman. She had been disloyal once, in a lifetime of loyalty. So why had she behaved so much out of character and to such devastating result? During the endless night, watching the shadows darken into unrelieved blackness, watching the dewy light of dawn creep gradually into the four corners of his room, he, too, had come to a decision. He had to know why she had betrayed him. He had to hear it from her lips. If he could understand that, he was certain that at last he would be able to lay the past to rest.

Silence stretched between them once more and again he was the one to break it.

'Are you on your way anywhere in particular? If so, may I escort you?'

'Thank you, but I am almost there. I am to pay a morning call on Lady Foyle.'

'Then let me offer you my arm,' he said briskly, nodding dismissal to Rosa. 'You may return home, your mistress will not need you.'

Before Cassie could protest, her maid had begun retracing her steps to Mount Street. She did not take the offered arm, but stood facing him on the narrow pavement. 'That was high-handed, Lord Trelawny. It is my prerogative to dismiss my maid.'

'I'm sorry if you disapprove. I have no wish to quarrel with you.'

'That would certainly be a change,' she returned acidly. His arrogance had helped her regain something of her poise.

'I hoped that I might speak with you alone.' His tone was level, giving no hint of what he was feeling. And for a moment he appeared unwilling to go on, unable to find the words he needed.

'Shall we walk?' he suggested at last.

She nodded and they began to stroll side by side, taking care to maintain a distance from each other. The move- ment, though, seemed to act as a release. 'After yesterday,' he said, 'I've done some thinking. In fact, a good deal of thinking.'

He paused and Cassie waited, her composure once more in danger of slipping away. What was he about to say? That he loved her? That after their impassioned lovemaking, he still cared deeply for her and could no longer consider marrying Marianna Marquez? What traitorous thoughts, what stupid thoughts, she chastised herself.

'I wanted to apologise,' he began again. 'I wanted to tell you how deeply sorry I am for any upset I've caused since my return to London.'

'*Any* upset? You have deliberately set out to distress me.'

'I won't deny it, but I am still sorry.'

He was looking contrite, unusually so, and she felt emboldened to question him. 'I don't understand why you have been so intent on hurting me. Why?'

He shook his head. 'I'm afraid I cannot answer with any

truth. I don't know myself. When I disembarked at South-ampton, I thought the past was dead and buried for me.'

'It seems that it wasn't,' she said flatly.

'No, it wasn't.' He paused and then said with delibera-tion, 'I've behaved foolishly, I'm willing to admit, but if I could understand the past, then I think it would finally die for me.'

He could see she was puzzled and he turned towards her, his gaze direct and searching. 'If I knew, if I could understand, why you did what you did.'

She gave a small, uncertain laugh. 'I could echo your own words. I cannot answer why with any truth, I hardly know myself.'

They rounded the corner of Curzon Street and, with an effort, she tried again. He deserved that at least.

'Put it down to naivety, youthful stupidity, if you will. When you are young and untried, it's easy to be dazzled by surfaces. I was living in a world I had never known before, a world heady with excitement.'

'But to be taken in by a creature such as Joshua,' he protested.

'You were equally taken in,' she reminded him sharply. 'He was your friend.'

'And that surely makes it worse. It makes me more stupid and you more venal.'

She flinched at the word. He made me feel special.' She was defensive.

'And I didn't?'

'I was just part...' and she strove to find the phrase which would adequately convey her sense of his indifference '... I was just part of the furniture of your world.'

'Never!' He felt stunned. He had been drowning in love for her and she hadn't noticed. 'How could you not know –?' He broke off, biting back the words of passion he had been about to utter.

But Cassie, deep in that distant past, had hardly noticed. 'Joshua made me feel that I mattered to him, really mattered. I know now that I was a fool.' Her voice was barely more than a whisper and she glanced down at the delicate kid sandals she wore, as though hoping she might be absorbed into the pavement. 'In fact, I knew that almost immediately.'

'You parted very soon afterwards? I never knew.'

'Why would you? I cannot imagine you wished to hear news from home.'

He grimaced at the truth of the observation.

'It was never going to work.' She gave a long sigh. 'Joshua was charm itself, but he was an opportunist.'

'A here and thereian?' It was doing Luke good to hear how miserably the affair had ended.

'If you like.'

'But someone that wreaked destruction wherever he went,' he pursued, his tone now one of quiet sympathy.

'I won't make him an excuse,' she said robustly. 'I caused damage to everyone who cared for me. I recognise that. But as you were happy to remind me yesterday, I cannot undo it. Any of it.'

'But you don't need to compound it.'

'What do you mean?'

'Don't make another bad choice.'

She bridled. 'And how might I do that?'

'I'm hardly the right person to give advice, but you must know the future you are proposing is wrong – for you, for everyone. You have earned your freedom, so live free.'

'You're quite correct,' she responded, her voice tart. 'You *are* hardly the right person.'

They had reached the door of Number Twelve and with this parting shot, she climbed the front steps. His face, as he raised his hat in farewell, was blank of all expression. He turned and walked away down the road, leaving Cassie bewildered.

He had shown himself sorry for his conduct, sorry for the distress he had caused. He'd conversed seriously, dared to talk about the past with her, and amid the barbs of resentment there had been sympathy. It seemed that he'd had a change of heart. But why? And what did he mean, that she should live free? How dare he presume to tell her how to shape her life? It was well enough for a man to say "live free". He had the luxury of choice, but, as a woman, she did not.

The door opened and she was ushered into Serena Foyle's drawing room. She knew most of the faces gathered there and it was an easy matter to smile sweetly and murmur the vacuous compliments required by the occasion. But while she observed the social rules, her mind was roving through every detail of the recent encounter. Was it just luck that she'd met Luke where and when she had? She thought not.

It was clear that he had been visiting Curzon Street himself. And he would have come, not to sit drinking tea with

Lady Foyle and her intimates, but to see Marianna. He had been visiting the girl he intended to marry. Naturally they would have wedding plans to discuss once his period of mourning was at an end, even now perhaps arrangements to make for Marianna to visit Madron.

Cassandra quailed at the thought, but that was something to which she must grow accustomed. It was possible Luke's forthcoming marriage had contributed to a new generosity of spirit, his willingness finally to forgive and forget the past. She should feel grateful for that, she supposed.

～

That night she slept better than she had for days. Whether it was sheer exhaustion or the fact that she and Luke were no longer enemies, she didn't know. His interference in her life was at an end, it seemed. So was his interest, another voice whispered unkindly, but that voice was swiftly quashed. She must bury the past as Luke was doing, bury it and move on to a new and different world.

For once she had spent the evening by her own fireside with plenty of time for reflection, and when she tumbled into bed, she was ready to fall into a deep and dreamless sleep. Not even Dominic's noisy return with the dawn had the power to waken her.

Chapter Fourteen

Dominic's mission to enjoy himself to the full had been so successful that when the next day, bleary eyed and slumped over the breakfast table, his mother reminded him that he'd agreed to escort his sisters to St James's Park, his only answer was a heartrending groan.

'We really don't need him, Mama,' Annabel chirped.

She was in fine form, still bubbling from the two long dances she had managed to extract from Sir Hugo at the Seftons' party. To add to her pleasure, Cassandra appeared of late to have lost her usual bloom.

'Stebbings will be with us and that will be sufficient. In fact, Cassie can stay home, too. She still doesn't look at all the thing,' she added solicitously.

'What nonsense. You cannot possibly go driving with just a coachman for company.' Lady Katherine looked anxiously across the table at her elder daughter. 'You will go with Annabel this morning, I trust?'

'Yes, of course, Mama. It's arranged that we meet the Misses Banhams at eleven.'

Cassie couldn't remember exactly why she had agreed to

drive with two sisters she privately considered bird-witted in the extreme, but managed to say brightly, 'It's a beautiful day for a drive in St James's.'

～

She went quickly upstairs after breakfast to complete her *toilette*. Annabel was already arrayed in midnight blue and she had no wish to challenge her sister's colourful palette. Instead she donned a robe of figured cream lace over an underdress of amber silk. Her auburn curls were brushed to a shine and threaded through with a simple cream ribbon.

She felt instinctively that this was an important day and she wanted to look her best in meeting it head on. A newly discovered sense of purpose brought back colour to her face and the porcelain cheeks now sported a delicate glow. She looked as fresh and as young as the spring morning into which the sisters were venturing.

Annabel glared at her in annoyance. A resurgent Cassandra was not what she wanted. Sir Hugo had mentioned at the rout that, though he must work for several hours on papers he had brought back to London, he would be riding in the park this morning and hoped to see both herself and her sister there. Annabel was under no illusions as to whose company he truly sought, but she had hoped to intercept him befor Cassie once more entered his orbit. She was anxious to exploit the friendship they had struck up two nights ago, and her sister's radiant presence would hardly further her plan.

Once out of the house, Dominic suddenly remembered a prior engagement and excused himself. He had made a casual promise to Marianna to ride with her this morning and this was likely to be more entertaining than plodding dutifully after his sisters' carriage. He was also feeling a little guilty at having abandoned the girl so cavalierly at the Seftons' rout.

Annabel was pleased to see him go. If she could think of a pretext to lose Cassandra, too, she would be free to seek out Sir Hugo and fascinate him as she knew she could. But Cassie was going to be difficult to evade: her sister had opted to take the reins, the coachman by her side, and further frustration followed when they encountered the Misses Banham waiting for them at the north gate of the park. Annoyingly they had remembered the arrangement to meet and, while Cassandra held the horses steady, they clambered noisily into the carriage. Arrayed in matching dresses of sprig muslin, they each carried a frilled parasol in contrasting colours, and positioned themselves on either side of Annabel, like two chattering bookends.

Laughing and giggling their way into the park, they exclaimed at Cassie's skill at driving the carriage through such busy thoroughfares, asserting with loud squeals their complete confidence that she could be trusted to tool them around the park without mishap. Most of what passed for conversation between them – the latest scurrilous *on-dits* circulating in town – went unanswered, but since they needed no audience but each other, they were not disconcerted by their hosts' silence.

When they'd finally exhausted current gossip, they turned their attention to their companions, complimenting the Latimer sisters on their looks, their dresses, their carriage. Everything that could be praised, was praised.

Unusually for Annabel she seemed not to notice their flattering remarks, even when they were particularly lavish in their admiration of her blue satin. Cassie thought she seemed distracted, excited almost, looking nervously from right to left and then behind, sometimes even hanging over the side of the carriage to gain a better view. It hardly seemed likely, but was it possible that Annabel had made an assignation?

'There's Lucy,' the elder Miss Banham suddenly shrieked. 'And with Petronella!'

'Our cousins,' the younger sister explained to the startled Latimers. 'Miss Latimer, Miss Annabel, would you mind awfully if we were to get down? It's an age since we've seen our cousins and there's so much to tell!'

The Latimer sisters readily assented. Both were heartily weary of the clamour that had accompanied their drive around the park. Annabel's face became intent. She had now only to free herself from her sister's company and she could at last seek Sir Hugo alone. But nothing happened to aid her plan, and just a few minutes later she saw him riding towards them.

He hailed them with pleasure, sidling his horse up to the carriage to greet Cassandra for the first time in nearly a week. For a long moment he sat in silence, gazing at her. He had forgotten just how beautiful she was and was suffused with eagerness to make his declaration instantly and win her as his wife. Belatedly, he remembered her sister's presence.

'Good morning, Miss Annabel. I trust you suffered no ill from your exertions at the rout?'

Annabel smiled a little sourly. Sir Hugo seemed not to notice and immediately turned his attention back to Cassandra.

'I was most sorry to hear of your indisposition, Miss Latimer, but I see from your looks that you are now fully recovered. I had hoped to see you at the rout, but in your absence your little sister kept me on my toes.'

'So I understand, Sir Hugo.' Cassie smiled, her green eyes warm and welcoming. 'And how did your business at Thorne Park prosper?'

'It went well, plenty to do you know, as always, but also plenty of time to plan.' His expression became serious. 'I am most pleased to find you here this morning. There is something particular I wish to discuss with you. I wonder if you would do me the honour of walking a short way with me?'

She knew this was the moment that had threatened for so long. Now that it had finally come, she felt calm and resigned. It was something she must do for herself, and for her family. It was no good imagining that a dashing white knight would ride to her rescue. Those were the foolish daydreams of an immature girl. This was the reality – a comfortable life with a comfortable husband.

Sir Hugo slipped from the saddle and, with a flourish, handed her down from the carriage. He was about to offer Cassie his arm when Annabel indicated that she also wished to alight. Sir Hugo was surprised by this lack of tact, but polite as always, he helped the younger girl down and all three began walking together over the luxuriant carpet of grass from which the dew had only just disappeared.

⌒

A little earlier Dominic and Marianna had manoeuvred their horses through the busy West End traffic. Pedlars, carts, every kind of carriage thronged the roads leading to St James's and all their attention had been taken up with gaining a safe passage through the maelstrom of noise and bustle. Twenty long minutes later they finally reached the safety of the park and trotted smartly through its eastern entrance.

Dominic glanced briefly at his companion. He was not the most acute observer, but she seemed unusually subdued. At first he had put it down to several late nights and this morning's early rising, but as they rode, he became increasingly aware of tension within the slight figure riding beside him. After a few abortive attempts at conversation, he gave up talking and they rode in silence.

The air was still and cool and shafts of sunlight filtered through the newly leafing trees. They were encircled by an island of natural beauty and it seemed to bring Marianna back to life. She took a deep breath; she would make a confession. And there was much to confess.

Her frustration at Luke's continued blindness had been replaced at the rout party by a new fascination. In that hot, enclosed little room she had been captivated by the ebb and flow of changing fortunes, the excitement of placing her stake, the rush of adrenaline as the cards sped from the faro box and the thrill of delight when the pile of rouleaus in front of her began to grow.

Not so delighted, though, when they began to disappear. But then Lord Amesbury had come to her rescue, had advanced her some of his own rouleaus for no more payment than her handkerchief. In the thrill of the game it had seemed perfectly normal for her to hand over this small personal possession. But the sly looks the other players exchanged had alerted her to the fact that his lordship's offer was hardly usual.

He had behaved impeccably, though, advancing more tokens without demanding anything further from her. At least for the moment. He had said that he would think of some way she could repay him, but that she wasn't to worry her pretty head. He was a rich man, a few losses meant nothing to him. At these last comments Marianna's immediate neighbour, apparently so correct and punctilious, had smirked knowingly. She caught both his grimace and Robert Amesbury's answering smile and a vague discomfort became a pressing anxiety to leave.

'What do you know of Lord Amesbury?' she asked, reigning in her horse.

Dominic came to a halt and gave her a cautious look, trying to gauge how much he should say. 'Not a lot.' His reply was hardly helpful.

He saw her biting her lip and relented a little. 'Why do you ask?'

'Only that I'm interested in the people I met at the Seftons' party. I understand it was Lord Amesbury who held the faro bank.'

'He often does. He's a very rich man.'

'Is he married?'

Where was this leading? thought Dominic. 'No, not married.'

'Yet he's quite old.'

'He's not that old. And he doesn't exactly lead the kind of life that goes with being married,' he added bravely.

'What kind of life?' came the inevitable question.

'Pretty rackety.' Better to be brutal to be kind if the girl had any idea of snaring Amesbury.

'Dominic, I lost money to him,' she disclosed in a sudden rush of words.

'We all lost money to him.'

'I mean I lost more – after you left.'

'You couldn't have lost much more. You only had a few rouleaus left – enough for just one more stake.'

'I borrowed more.'

Dominic urged his horse forward and it was seconds before he spoke. He seemed to be struggling to take in Marianna's words and his face wore the beginnings of unease.

'Borrowed? From him?'

'It was not a good idea?'

'Definitely not. What did you pledge?'

'Pledge?'

'What did he ask for?' Dominic was becoming seriously alarmed.

'My handkerchief, first, but then he gave me rouleaus for free.'

'He never gives anything for free.'

'That's what I'm thinking now,' she said miserably. 'What will he do, do you think?'

Dominic hardly liked to put his thoughts into words and his vague feelings of guilt found vent in scolding. 'Whatever made you do such an idiotic thing?'

'I didn't realise it was wrong until later. You were not there to advise me,' she accused him.

'It shouldn't be me advising you. It should be your aunt. You must tell her what you've done and she must repay Lord Amesbury his debt.'

'I can't do that. She will be angry and send me immediately to Spain.'

'I wouldn't blame her. You're too much of a responsibility. Anyway you're leaving for Spain at the end of the Season, so why not now?'

'I have my reasons,' she said gravely. Then, following her train of thought, she asked in a falsely bright voice, 'Is Miss Latimer riding here today?'

'She's out driving with my sister. I'm supposed to be with them, but Annabel's screeching sends me insane. I thought you were the better bet, though now I'm not so sure!' He couldn't repress a grin.

She ignored the witticism. 'Is she here right now? Perhaps we should go and find her.'

'We won't have to look too far.' He raised his arm to point ahead. 'She's there, just to the right of that clump of trees.'

They reined in their horses once more. A carriage had been drawn up beneath the trees and to one side they saw Sir Hugo Thorne talking animatedly to Cassandra. He had her hand raised to his lips and then, as they watched, slipped what looked like a ring on her finger.

'Perhaps not the right time to interrupt,' Dominic commented drily.

Marianna felt considerable surprise, but also a warm

pleasure. If Cassandra were pledged to another man, it might mean Luke would look more kindly on her.

'They are to be married?'

'My mother's been waiting an age for this – Cassie must have finally decided to put the man out of his misery.'

'It's a very happy day, then. Let's go and congratulate them.'

'I don't think we should right now,' he prevaricated. 'Just look at Annabel!'

They looked across from the betrothed couple and saw a figure in bright blue satin some distance from the carriage, standing rigidly with averted head.

'Like I said, perhaps not the best time to interrupt.' He gave a mischievous smile. 'Come on, let's have a gallop. No one's around to tell tales.'

'I must not, Dominic. I am already in trouble for that.'

He set himself to persuade his companion that a gallop was just the thing to blow away her megrims when a large black stallion cut across their path and Luke Trelawny was hailing them with a smile.

Chapter Fifteen

'Good morning to you both. I'm very glad to see you, Marianna, though I didn't expect to meet you so early in the morning.'

'It's such a beautiful day I couldn't lie abed. Did you want to see me particularly, Luke?' Her tone was eager, almost breathless.

'I was worried I might miss you, knowing what a crowded social calendar you have,' he teased. 'I wanted to tell you that I'm leaving for Cornwall tomorrow.'

'Cornwall? But why tomorrow?' Her dismay rang out clearly.

'Why not?' he said bracingly. 'I've tarried too long – and my mother deserves better. I should be at her side, don't you think?'

'Yes', she stuttered, 'of course, but it seems a sudden decision.'

'Hardly sudden. It's taken time to organise my affairs, but the lawyers are ready at last and there's no longer any need for me to stay in London. I have written to my mother to expect me very shortly.'

Dominic saw his companion's face and knew instantly

that his supposition over Amesbury had been false. But this relationship didn't look much more promising. There was an awkward silence and he felt it incumbent to oil the social wheels.

'I'll be returning to Cornwall myself pretty soon, Luke. We must be sure to ride out together – if you can spare the time.'

The older man smiled his assent. 'There's always time for a decent gallop.'

Marianna had been following her own thoughts and blurted out, 'But won't you stay for the Vauxhall spectacle? It's only a few days away.'

'I think not, but you're sure to enjoy yourself. I remember seeing the fireworks for the first time when I was about your age and they were truly magnificent.'

The reference to her youth had Marianna dig her nails into her hands and scream silently. Wanting to hit out, she said as casually as she could, 'If you're leaving so soon, you'd better make haste to congratulate Miss Latimer. She is close by, I believe.'

Dominic looked at her with surprise, wondering what her game was. Not for the first time he felt completely out of his depth in trying to fathom females.

'Congratulate Miss Latimer?'

'We have just seen her with Sir Hugo Thorne in a most romantic situation, haven't we, Dominic?' Her companion looked suitably revolted. 'Dominic tells me the betrothal between Sir Hugo and his sister is something the whole family has been expecting, and it looks as though it's happened this very day.'

Luke was far too self-controlled to betray his feelings, but his face grew austere and the light went out of the smiling grey eyes.

'I had better do as you suggest then and seek Miss Latimer out.'

He wheeled his horse sharply around and rode away. His face might wear an impassive mask, but inwardly he was racked by fury. She was going to marry the man! How could she even consider it? Just a few days ago she had kissed him, caressed him, laid herself open to his lovemaking. The thought almost tore the breath from his body.

Only yesterday in Curzon Street he'd felt certain he could leave their old history behind. He'd been stunned that Cassie had not known the depths of his youthful love, but begun to understand just how easy it had been for Joshua to mislead her. The familiar, nagging hurt hadn't disappeared completely, but the pain become more bearable. Now, though, the wound had opened again and laceratingly. Yet another man was to smile into those startling emerald eyes, to run his hands over that beautiful, lithe body, to laugh and tease and fun with her.

No, *that* he wouldn't do. Sir Hugo Thorne was not a man made for fun. Nor was he a man made for love, not the kind that she needed. If *he* were still in love with her... But he wasn't, was he? Her betrayal might have been an act of youthful folly, but she had damaged him too badly for him ever to trust her again. And now she was to marry this dull do-gooder and be lost forever. How could she? The question thrummed through every particle of his flesh.

Behind a veil of tears, Marianna watched his figure as it grew slowly smaller in the distance. Riding alongside, Dominic maintained a discreet silence. He trusted that he would not be called upon to become a confidant and waited for her to recover herself. With a great effort, she turned to him with a show of enthusiasm.

'That was exciting, wasn't it, but can we return to my problem? I need to win back the money I lost to Lord Amesbury. Will you help me do that?'

'You want me to win it?'

'*I* want to win it. It's my debt. But I need you to introduce me to a place where I can do that.'

'You're asking me to take you to a gambling den?'

'Yes.'

'I won't,' he said flatly.

'Why not? If you're scared we might be recognised, I could go in disguise.'

'It gets worse.'

'No, it doesn't, I can disguise myself very well as a boy and go as your friend.'

He looked at her slim figure appraisingly. 'I'm sure you can, but I'm not taking you to any gaming hell.'

'I don't want to go to a hell, just a place where I can win back the money.'

'That's a gaming hell.'

'Please, Dominic.'

'No, no and definitely no.'

'Then you won't help me?'

'I've told you what to do. Go to your aunt and confess. The worst she can do is to pack you off to Spain. Would that matter so much now?'

She flushed at the inference, but knew that he was right. She supposed that she must find the right opportunity to tell Lady Foyle what had happened. But then her aunt would be sure to tell the Spanish relations of Marianna's disgrace and from the moment she arrived in Madrid, they would be watching her every movement. She wished she had never left Argentina.

⤳

In the distance Luke had ridden up to the small group standing beneath the trees. Annabel had joined her sister and Sir Hugo near the carriage, as anxious now to leave as she had been earlier to find him. She scowled even more ferociously as she recognised the man seated astride the glossy black horse picking its way towards them.

Luke Trelawny slid from the saddle as Cassandra turned. He came forward and bowed just a little too deeply.

'I understand from your brother that felicitations are in order.' His voice was harsh, slightly disdainful. 'May I take the opportunity, Miss Latimer, to congratulate you and Sir Hugo, on your forthcoming marriage.' And here he bowed extravagantly towards the other man. 'I wish you both all the happiness you are capable of.'

Cassie flushed, knowing the double edge of those words, but executed a dignified bow in response. Her fiancé smiled happily and without guile.

'Thank you, Lord Trelawny. Your good wishes are most welcome. I consider myself to be blessed indeed to have won this remarkable lady for my future wife, a gift beyond anything I deserve.'

Luke's expression was sardonic. 'You must not sell yourself short, Sir Hugo. I'm sure Miss Latimer would be the first to agree that your honesty and loyalty are qualities to aspire to.'

Sir Hugo blinked at this sentiment, but his smile broadened even further. He felt supremely happy and nothing was going to spoil this wonderful day for him.

Annabel stood close by, an interested observer. Luke's comments appeared to be coming from between gritted teeth and offered a small hope. She might yet salvage something from a day that had gone so badly awry.

Pinning on her most enticing smile, she turned to the happy lover. 'I believe, Sir Hugo, that you were involved in plans for the canal that has been constructed to feed the lake. I would love to see it and understand exactly how it works. Would you be good enough to take me?'

If Sir Hugo felt this was a strange request coming at the very moment of his betrothal, and from a girl who had hitherto not shown the slightest interest in engineering, he was far too polite to show it. Willing to do anything for anybody on this glorious morning, particularly a close relative of his beloved, he immediately agreed.

'It appears we must leave you, sir. He bowed his farewell. 'Thank you again for your good wishes.'

He began to walk towards the Chinese bridge with Annabel in tow, already beginning a complicated discourse on his understanding of the water-management system. Equally bewildered by her sister's request, Cassie turned to follow them, but was stopped in her tracks by Luke's rough grab of her arm.

He hardly waited for the others to be out of earshot before he said wrathfully, 'You cannot really mean to marry that man!'

'I beg your pardon!' She was shocked.

'I think you understand me, but to avoid any doubt I was questioning your sanity in agreeing to marry Hugo Thorne.'

'How dare you presume to question whom I marry?'

'I dare to presume because I seem to know you better than you know yourself. But even you must be aware of how unsuited you are to each other.'

The red cascade of curls trembled with anger. 'You are insulting, sir.'

'I would call it honest rather than insulting, but it is better to be insulting than concur in this charade.'

'You are misinformed, my lord. There is no charade. Sir Hugo and I have known each other for many months and have agreed that we will suit admirably.'

She wondered why she was defending her choice of husband to Luke of all men, but she felt compelled to continue and found herself declaring, 'Sir Hugo is a man of the highest honour and integrity.'

'I'm sure he is. He is also a gudgeon if he thinks he can control you.'

'No man controls me and Sir Hugo is far too wise to wish to do so.'

'But not wise enough to refrain from marrying you,' he retaliated.

She glared furiously at the tall, elegant figure in front of her and responded in a voice crackling with ice. 'This is mere ranting and I will listen no more. I bid you good day, sir.'

Her cream skirts swished to one side as she made to walk away. But Luke would not concede. Ignoring her cold fury and the summary nature of his dismissal, he called out, 'If you value his happiness as much as your own, don't do it.'

She retraced her steps and stood looking directly up into his eyes, now dark and glittering.

'If we are to give each other marital advice, I would suggest that wedding a child fresh from the nursery is unlikely to guarantee success. At least I intend to marry a man of my own age and one I have known for many months.'

Brushing aside his supposed alliance with Marianna, he countered coldly, 'How much of a guarantee is that? You once agreed to marry another man of your own age and one you had known a *very* long time, but that alliance wasn't too permanent, was it?'

He smiled derisively at her. 'At the moment Sir Hugo is living in his own little paradise, but how long do you give him? He would be well advised to grow steel armour in the very near future – say three weeks from his wedding day.'

'You have been as offensive as it is possible to be, but nothing you say can touch our happiness.'

Luke grimaced. 'How charming! And how strange there was a day when I felt that, too. I looked deep into your green eyes, touched your luminous skin, tangled my hands in that wild red hair – and what a premonition that was – and believed that I was as happy as it was possible to be, that nothing could ever touch that happiness. How wrongly can a man judge!'

Cassandra swallowed hard. 'Yesterday you assured me that you considered the past dead. Can you not accept that we made a mistake and forget?'

'*You* made a mistake, Miss Latimer, and you are about to make another. About to hurt others once more. For myself, the past is nothing. But I find it difficult to forget those for whom the pain still lives. But then you never cared too much about them – friends, parents, all could be sacrificed. All that mattered was that you had your desire. A desire, it seems, that died almost as soon as it flickered into life.'

He was being unjust, deliberately stoking his anger against her, but he found himself powerless to stop.

'You are unfair to accuse me of not caring for the pain I caused. You must know otherwise. It has been an open wound for all these years.' Her voice faltered and unshed tears stung her eyelids. She steadied herself and tried for a calm she was far from feeling.

'In my youth I made a mistaken attachment – I have freely confessed it – and paid for that mistake. If you once cared anything for me, can you not find it in your heart, if not to wish me well, at least not to wish me ill.'

For a moment Luke felt an overpowering weariness. Only hours ago he'd made the decision to forget her betrayal, to walk away from the pain that had dogged him. So why was he continuing to haunt this woman, to pile hurt upon hurt?

Chapter Sixteen

She saw the trouble in his eyes and the frown between his dark brows and pushed her advantage.

'Because *our* betrothal did not succeed, it is no reason to suppose that my marriage to another will not.'

'If so, that other will need to be a very different man from the one you have chosen. He will need to be a man who matches you in strength of character and depth of feeling. For all his honour and integrity, Sir Hugo is not that man.'

He spoke the words slowly and deliberately, his gaze intense and tugging at her soul. For what seemed an age their eyes devoured each other while their lips remained silent; it was easy to forget they were antagonists engaged in a bitter conflict.

Then recovering her former iciness, Cassie snapped back a response. 'And who would you suggest, Lord Trelawny? Where is this model of manhood I must aspire to? Surely not yourself?'

'Have no fear, I would never again submit myself to such an ordeal.' His voice broke apart the shell she had tried to build for herself. 'You say *you* have suffered. I hope so indeed, for my years have been every bit as painful.'

'I know nothing of your life in Argentina, but I cannot imagine it was devoid of all pleasure.'

'Argentina?' he questioned bleakly. 'I refer to the constant pain of living with betrayal.' And then in a searing aside, 'But naturally you would know nothing of that.'

'On the contrary, I am no stranger to betrayal,' she said in a low voice, 'though you would judge it well-deserved.'

She found herself moving towards him, drawn by the warmth of his body and a strange need to offer comfort. She resisted the urge to take his hand, but could not stop herself pleading. 'I thought we had agreed, Luke, to put injuries aside. I wish you well in the alliance you are about to make. Can you not wish the same for me?'

His eyes found hers and for an instant there was an answering warmth. The taut lines of his face relaxed and his mouth softened in the way she remembered so well, a prelude to his kiss. She waited, hardly daring to breathe. But then his whole body visibly tightened and his face resumed its hardened expression. When he spoke, it was clear that anger had reasserted itself.

'My relationship with Miss Marquez has nothing to say in the matter. The truth remains that the man you propose to marry is not worthy of you.'

She took a step back as though he had slapped her in the face, and observing her shock, his anger flared again. 'Good grief, can you not see what a travesty this marriage is? Have we suffered so much for so little?'

His wrath was answered by a newly awakened fury in her. 'I find your sentiments abhorrent and your conduct highly improper.'

They stood facing each other so close they could taste one another's breath. Both had been shaken by the ferocity of their anger. Both had felt the familiar throb of desire which neither could acknowledge. Cassandra drew her slim figure erect and confronted him with eyes glittering like green glass.

'I have borne much in this interview, but will not do so again.' Her voice was brittle with feeling. 'I ask that you leave me now and never again speak to me.'

His face expressionless, Luke turned on his heels and scooped up the reins of his mount grazing quietly nearby. Without a backward glance, he flung himself into the saddle and dug his heels into the flanks of the startled beast. Cassandra remained where she stood as the horse bounded forward, her face equally impassive, but her heart beating far too hard.

Sir Hugo, having by this time exhausted his knowledge of canal engineering, was in time to see Luke ride furiously away. Clearly there had been an altercation.

'Let us make haste, Miss Annabel,' he said in a worried tone. 'I fear all may not be well with your sister. That man – Lord Trelawny – appeared extremely angry and I am concerned she may have suffered some mischief from him.'

'That man has known Cassandra all her life, Sir Hugo, and is unlikely to be a threat. In fact, he knows her so well...' and here Annabel produced her trump card with a fitting display of naïve innocence '... that they were once promised to each other.'

'Promised! Betrothed?' Sir Hugo looked bewildered.

'How is this?'

'Oh, I do beg your pardon. You didn't know? How stupid of me. I assumed that Cassandra would have told you or that you would have heard mention of it – it was the town's biggest *on-dit* for many weeks. But perhaps you were away from London at the time?'

'What happened exactly?' he asked weakly.

Annabel was admirably succinct. 'She jilted him three weeks before the wedding.'

'Good gracious,' was all he could utter before Cassandra joined them. He managed to smile solicitously down at the lovely face, trying to blot out Annabel's last words.

'My dear...' he patted her hand ineffectually '... I do hope all is well.'

Still reeling from the encounter with Luke, she withdrew her hand with a small shrug of impatience. 'But of course, Sir Hugo. What could be wrong?'

'Then shall we continue our stroll in the park? The weather looks as though it will hold for some hours.'

His face was hopeful, but Cassie longed for solitude and the latter won. 'Will you forgive me if I cut our walk a little short today? There are things awaiting my attention at home.' It was a feeble excuse, but it would have to do.

'Annabel, are you coming?' Cassandra was already climbing into the waiting carriage.

Her sister was equally quick with her response. She rather fancied a walk and would return to Mount Street on foot. She was sure that Sir Hugo would escort her. 'For I don't doubt that he could do with the company,' she said repressively.

Cassie stared hard at her sister, but the bland face gave nothing away. Sir Hugo stood close by looking dazed, even shocked, but she knew she could no longer bear to be in his company. Luke's strictures rang ceaselessly in her ears and she had to get away. She gave a sign to Stebbings that she wished him to take the reins and in a moment the carriage had jolted forward.

⌒

The journey to Mount Street was accomplished in less than a quarter of an hour, but she hardly noticed. She should be used to Luke's animosity by now. From the moment they had met again, it had been plain there was to be no truce between them. Yesterday's interlude had simply been a pause in hostilities. His conduct had swung between discourtesy, even aggression, and small moments of rekindled desire. But whatever extremes he'd loosed upon her, they seemed always to proceed from a deep-seated antagonism, a fierce desire to make her regret what she had done all those years ago.

Yet even when she was thinking the worst of him, she had sensed a kindness that he couldn't suppress, feelings from the past he couldn't dismiss. And today he had confessed for the first time that she had hurt him badly. It meant, did it not, that he had loved her once, not as a sop to parental wishes, nor as a trophy, but deeply and heartfelt. If that were true, she had judged him very wrongly. If that were true, it would explain why he could not overcome his anger, why he was still her enemy.

And now his love was no more: he'd made that plain. He didn't want her for himself, but had no intention of letting her go quietly into a new life. He was seeking to destroy even that solace. Until this morning she had never truly grasped the power of his ill will. He had made a mockery of her wish to consign the past to oblivion – it would always be with her. Despite the sun's warmth flooding through the open carriage, the thought made her hands shake and her teeth start to chatter as though she suffered a severe chill.

At home she climbed to her room with a bone-weariness, her feet dragging from stair to stair. Once in the safety of her chamber, she flung herself on the bed and lay there in a state of utter fatigue. The day's events – Luke, Hugo, even Annabel – rushed past her unseeing eyes in a chaotic blur. Even Annabel! Her sister's behaviour was not the least odd thing that had happened. She wondered what ailed the younger woman.

An hour later the front door slammed and purposeful steps sounded outside her room. Annabel jerked her head around the door, looking unbecomingly flushed, but with a smug expression on her face.

'I'm sure you'll be pleased to know that I more than compensated for your absence,' she taunted.

Cassie stared at her uncomprehendingly. Her head had begun to ache. 'What are you talking about?'

'I'm talking about your fiancé. I presume he still *is* your fiancé. I've just returned with Sir Hugo and it's clear to me that your conduct has upset him deeply. I've tried to smooth things over but I can't be sure how successful I've been.'

Cassandra sat up swiftly, her indignation banishing the incipient headache.

'I don't understand what right you think you have to speak in this fashion or indeed to discuss me with Sir Hugo, but be very sure that I have given you none.'

Annabel remained in the doorway, her arms crossed in defiance. 'I know nothing about rights,' she declared truthfully, 'and it's true I don't possess your rather obvious enticements, but I think I know a little better how to treat a man. And it's not with the contempt you deal out.'

'What nonsense you talk.'

Cassie laid her weary head back on the pillow. There was a grain of truth in Annabel's pronouncement, but only a grain. And why was her sister so exercised on Sir Hugo's behalf?

'Contempt!' Annabel reiterated ringingly. 'You become engaged to an honourable man and immediately consort with your old lover. You accept Sir Hugo's ring and then refuse to spend time with him.'

Cassandra seemed not to be listening, but this did not deter her sister. Annabel was becoming ever more agitated, her face working furiously.

'How do you think that makes him feel?' She took angry strides into the room and pointed dramatically at her guilty sister. 'You don't deserve his love.'

'And you do?' Cassie suddenly understood the drift of her sister's conversation. It made sense of her earlier actions. She had evidently been on the look-out for Sir Hugo, hoping to meet him alone in the park.

'More than you at any rate,' Annabel snapped back. '*I'm*

not made of ice!'

And with that she banged the bedroom door behind her, leaving Cassie to wrestle with this new and unwelcome development.

Chapter Seventeen

Sir Hugo had made elaborate preparations for an evening's visit to Vauxhall. It was not a venue he would ordinarily have patronised – the Gardens had a reputation for encouraging wanton behaviour – but the Prince Regent himself was to sponsor a fête there and nothing else had been talked of among the *ton* for days but the magnificent firework display to be mounted in his honour. So it was that with great care Sir Hugo planned every detail of the evening's entertainment. His carriage was to call at Mount Street at seven o' clock and take up Cassandra and her siblings. Lady Katherine had cried off at the last moment, citing the burden of preparations for Annabel's ball.

The party would drive to Westminster Pier and from there take a boat over the Thames, approaching the Gardens by the water entrance. Sir Hugo had already hired one of the hundred supper boxes available in the central amphitheatre and looked forward to serving his guests the wafer-thin ham for which Vauxhall was famous, washed down with the very best champagne. A fifty-strong orchestra would entertain them throughout the meal, but their box was sited far enough away for conversation not to be unduly disturbed. Reserved places at the fireworks arena were also secured. Nothing had been left to chance. He was determined to make the evening a fitting celebration of his recent engagement.

To his dismay the expedition got off to an uncomfortable start. Cassandra was already waiting in the hall when he arrived at Mount Street, looking voluptuous in a low-cut silk robe of the deepest gold worn over a flimsy underslip of ivory gauze. He had never before seen her dressed so seductively and, after his initial surprise, felt himself falling deeper under her spell, the strain of their last encounter forgotten. His enchantment, though, was soon fractured by the storm raging above.

'You foolish boy, look what you've done!'

It was Annabel thumping down the main staircase in an unladylike fury. Hardly able to speak, she glared at the two patiently waiting and pointed a trembling finger at the hem of her dress.

'Do you see that? It's torn beyond repair! And all because he can't keep his clumsy feet to himself. He's not content to stand all over my dress, oh no, he has to tear it to shreds.'

'If you hadn't got into such a temper and pulled against my foot, it would never have torn.' Dominic arrived down the stairs two at a time, looking as cross as his sister.

'I didn't pull it, idiot. I was trying to free it. Why did you stand on it in the first place?'

'Why does the sun shine? Why do you wear ridiculous frocks? There's no answer.'

She was about to loose another tirade when Cassandra

intervened. 'You could change into your lilac silk, Annabel. It will be perfect for the Gardens and then tomorrow you can ask your woman to restitch the hem.'

'How can she mend such a huge tear. And why should I wear the lilac? It's completely insipid and I hate it. I shan't go to Vauxhall and it will be your fault.' She rounded angrily on her brother.

Sir Hugo, ever more aware of the advancing hour, thought it time to try his own hand at peacemaking. 'Miss Annabel, you have a wardrobe of beautiful dresses from which to choose. Please do so and favour us with your company this evening.'

Dominic snorted derisively, but his sister allowed herself a glimmer of a smile in Hugo's direction before she retraced her steps to the bedroom. Annabel's infatuation still flourished, Cassie noted. Her sister's passions had a tendency to disappear almost as quickly as they erupted and she hoped this would prove the case with Hugo. If she made sure that Annabel knew their engagement was happy and secure, she was hopeful her sister would transfer her affections elsewhere.

⸺

They were late for the boat and Sir Hugo had to pay a hefty waiting charge, but was relieved simply to have got all of them to the Gardens. Annabel and Dominic kept up a low level sniping for most of the journey, but Cassie blocked her ears to their wrangling. She was determined to make the evening a success, to make amends for her earlier dudgeon and show Sir Hugo that she appreciated the considerable thought he'd expended on the evening.

And she was enjoying herself. She had never before visited Vauxhall, even though between April and June it was a popular pleasure haunt of the *ton*, and when they stepped from the boat and began to make their way along the Grand Walk, she was entranced.

Tree-lined promenades and gravelled pathways led off from the main route and everywhere fountains, statues, even artificial ruins, dotted the landscape. The evening light had by this time darkened and they walked in a fairyland of a thousand lanterns hanging in festoons from the trees and between the cast-iron pillars of the vaulted colonnade which ran alongside the Grand Walk.

'What a magical place,' she said, her eyes deep pools of turquoise in the shadowy light, 'and how good of you to think of this excursion.'

Sir Hugo, suffused with happiness, smiled benignly and tucked her arm tightly into his. Dominic had disappeared almost as soon as they had reached dry land, and although Annabel maintained a forbidding frown, a degree of peace was restored. Lavish praise of a particularly fetching loo mask she had bought for the occasion mollified her sufficiently to consent to explore the Gardens with her sister and future brother-in-law.

For an hour or so the three of them strolled along the walkways, listening to the bands of Pandean minstrels which played on platforms scattered around the Gardens. Even Annabel was intrigued at some of the innovations that had been designed to interest visitors, marvelling for some time at the mechanical Cascade that played endlessly at the centre of the South Walk, another stately avenue spanned by three triumphal arches.

Eventually they made their way to the two central semi-circles around which supper boxes provided places to eat, to listen to the orchestra or simply to watch the strolling crowds.

Sir Hugo, all attention, made his two guests comfortable. A shawl here, a cushion there, and a hovering waiter despatched to fetch the supper he had ordered. Dozens of waiters ran from box to box, bringing platters of chicken or ham with salads for the guests to mix themselves and bowls for them to brew their own very potent arrack-punch.

This was already having some effect in a few of the supper boxes, their inhabitants masked and feeling free to conduct themselves with abandon. The masqueraders were laughing immoderately at their own jokes or cavorting to the music which played nearby. A few of the women already looked dishevelled. Sir Hugo's box was set back slightly from the majority and he was relieved that the ladies under his charge would not be incommoded by such improper behaviour.

'What curious murals.' Cassandra pointed to a rear wall, hazily illuminated by the globe of light hanging from the roof and covered with paintings.

'I believe they were done by a Francis Hayman in the last century,' Sir Hugo intoned. 'But they have constantly to be repaired because so many examine them a little too closely!'

'I do believe you've been researching this for us,' she teased.

He smiled and admitted as much while Annabel

scowled, then yawned ostentatiously.

It was fortunate that a distraction soon materialised in the form of supper and with it, Dominic, who appeared out of nowhere to eat his share. He didn't stay long, however. As soon as the chicken and ham had been despatched, he excused himself with the words that he thought he might try a little jaunt around the dance floor. At this Annabel scowled even more ferociously and began pointedly to tap her feet.

Cassie was by now wholly out of patience with her sister though she knew well the cause of Annabel's bad temper. But Sir Hugo, blissfully ignorant, offered his arm to the younger girl, saying genially, 'I think it must be time for us to repeat our efforts of the other evening, Miss Annabel – that is, if your sister has no objection.'

Cassie was only too pleased to be left in peace. There was now quite a crowd of people dancing to the infectious music of the orchestra and she enjoyed watching them twirling and spinning beneath the trees, the lanterns dusting the moving figures with sprinkles of light. A carnival spirit was abroad, many of the dancers dressed in full disguise. Among the crowd of harlequins, cavaliers, jesters and shepherdesses, she thought she saw Marianna and her aunt.

She could have been mistaken, but it was possible that Lady Foyle had been persuaded after all to bring her charge to this den of iniquity. If so, it was strange that Luke was not with them.

She fell to wondering why she and Luke had never visited Vauxhall when they were a betrothed couple. But those had been awkward months in London when her decision to marry had begun to seem hideously wrong. The growing influence of Joshua had seen to that. He, of course, would have leapt at the chance of meeting her at Vauxhall. Masked and disguised, it was a perfect opportunity for the kind of underhand lovemaking he was so good at.

But Luke would have shrunk from it. He was too upright, too conscious of what was deemed proper conduct. Or had been, she amended. The Luke she had encountered in the past few weeks was anything but proper. He was unpredictable and passionate and his tirade in the park just a few days ago had gone well beyond the bounds of correctness. Had he really changed so much and Argentina made him into a new man? Or had that streak of recklessness, of fervour, always been there just waiting to be lit? Six years ago she had chosen not to apply the flame, but instead had turned away to Joshua. It was a sobering thought.

'All alone, sweetheart?'

She looked up startled. A man dressed in a scarlet domino had suddenly appeared at her side. She had been so deep in thought that he must have leapt the wooden barrier without her realising.

'We can't have that, can we, not on a night made for merrymaking?'

The man let out a harsh guffaw and breathed fumes into her face. Repulsed, she rose from her seat, thinking to escape down the staircase at the side of the box, but he was too quick for her. Grabbing her arm, he pulled her close and began to rub his face against her cheek. With a mighty wrench she snatched herself away and desperately made for the stairs, but her flimsy slipper caught in the table leg and he was on her again almost immediately. His arms encircled her waist and dragged her into a clumsy embrace. She shrank back against the wall of the box as his fleshy mouth hovered over her lips.

But then a hand appeared out of the darkness. It alighted on the man's shoulder and jerked him roughly backwards. He let go in surprise and turned to face the cause of this intrusion. Grey eyes gleamed behind a black velvet mask and a steely voice commanded him to leave immediately. Cassandra knew the voice and the figure instantly.

'Who d'you think you are to tell me what to do?' the man in scarlet protested.

The grim figure stood tensed, his hand now on the man's collar. 'Unless you leave now,' he hissed into his ear, 'you will find out soon enough.'

Chapter Eighteen

The man put up his arms in readiness for a brawl. Dreading the scene to come, Cassie looked wildly around for Sir Hugo and her sister. Even Dominic might be of use in this situation. Then quite suddenly it was over. The intruder had been picked up bodily and tossed over the barrier he had earlier jumped.

At the first sounds of the quarrel people had begun to emerge from the neighbouring supper boxes to see what was amiss and now a small crowd gathered around the prostrate man. Those revellers who had imbibed most seemed to think the whole thing a drama put on for their entertainment and were loud in their praise of the acting. But the more sober were plainly concerned with this breach of the peace and began to mutter ominously amongst themselves.

The black-masked figure grabbed Cassandra's hand and propelled her swiftly down the stairs and out of the box. He carved a path for them through the now restive crowd, holding tightly to her, and a few minutes later she found herself running with him up the Dark Walk. No lanterns hung here, the only light that of a crescent moon barely visible through the lowering clouds.

The air was heavy with the scent of lilacs now in full bloom, their abundant foliage casting inky shadows on the gravelled pathway. She could hardly see a foot in front of her, but her rescuer's firm hand kept her from stumbling.

The crowds gradually dwindled and the sounds of music faded into the distance. Breathless, they came to a halt outside a small rustic shelter cleverly hidden within a clearing between surrounding trees. It was invisible, except to those standing immediately outside. Luke pulled her into its sanctuary, hardly allowing her to catch her breath before he began to berate her.

'Where the hell is your fiancé?' he uttered explosively.

She bridled immediately. 'How dare you use such language to me?'

He ran his hand through his already dishevelled hair and attempted to gain control of himself.

'I apologise for my intemperate speech, but I repeat – where is your supposed fiancé?'

'He is not supposed, he *is* my fiancé,' she retorted coldly.

'Then why isn't he taking care of you?'

'Sir Hugo has taken every care of me. He was absent for a short time only while he danced with my sister.'

'And while he placates that bad-tempered vixen, he leaves you exposed to the attentions of any rake on the cut.'

'You exaggerate. The man was a nuisance, no more.'

There was silence while they glared furiously at each other. Then she challenged him. 'I thought I'd made it clear that I never wished to speak to you again.'

'And I'm most happy to concur, but what am I to do

when I see a woman, any woman, menaced by a scoundrel?'

'You make too much of the incident – there was no cause to intervene.'

'Really? Then why were you cowering in fear?'

Cassie clasped and unclasped her hands, trying not to show her agitation. 'I was not cowering,' she said staunchly. 'Nor did I wish to become embroiled in an unseemly wrangle. Did you have to be quite so brutal?'

'Would you have preferred to be ravished?'

'That was hardly likely. The man was clearly drunk.'

'But sober enough to see the prize he was winning.'

She said nothing and again a long, tense silence filled the air between them. The moment of danger had passed and they were both acutely aware of their seclusion.

But still he could not resist looking at her, his gaze growing rapt as the seconds passed. The soft contours of her body seemed to cry out for his touch and he longed to unpin her curls and bring that flaming curtain cascading down. Exerting all his self-control, he made his face expressionless, and when he spoke his voice was heavy with irony.

'Evidently I misjudged the situation. The man was no threat to you and I have done him ill. I'll leave you to convey my apologies to our unfortunate friend,' and he gestured back the way they had come. 'You will doubtless make a better job of it than I.'

Cassie followed the direction of his hand and looked quickly behind her. 'Has he come after us?'

He shook his head. 'There is no one there.' He knew he should leave it at that and walk away, but his frustration impelled him to carry on the fight.

'You can relax, you are quite safe. But then you always have been with me, haven't you? A little too safe.' He looked down at her with a cynical smile. 'For someone who despises the familiar, it's strange how little you enjoy excitement when it comes knocking.'

The energy drained from her. She had been forced to brave the unwanted attentions of a stranger, and now must rekindle her strength for yet another battle. The night air was warm but she could not suppress a shiver.

He saw and said tauntingly, 'Perhaps you should have worn a little more this evening. Or was this a special treat for Sir Hugo?'

She ignored the gibe, but her anger was growing.

'Or perhaps,' he continued to harass, 'this is just the old Cassandra, the one who likes to offer a special treat.'

The blood whipped her cheeks pink and she turned savagely towards him, her hand raised. She hardly knew what she was doing. This was more than justified fury; all her suppressed desire fuelled the flight of her hand. He caught her arm mid-air and pulled her towards him.

'What happened to the ice maiden?' he goaded.

Then his hands were in her hair, tangling the wild red curls in his fingers and kissing them fervently. Unresisting, she allowed him to liberate her carefully fashioned locks until they tumbled across the smooth swell of her breasts. She knew she was a lost woman.

She wrapped her arms around his neck and inclined her face to his. Hungrily, her lips sought his mouth. She needed his touch with a desperation she had not thought possible. His lips grazed her cheeks, her neck, and glided downwards to the smooth whiteness of her breasts. She moaned with pleasure and he pushed her against the warm wood of the shelter, fitting himself to her body. She tore at his shirt, burying her face in his bare throat. She wanted only to feel his naked skin, the hardness of his body against her. Neither heard the footsteps running up the Dark Walk.

'Cassandra? Cassandra?' Sir Hugo's plaintive cry echoed along the deserted path.

Then Annabel's impatient tones. 'She will hardly have walked here alone in the dark.'

'She may have fled this way. I shall never forgive myself if anything has happened to her.'

'Nothing will have happened, Sir Hugo. My sister is well able to take care of herself.'

'We should not have left her alone. I had no idea of such a dreadful event occurring.'

'How could you? You must not blame yourself. She was alone for a few minutes only and we were dancing close by.'

'But not close enough. We should have waited until Dominic returned to the box.'

'Dominic!' Annabel snorted. 'In that case, we would have been waiting until the Gardens closed.'

The two stood motionless in the dimness of the shelter, their pulses racing and their breathing irregular. Cassie was the first to emerge from the sultry haze, fumbling with the ties of her bodice and desperately trying to smooth the creases of her skirt. Luke was still gazing down at her with a look that turned her knees to water, but she made a monumental effort to regain her composure and gave him a hurried push towards the entrance. With a last, lingering glance, he gathered up his loo mask and slipped out of the shelter into the darkness beyond.

'Cassandra!' They were still calling as she stepped out onto the Walk.

'I'm here, don't worry. I'm safe.'

Sir Hugo almost ran to her side. In his agitation his cravat had become untied and his carefully styled hair was ruffled beyond repair. He clasped her hands tightly.'Thank goodness. Thank goodness we've found you. I have been out of my mind with worry.'

'I'm sorry to have caused you such concern, but I had to leave the supper box unexpectedly.' There was hardly a tremor to her voice.

Sir Hugo still wore a worried expression. 'You gave us a serious fright, my dear. When we returned to the box, it was upside down - plates broken, tablecloth askew and chairs strewn everywhere. And you had vanished. Whatever happened?'

'Just a little unwanted notice from someone who had drunk too much punch, but a passing gentleman intervened. I've come to no harm so let us forget it.'

'But why did you choose to come here?' Annabel asked curiously. 'The Dark Walk is so gloomy and there's no one around.'

'I didn't choose the Dark Walk, Annabel,' she replied with a touch of asperity. 'I wasn't thinking where I was going. I was trying to escape.'

'Of course.' Sir Hugo soothed. 'And thank heaven you were able to. This unfortunate business has been entirely my fault. I was most remiss in leaving you without an escort.'

'Are you all right, Miss Latimer?' Lady Foyle and Marianna were hurrying up the gravelled pathway to join them. 'We heard Sir Hugo and your sister searching for you and thought we could help.'

'How kind you all are,' Cassie responded. 'Please don't be concerned. There was a slight incident, but nothing too troublesome.'

'What a relief! I told you these Gardens were not at all the thing, Marianna. I hope you will believe me now.'

Marianna hardly heard her aunt. She was looking around her uncertainly. 'Are you sure everything is well, Miss Latimer? I thought I saw a figure among the trees just now.'

'I don't think you can have. I'm certain I outran the man who was pestering me.'

'If he's lurking nearby, I will find the blaggard.' Sir Hugo was feeling a lot stouter now that his beloved was safe.

'There's nobody here except myself. I expect you saw the shadow of a tree, Marianna. There is so little light.'

The girl looked unconvinced, but remained silent. The firework display was imminent and she wanted to find Dominic and speak to him urgently under cover of all the noise. Another bruising encounter with Lord Amesbury that evening had made her desperate to exact help from her only friend.

Annabel, too, was anxious not to miss the pyrotechnics and said grumpily, 'I think we've spent long enough in this miserable spot. For goodness' sake, let's find our places for the display.'

She had enjoyed two whole dances with Sir Hugo before he remembered they had left Cassandra alone. Surely that proved his love was weak. He might be enthralled by her sister's beauty – men could be unbelievably stupid – but it was only a sense of duty that had prompted him to return to the supper box. He didn't truly love his fiancée, Annabel was certain.

Chapter Nineteen

Cassie took her place in one of the front rows of chairs. Her heart was still hammering and the promised spectacle held little appeal after the turmoil of the last hour. She noticed Marianna seated a little to the right. The girl must have seen Luke as he made his way back through the wood – she must know his form by heart. How truly dreadful. How could Luke, how dared he, make such abandoned love to her even as his betrothed was walking close by? And after all her promises to herself, she had succumbed without an instant's hesitation. They had both behaved disgracefully.

She would never have accepted Sir Hugo's invitation if she had known Luke was to be here this evening. And surely he should have escorted Marianna and Lady Foyle. Instead he'd chosen to come alone and in disguise, and there could be only one reason – the freedom it conferred on him to act badly, the chance to continue her punishment. His fury when he'd first learned of her betrothal was fresh in her mind and she knew he would look for any opportunity to torment her. Not that he'd had to search very hard. Disguise and darkness was the perfect mix. And she had offered herself, all of herself, without restraint.

She could still see the deep grey of his eyes, glowing and intense in the shadows, the strong curves of his face sculpted by the moon's silvery haze, and then the feel of his skin on hers, the feel of his touch as he explored her body for the first time. But in the warm darkness he had seemed as caught up in the moment as she, in thrall to this intoxicating passion that had flamed between them.

But that couldn't be. Cassandra lived in daily expectation of reading the notice of his forthcoming marriage. Once he had confessed this new love to Lady Emma Trelawny, he would publish it to the world.

A few seats away Marianna had already forgotten the shadowy figure in the Dark Walk; she had more pressing matters on her mind. As soon as the first cluster of fireworks had traced its multi-coloured pathway through the sky, she slipped quietly away, leaving her aunt looking skywards. Dominic wasn't hard to find. He was on the outer circle of people, laughing and talking with some choice spirits he had managed to befriend during the evening. She recognised his slim, rangy figure immediately. He need not have bothered to don a loo mask.

The touch of Robert Amesbury's hands earlier that evening was still on her and she felt slightly sick. She knew she had brought this trouble on herself. She'd set out to win back the favour that Amesbury possessed and free herself of his presence forever. Instead she had fallen into even deeper debt and he now held her vowels for a sum of money she could never hope to repay.

Tonight when he'd tracked her down and skilfully detached her from her aunt, she had been forced to submit to his caresses. Under cover of darkness and in the midst of the boisterous crowd, he'd taken liberties that Marianna was desperate to blot from her mind. It was a piece of great good fortune that at that moment Sir Hugo had raised the alarm. Amesbury had melted away and she had been reunited with Lady Foyle.

But not before he had whispered a very clear threat into her ear. A handkerchief was but a poor return, he'd said, for the friendship he had extended. Marianna owed him money and he would be paid one way or another. The time for settlement had come, but this was by far too public a place. His house would prove a much cosier love nest. They were both bid to Annabel Latimer's come-out ball on Friday. He would see her there and when the dancing was at its height would send a signal to her to slip away and meet him outside. A carriage would be waiting to take them to his town mansion for a dinner *à deux* followed by... well, he would no doubt think of something. She would be returned to the ball in time for Aunt Serena to take her home and no one would be the wiser.

Marianna was in despair. When she'd first met Robert Amesbury he had seemed a dashing, experienced man of the world, whom she had managed to attract despite being little more than a schoolgirl. But very soon she'd been forced to confront the frightening reality that she was at the mercy of a predator with a perverted taste in young girls. She knew herself to be too naïve and inexperienced to deal with the situation alone and she could only hope that Dominic would prove her saviour.

'You must come away with me at the ball,' she announced abruptly, hardly waiting to exchange the customary pleasantries with him.

He gaped. 'Come away with you? What are you talking about?'

'At your sister's ball. I will be there and so will Amesbury. You must take me away or I'll be forced to go with him.'

'Are you crazy? Have the fireworks fried your brains?'

'I couldn't be more serious, Dominic. Amesbury will make me go with him if I don't escape.'

'Don't be so bird-witted. He can't force you to do anything if you don't wish it.'

'He has my handkerchief – you know that – and now he has my IOUs, too.'

'What!'

She hung her head, not daring to meet his gaze. 'You wouldn't help me and I tried to win back the handkerchief and lost even more money. If I don't do as he says, he will go to my aunt with my vowels and tell her how dreadfully I've behaved.'

Dominic shook his head in disbelief. 'Then speak to her yourself before he can. I told you before that your best hope is to be honest with her. Throw yourself on her mercy.'

'But now it's worse. It's not just the money – she'll suspect that I've behaved, well... not very properly,' she finished lamely.

'Of course you haven't behaved properly,' Dominic exploded. 'But she must know what kind of fellow Amesbury is and she won't judge you too harshly, I'm sure.'

'She will send me to Spain without a second thought and I'll go there in disgrace. Amesbury will make sure my aunt knows about the debt *and* the liberties I've allowed him, and when I arrive in Madrid my family will say I've brought shame on them. They might even lock me up!'

'And how will going away with me be less shameful?'

'I won't really go away with you, or at least not far, but I need you to make arrangements for me. A carriage to Dover and then a passage across the Channel.'

'You can't travel all that way alone, a chit of a girl like you.'

'I'm not a chit.'

'You're seventeen and the biggest wet goose I've ever met.'

The conversation was not turning out the way she had hoped and Marianna could see her chance of securing help fading away.

'Dominic, please, please, help me. If you don't think I should travel alone, come with me as far as Paris. My father has friends there and I could stay with them. They'll help me travel on to Spain.'

The pleading in her soft brown eyes was having its effect, but he still couldn't grasp what she would gain from her plan.

'But don't you see,' she said trying hard to remain patient, 'I can leave a note for Aunt Serena saying that I've left London because I'm so unhappy. Someone I met has hurt me.' That at least was true. 'I'll ask her to keep my confidence and not discuss with anyone why I've left. She won't know about the debts or about that dreadful man, and neither will my relatives in Spain. All they will think is that I've arrived a little earlier than expected.'

'And when Lord Amesbury knocks at your aunt's door after you've left with *his* story and *your* IOUs?'

'Do you think he will?' A scared look had returned to her face and Dominic relented.

'Probably not. It's you he wants, not the money. Once you've fled, there won't be much point in trying to harass Lady Foyle.'

'There you see, I'm right. All we have to do is to get to Paris and then everyone will be happy.'

'Oh yes, everyone,' he said acidly. 'And how do you propose that we get to Paris? Hiring a carriage to Dover costs money and if you think I'm travelling with you on the common stage, you can think again. And when we get to the port, there'll be money needed for a boat ticket and you might not get a berth straight away. That will mean laying down more blunt to pay for accommodation.'

'I don't think I'll stay overnight in Dover,' she said hurriedly. There would be little point in rescuing her reputation from Robert Amesbury's clutches to have it shredded by keeping company with a different man. 'We'll go on board straight away.'

Dominic wasn't at all sure that would be possible. He imagined that berths on ships crossing the Channel had to be booked some time in advance, but Marianna seemed to know what she was talking about. He had never travelled beyond England and the girl's assurances that she still had a large sum of her father's money intact and that she spoke passable French finally convinced him. He was still feeling guilty that her troubles had begun when he'd introduced her to gambling. He cursed that evening heartily. If he'd had a clue what she would do, he would have kept dancing that night until his feet dropped off. Wearily he agreed to ride with her the next day and make detailed plans for her escape on Friday evening.

Cassandra heard her brother coming in a few hours later. He made no attempt to be quiet, banging the front door behind him and thudding loudly up the stairs to his room. Presumably his night at Vauxhall had gone little better than hers.

Her evening had been ruined. Not by the drunken intruder since her fear of him had been fleeting. Almost as soon as she'd realised that he could be a real danger, Luke had knocked the man down and thrown him over the barrier. Then in swift succession their escape from the crowd, the breathless journey up the Dark Walk and finally those moments of sweet delight. Once again he'd set her body alight and left her yearning and confused. Once again she had known no caution. And all these hours later, she could feel her heart pounding still.

But he was playing with her – his affections lay elsewhere. He was simply intent on proving her unfaithful, especially now she was to make a marriage he abhorred. He wished to expose her as a woman who accepted one man while making impassioned love with another. Her betrothal should have protected her from folly, but she had betrayed Sir Hugo. While he was frantically searching for her, she was being caressed by another. She had wanted Luke as badly as she would ever want a man and had shown him so just as plainly. If they had not been interrupted, she knew she would have given herself to him completely.

He had proved her forthcoming marriage was nothing more than a sham, proved she was the inconstant woman he'd always thought her. He had won their battle of wills.

Chapter Twenty

If Cassie thought it dishonourable that her old lover had chosen to roam the gardens of Vauxhall alone, Luke was thinking the same. He had refused Marianna's invitation to escort her to the fête and with good reason – accompanying her to a masked revelry was unlikely to discourage her infatuation and he had already been at pains to bid her goodbye.

The legal papers he'd tarried for were now stamped and signed and while Marianna was enjoying the party, he should have been well on his way to Cornwall. Yet last night he'd lurked in the shadows, eager to avoid detection, his cloak and loo mask a flimsy disguise. Why on earth had he done so?

The news of Cassandra's betrothal had fallen on him like a bludgeoning hammer. He had felt himself disintegrating from the force of his anger and had needed immediate action, immediate distraction, to free himself from the fury that had him in its grip. He had ridden swiftly from the park to the livery stables, then marched straight to Jackson's Boxing saloon where half-a-dozen rounds with the Gentleman himself had left him physically bruised and battered, but feeling a good deal better. At least for a while.

But then that old haunting refrain began again and a fervent need to see her swept over him. She had been adamant that he stay away and he dared not risk an open confrontation. If he had, the temptation to grab her and show her just why she shouldn't marry Sir Hugo would have been irresistible. Yet the need to see her was like a drug. It had him in its grasp and would not let go.

The fireworks at Vauxhall had been talked about for weeks and he knew she would be there. In the event he'd been reduced to watching her from afar. He had seen her take her place in the supper box with her irritating sister and that stuffed shirt, Latimer. She had looked magnificent: her wayward curls had seemed almost alive, a cascade of fire, and the fall of her gold silk gown had transformed her slender figure into voluptuous beauty. He had stood transfixed, desire touching every one of his senses. He'd felt himself galvanised into action, urged forward to leap the barrier and pull her into his arms. Almost but not quite. Self-discipline had somehow prevailed and he'd continued to watch from the shadows.

But when an intruder had appeared out of nowhere and threatened her, prudence had been thrown to the winds. There had been immense satisfaction in taking out his frustration on the miserable unfortunate who had dared to frighten this goddess. And then the whirlwind run with her up the Dark Walk to elude the attentions of the gathering crowd.

Looking back, he recognised their flight had been more than a response to menace. It was an attempt to escape with her, to run away and leave behind the mess they had jointly made and just simply be together. The memories of their tryst were still with him: the soft rustle of foliage, the sweet odour of lilacs, and her body inviting and responsive beneath his hands. He was her prisoner and the ferocious desire she aroused in him was causing as much suffering as he had ever inflicted.

For she belonged to another man. She could not break the engagement she had entered – the label of jilt would not be so easily shrugged off this time. She would have to marry Sir Hugo. Already she was progressing steadily towards the altar, preparing herself for a calm and uneventful life with a calm and uneventful man. That was the choice she had made and, for her sake, he must stand back and let her follow it. Wasn't true love selfless?

Somehow the injuries of the past had dissolved to nothing. She had failed him, but she had been the victim of a master seducer against whom her inexperience was no match. And he, Luke, was partly to blame. He had been her betrothed, her lover, but he'd not shown her the love she craved. He'd been stiff, awkward, shy almost. She hadn't guessed, maybe couldn't guess, the depths of his feelings for her.

He saw her now in his mind's eye, a young, vital girl, saw her at the very moment that she'd agreed to marry him. They had stood on the cliff top, the waves thundering beneath, random spray misting the very air between them. She had gazed up at him, her face warm with happiness, and said yes. Then she'd reached for his hand and tugged him along the path to the cove, her smile urging him on, her eyes laughing with pleasure. Her heart had been true, he was sure.

After years in which he'd kept the past under lock and key, meeting her again had released a great dam of emotion. He'd thought he would never feel so deeply again, but he'd been wrong. And why was that? He could pretend no longer. It seemed that he had always loved her, from the days of callow youth through the years of exile to this very moment. His clumsy plan to teach her a lesson and free himself from her power was simply hurt love.

He longed for her, burned for her, but he must subdue those feelings. Tomorrow there would be a ball at Mount Street in honour of her tiresome sister and he had been invited. He would bid her farewell in a crowded room and bow out of her life as gracefully as he could. His luggage would be packed and waiting for him at the inn. Early the next morning he would be on his way to Cornwall.

‿

Number Six Mount Street was a house in upheaval and if Cassie were tempted to dwell on her transgressions at Vauxhall, the preparations for the ball effectively banished all such remorse. For days the housemaids had been dusting and sweeping every corner of the house, shining silver and polishing chandeliers. Every spare glass had been unearthed and washed until it sparkled. The house was a modest size and to hold a ball for up to fifty people, though small by the Season's standards, was an immense undertaking. The two first-floor salons were to be made into one by the simple expedient of sliding back the wooden partitioning. This would be the ballroom.

'We must roll up the carpets,' Lady Katherine instructed three panting footmen early on the Friday morning. 'They will have to be taken to the cellar, I fear, but the parquet floor will be excellent for dancing.' The men, perspiring down three flights of stairs, did not appear overly impressed by this information.

'Cassie,' her mother called urgently to her from the drawing room. 'Do you think the quartet we've hired could be stationed at one end of this room?' She indicated the window enclave.

Cassandra wrinkled her nose. 'Not really. It would mean that we cannot open the windows behind them, and it looks set to be a very warm evening.'

'The room is already uncomfortably stuffy, I agree, but I cannot see where else to put the musicians.' Lady Katherine frowned. 'It will have to do.'

'It might not matter,' her daughter comforted. 'We can fling the windows wide at the far end of the second room and if people become overheated, they can step out on to the balcony to refresh themselves.'

'Not too many people,' her mother said wryly. The iron-work balcony which overlooked the gardens to the rear of the house was no more than six feet wide.

⌒

As the day wore on, Cassandra became very aware of her mother's increasing anxiety. This evening's event had been planned as a modest introduction of Annabel to the *ton*, but somehow it had escalated. More invitations had been issued than Lady Katherine had bargained for and some of these to the most fêted in society. Refreshments had been ordered from Gunter's in addition to those being produced in the kitchen by Cook and her helpers, and the best champagne had been ordered at a ruinous cost.

What should have been a simple occasion had been transformed into a major undertaking. Lady Katherine could not decide just how this had happened, although Cassie could have enlightened her. She knew her sister had been busy.

Annabel was not content with what she had described privately as a paltry affair and refused to be put off with the promise of a much grander ball in her honour the following year. She was partaking of London society now and she wanted her official launch to be talked of for weeks to come. She had been unable to persuade her mother to hire a more prestigious venue, but she was determined that everything that could be done to make the party memorable would be done. It was she who had chosen the champagne and ordered the additional delicacies and she who had ensured that invitations had gone out to the very highest of the *ton*.

That was her sole contribution to the evening's success. Her day was spent in her room preparing for her grand appearance. The dress she had originally chosen for this momentous occasion was deemed that morning to be commonplace and she was engaged in a frantic and increasingly bad-tempered search for the perfect ensemble.

It was left to Cassandra to assist her flurried parent in the hundred-and-one tasks that had to be accomplished. Had the flowers arrived and how were they to be arranged? How many musicians had arrived and was there sufficient room for all of them in the window enclosure her mother had chosen? And what should the order of music be? Where were the dance cards that had been ordered at least three weeks ago and why had the ices been delivered so early that they were bound to melt well before they could be served?

So it went on as the hours of the day ticked by, Cassie and her mother scurrying from ballroom to dining room to kitchen to hall, solving problems, settling disputes, until they were both so fatigued that all they wanted was to retire to bed and let everyone else dance the night away.

In the confusion that permeated the house, they hardly noticed Dominic. He had quickly been pronounced useless in preparing for the ball and advised to lose himself for the day. That suited him perfectly. He had plenty to do if he were to carry off Marianna early the next morning and his family's abstraction meant that his constant comings and goings went unremarked. It struck Cassie that he looked unusually serious, but she was too busy to enquire further. Meanwhile upstairs Annabel continued to drive her maid-servant to distraction until finally she had decided on the outfit which would eclipse all others and the entire house breathed a sigh of relief.

~

At nine o' clock Annabel, primped and pampered, took up her place in the entrance hall at the head of the family, waiting to greet her guests. Cassandra, standing slightly behind her, hoped that her own appearance was not too disordered. She had completed her *toilette* with only a few minutes to go, scrambling into her dress as the first of the carriage wheels were heard rumbling across the cobble-stones outside.

She need not have worried since her beauty was undi-minished. In the short time available Rosa had given up any idea of achieving the latest elaborate style known as *à la Méduse* and decided on a simple arrangement of soft curls around the face with the rest of her mistress's unruly hair pulled back into an orderly chignon. Diamond clips on either side softened any severity and matching diamonds sparkled from her ears and nestled in the curves of her bosom. The Pomona-green gauze she wore over a paler underdress accentuated the emerald of her eyes and the small diamond fastenings to her bodice made her seem alive with light whenever she moved.

Cassie had made little attempt to appear anything other than acceptable, yet she easily outshone every other woman in the room. Those daring young damsels who had worn gauze dresses over damped and transparent petticoats in order to attract attention, looked frankly tawdry in the face of such transcendent beauty. Fortunately Annabel was so immersed in her own absorbing bubble of pleasure that she had no eyes for any of her family, least of all the sister she hoped to supplant.

Marianna and Lady Foyle were among the first to arrive and Cassandra noticed once more how very pale and quiet the young girl was. Something ails her, she thought, but what? Robert Amesbury followed close behind, suave and debonair as ever, but exuding a sense of threat, subtle and unexpressed. Cassie was at a loss to understand why he'd come since he was not a particular friend of the family, but seeing Annabel's blush as she curtsied to him, she knew immediately who had pushed for his invitation. Lord Amesbury's attendance at one's coming-out ball was a fine prize to win.

She had little time to contemplate the oddities of the guest list before Sir Hugo was before her, splendid in black satin knee breeches and long-tailed coat, and reverently taking her hand.

'How good to see you, my dear. And looking breathtaking as always. I seem hardly to have managed a word with you of late.'

She looked guiltily up at him. 'I'm sorry. This week has simply sped by – there has been so much to do for Annabel's come-out and Mama is without my father's help.'

'I know how busy you must have been, my dear Cassandra, and that is only right. Your mother needs your support and I would expect nothing else from such a loving daughter. But when this evening is over, I hope we will have the chance to spend time together.'

'We will, of course,' she reassured him hastily.

'I am very much looking forward to introducing you to Thorne Park, as soon as ever it is convenient for you – and for your mother, naturally. I am sure you will both enjoy the country air, and I hope it's not too boastful to say that you will be well pleased with the home you find there. Every member of my staff is ready and eager to welcome the new Lady Thorne.'

Cassie brushed aside this reference to their marriage, but tried to sound enthusiastic about the forthcoming visit.

'I'm looking forward to seeing Thorne Park as much as you are to showing me.' This was only half a lie at least. 'But until Annabel and Dominic return to Cornwall, you must see that it is impossible.'

Annabel, who had moved towards Sir Hugo as soon as she saw him enter the room, caught the tail end of the conversation and looked thunderous. Only the arrival of a new dance partner prevented an outburst. She smiled extravagantly at the young man who stood before her and made a play of ticking off his name on her dance card. With a withering look at her sister, she allowed herself to be swept back on to the ballroom floor.

Chapter Twenty-One

It was halfway through the evening before Sir Hugo caught up with his beloved again. Her duties had not stopped with the arrival of guests; she and Lady Katherine had constantly to mingle, to introduce, to smooth the social waters. He finally ran her to ground just as she had finished giving instructions to one of the footmen to begin opening the final crate of champagne.

'Cassandra –' he pounced on her – 'this dance must be mine!' The musicians were tuning up for the first quadrille of the evening.

She found herself having to apologise yet again. 'I'm sorry to disappoint you, Hugo, but there are a hundred-and-one things I must check before I can think of dancing.'

His face fell and she glanced hurriedly around. 'I see Annabel is temporarily without a partner. It would be most kind of you to ask her to join the quadrille.'

Sir Hugo gave a resigned smile. 'If you wish it, my dear. It's well that your sister dances so creditably.'

He moved obediently to where Annabel stood disconsolate. The name on her dance card had failed and she lacked a partner at her very own party, but Sir Hugo's arrival transformed the miserable situation. Seeing the genuine smile of warmth directed at him, he felt that his sacrifice had not been in vain. They were soon dancing easily together, chatting almost as old friends, Cassie noted. She was satisfied. The better Annabel knew Hugo, the less likely she was to weave fantasies around him.

⌒

By eleven o'clock the ball was in full swing. Almost every guest who had been bidden to the party had arrived and those who were planning to go on to other and grander events had not yet left. The dance floor was crowded, a jewelled kaleidoscope of colour as the women twirled and pirouetted in their partners' arms. If the musicians felt stifled in their enclosure, they did not show it, playing without pause for the eager dancers. The temperature of the room had been rising by the minute and the copious banks of flowers, which decked the walls on either side, were beginning to wilt. The starched shirt points of the gentlemen showed a definite tendency to limpness and even the most elegant of the women had recourse to their fans as the evening wore on. The call to partake of refreshments, when it came, was greeted with some relief.

Supper was a sociable event. The Latimers' dining room had been cleared of furniture and in its stead trestle tables set up, covered in starched white linen and furnished with white porcelain and silver cutlery. Small crystal bowls of deep pink roses dotted the length of the buffet and a splendid centrepiece of mauve and white lilies towered majestically over the whole. The table groaned with every conceivable dainty that the combined efforts of Cook and

Gunter's could produce.

It was an intimate space and people gathered in groups around the table or arranged the few chairs still remaining in small clusters. The flushed, happy faces and the buzz of chatter was evidence that the event was deemed a success and Cassandra could relax.

At last she had leisure to look around her. Annabel was in high gig sitting with Sir Hugo and two of her female confidantes. She was evidently pleased to have netted the man she clearly considered the beau of the evening. Dominic hovered in the background, a jumpy look on his face. Cassie watched him for a while, feeling concerned, but unsure why. She saw that he was staring rather too fixedly at Marianna, who seemed to be involved in some kind of altercation with Lord Amesbury. How extraordinary! Robert Amesbury rose from his seat at that moment and made for the door.

Immediately she sped into the hall to bid him goodbye, her brain teeming. 'Are you leaving us already, Lord Amesbury?' she asked lightly.

He turned, smooth as always, his face giving no inkling of his thoughts. 'I regret, Miss Latimer, I have business elsewhere. Do accept my thanks for a most enjoyable evening.'

His tone was genial, but there was a metallic ring to his voice and his smile was tight and controlled. What could have upset him so much that he would risk gossip from an angry dispute and an early departure? Cassie noticed that his adversary, too, was making her way to the door. Marianna, still pale faced, had persuaded her aunt to leave betimes.

The musicians struck up again and the ballroom filled with couples still determined to enjoy the evening. Cassie had just decided this might be an opportune moment to offer Hugo the dance he desired, when a tall and striking figure was ushered through the door. The man wore the black satin knee breeches of the gentleman of fashion and a black tailcoat which fitted him to perfection. A white frilled shirt set off the lean, tanned face and a single diamond stud held in place a neckcloth tied in the intricate Oriental style.

It was Luke and he looked superb. She could hardly believe her eyes. Luke! Who on earth could have invited him? Her sister's cunning smile told the story. Of course, Annabel would hope to cause trouble if she could and this was her master stroke. Well, she would not succeed.

'Good evening, Lord Trelawny.'

Cassie's voice strove to remain unhurried and calm, though her eyes lingered on the seductive picture he presented. But the remembrance of their last encounter came rushing back and she gave herself a mental shake. She could not afford to show weakness, nor any sign of the feelings he aroused in her.

'Good evening, Miss Latimer. I hope I see you well?' His tone was crisp and businesslike. It helped to steady her.

'Yes, my lord, very well,' she responded formally.

They stood, unable to continue the conversation, unable to stop their eyes from feasting on each other. He was the first to recover.

'I regret that I am unable to stay. I came only to say goodbye.'

'You are leaving London?'

'I have always had the intention of returning to Cornwall as soon as I could, but circumstances have made it difficult.'

'Really?' There was challenge in her voice. 'I imagine Lady Emma must be very glad that "circumstances" now allow you to return home.'

He bowed his head, acknowledging she had hit home. She looked at him again. His eyes held a wistfulness she had not seen before.

'Won't you stay to dance a little while?' she managed. 'Unfortunately Miss Marquez has just left – she could not have known you were attending – but there are many others who would be delighted to partner you.'

He blinked at the mention of Marianna's name but then recalled that Cassandra still believed in the fiction of their relationship, a fiction he had been at pains to foster.

'I need no other partner, but if *you* will dance with me, I would be delighted. A waltz is just beginning.'

Mindful of having refused Sir Hugo earlier in the evening, Cassie demurred. If she accepted, her fiancé would feel justifiably offended and she had no wish to snub the man she was soon to marry. More truthfully, she knew that dancing with Luke would unleash feelings beyond her control and tear apart the social façade she had been so careful to cultivate.

'I am not dancing this evening, Lord Trelawny.'

'Come – a few steps only and then I will leave.'

She hesitated. The temptation to find herself in his arms again, and for the last time, was overwhelming. But she must not succumb to this insistent longing; she must put such feelings behind her for good. Her hand was trembling as he took it and raised it to his lips.

'A few minutes of the waltz should not take up too much of your time.'

As if in a dream, she allowed herself to be swept onto the dance floor. He held her tightly, moving to the strains of the music, his form fitting hers, two halves making a whole. Locked in a private intimacy, they heard and saw nothing other than themselves. The passion that flowed between them mounted inexorably until neither could bear to keep dancing. And so it was that as they neared the far window, Luke pulled the curtain swiftly to one side and danced her on to the balcony.

Cassie gasped. 'Whatever are you doing?'

His eyes shone in the moonlight that lapped the ornamental balustrade; when he spoke, his voice was rough with desire. 'I came to say goodbye, Cassandra, but I find I can only do so in private, just you and I alone together for a few moments.'

The soft air of evening washed over them and the smell of Albertine roses on the wall below drowned them in a sweet perfume. A slight breeze flicked her curls across her cheek and his hand went automatically to brush them back. He stopped himself.

'I came to say goodbye,' he repeated, 'and to wish you well for the future.'

The sincerity in his voice was unmistakeable. His anger had gone, Cassie realised. He had accepted her betrothal and whatever schemes he'd been devising were finished.

This was the outcome she had craved during the past days of misery. Yet she was filled with the greatest sorrow – in a few minutes she must watch him walk from the room and out of her life forever.

As if reading her mind, he said gently, 'You deserve happiness. I should not have hurt you, you of all people.'

She could see this sentiment came from deep within his heart and wondered what other feelings might lie beneath that calm, elegant exterior. It took her a while to answer and when she did, her voice sounded barely above a whisper.

'I am not free of blame either, as we both know.'

'All that is past. We were young and foolish, and there I should have left it. But when I saw you again...' He shrugged his shoulders expressively. 'It was all up with me. The old grievances began to live again and I seemed powerless to slay my demons.'

'And now?'

'I've not completely slain them, but they are back under lock and key.'

His smile was awry, his face shadowed despite his best efforts. She had a crazy urge to take him in her arms and kiss him back into happiness. The shocking thought rendered her silent for a moment.

'You need fear no more intrusions from me,' he said, thinking she required reassurance. 'You will have a splendid future, I'm sure, and I wish you the happiest life possible.'

'You were always a generous boy, Luke,' she whispered.

'And you were always a loving girl, as I'm sure Sir Hugo will find. He once said that he considered himself blessed to have won you for his wife and he was right to think so.'

Luke moved slowly towards her. She felt herself tremble when his fingers lightly touched her hand and trailed their way up her bare arm. Then they were in her hair winding, stroking, caressing the fiery curls. Both hands moved to cup her face and he gazed intently into her eyes, absorbed in their emerald depths.

'One last kiss,' he murmured.

She raised her face to his, her mouth soft and yielding beneath the hard pressure of his lips. His arms were round her pulling her body into his, moulding her to himself.

'Cassie,' he groaned, 'what have we done?'

His use of her pet name demolished any remaining resistance. His mouth once more fastened on hers, his lips exploring, insistent, until she wanted nothing more than to feel him, all of him, close to her and forever.

For long minutes they were oblivious to everything. They saw nothing of the curtain being quietly lifted and two pairs of eyes staring at them, Sir Hugo's in horror and Annabel's in jubilation. When they emerged from the enclave, shaken from their encounter, neither observer was to be seen. Sir Hugo had taken a hasty leave of Lady Latimer and Annabel, the picture of innocence, had joined a new set for the country dance which was just then striking up.

Chapter Twenty-Two

For the few hours that remained of the ball, Cassandra was glad to have plenty to do. There were still refreshments to be ordered from the kitchen, damsels to partner, coats to be retrieved and farewells to say; almost anything would do to keep the pain at bay. Luke had gone. Those words danced blackly in her mind's eye and had constantly to be repressed. It was only when the last person had been escorted to the last carriage that she could no longer hide from her grief: Luke was gone and his leaving was forever.

There was no sign of Dominic, but her mother and sister were in the hall, looking tired from their individual exertions, but both pleased with the evening's success.

'Thank you, Cassie, for all your hard work today.' Lady Katherine clasped her hand warmly. 'Without you things would not have gone so smoothly. I'm sure Annabel is most grateful.' She looked meaningfully at her younger daughter.

Annabel did not respond and there was an uncomfortable silence.

'What happened to Sir Hugo, Mama?' Cassandra asked. 'He seemed to disappear in a puff of smoke.'

Her joke fell somewhat flat, but her mother smiled. 'He left shortly after supper, my dear,' she said mildly. 'I'm not entirely sure why. He said something about another engagement, though it seemed rather odd to me. I thought you might know.'

'No, indeed. I understood he would be present for the whole evening. How very strange.'

'He seemed a little distressed.' Lady Katherine was thoughtful. 'But I could be wrong.'

'You're not wrong, Mama. He *was* distressed.' Annabel had come instantly to life.

'Why, whatever has happened?' her sister queried in astonishment.

'I don't know how you have the nerve to stand there and ask that!' Annabel was almost jumping with annoyance.

Her mother looked questioningly at a bemused Cassandra, but no help was forthcoming. 'Explain yourself, Annabel,' Lady Katherine commanded crossly.

'If you really want me to I will, but I would think Cassie should be the one to do the explaining. She's the one who's engaged to Sir Hugo, but can't stop kissing other men.'

'What!' Cassie and her mother exclaimed in unison.

But it was Cassandra who turned pale. Sir Hugo must have seen her kissing Luke and naturally it was Annabel, who would have led him to that window and ensured her disgrace. Her sister must have been watching them all the time and seized a golden opportunity the minute it came.

'What is this, Cassie?' her mother was demanding.

'Luke came to say goodbye, Mama,' she began calmly. 'He was bidding me farewell.'

'Hmph!' Annabel interrupted crudely. 'Some farewell! You were in his arms and he was kissing you in a quite scandalous way.'

'Cassandra, is this true?'

She did not answer her mother, but turned away and began to climb the stairs to her room. She was sick at heart and there was nothing she could say in her defence.

⌒

At eleven o'clock the next morning Sir Hugo Thorne presented himself at Mount Street and asked to speak to the eldest daughter of the house. He was in a chastened mood but also determined. He had sat up late into the night, thinking through his predicament, and had come to a decision. He must see Cassandra Latimer immediately before he changed his mind. He only hoped that meeting her again would not throw him off track.

When the maidservant scratched at the bedroom door with Sir Hugo's name on her lips, Cassie braced herself for what she knew would be a distressing interview. She had been up and dressed for many hours; in fact, she'd hardly slept, going over the events of the previous evening in her mind and preparing herself for the likely outcome.

Now the moment had arrived. She walked slowly down the stairs, her expression serene and her graceful carriage masking the distress she felt. Sir Hugo, looking towards the staircase, saw a vision of the palest pink tulle. Resolutely, he squared his shoulders.

'Good morning, Miss Latimer.' No Cassandra now, she reflected.

'Good morning, Sir Hugo.' She was equally formal.

'You wished to speak privately with me?'

He was grateful that she had come straight to the point. 'Would that be possible?' He cleared his throat nervously.

She led the way into the library, a room normally deserted for most of the day. They were unlikely to be disturbed since the servants had already cleaned. In any case, she imagined the discussion would not take very long.

'Miss Latimer,' Sir Hugo began, clearing his throat again. 'We have known each other for many months now and you must be aware that I have grown to esteem you highly... and to love you.' He almost mumbled these last few words. Cassie inclined her head slightly.

'I had hoped,' he began again with difficulty, 'that we were well enough suited to contemplate making our future lives together. When you accepted my proposal, I was the happiest man alive. However...' and he appeared to be choosing his words carefully '... it would seem that you were not of the same mind.'

She bowed her head. She must say something to this honourable man who was clearly struggling to make sense of a world turned upside down. The future he had so blithely anticipated lay in ruins.

'Sir Hugo, please believe me when I say that I also shared that hope.'

'Then I do not understand what has occurred.' His face lost its fixed expression and collapsed into a bewildered sadness. He looked hopelessly out of his depth and Cassandra's heart smote her.

'I fear it will be no comfort for you to learn that I am as confused,' she offered. 'However you should know that this painful situation is no reflection on you. You have been wholly generous in your conduct. It is entirely my fault.'

'You are most kind and it relieves me to know that I could not have done anything more to make our betrothal a success. But it leaves us with a problem.'

'There is no problem. In the circumstances it is impossible for us to marry and I imagine you came here today to tell me so.'

Sir Hugo looked pained. 'I regret that you are right in your surmise. After what has occurred I feel that neither of us could give ourselves wholeheartedly to a marriage.'

She nodded and put on her best smile. 'It is helpful that the notice of our betrothal has not yet been sent to the papers and only a few people know of our plans.'

'But what shall we say to those people who have been told we are to wed?'

'We will simply say that we found that after all we were not suited to each other.'

Sir Hugo turned this over in his mind and then smiled faintly. 'That sounds pleasantly vague. And people can pick it over at will and make what they wish of it.'

'Exactly.'

'As always, Miss Latimer, you have the perfect touch.' He looked regretfully at the beautiful woman who stood before him.

'Not always, Sir Hugo,' she reminded him gently.

'Quite so,' he said, and hurried towards the door.

The interview was at an end. They had survived it and without permanent scars on either side. Cassie breathed a sigh of relief. Now that it was done, a burden seemed to have been lifted. Her future would be difficult, but she would no longer be living a lie.

She followed him out into the hall and almost fell over the figure of Annabel, who had clearly been loitering outside the library door, agog to see what happened and ready with sympathy for Sir Hugo.

'Miss Annabel, good morning,' he said without much enthusiasm. The strident tones of violet silk hit him in the eyes and he winced. He had been hoping to escape from the house without having to encounter any other of the family.

'How nice to see you, Sir Hugo,' Annabel chirruped gaily, as if nothing of any import had happened. 'Are you intending to walk in the park? It would be such a waste to spend this wonderful weather indoors.'

He had been planning to return to his own home and lose himself in paperwork. Anything to obliterate this most painful meeting of his entire life. But Annabel was smiling encouragingly and shafts of sunlight lit the hall. Perhaps after all a walk in the park with a congenial companion might be beneficial.

Annabel had shown great enthusiasm for his latest project, the foundation of an orphanage in Lambeth, and her opinion on a number of pressing issues which had emerged since their last discussion might be valuable.

'If you would care to accompany me to Hyde Park, I would be delighted, Miss Annabel,' he responded obligingly.

She snatched up her bonnet from the chair and was at his side in an instant. It was evident she was prepared for this moment and Sir Hugo was flattered that she had planned to devote herself to keeping him company. At least one of the Latimer sisters held him in esteem. He reflected on how much time he had spent with Annabel lately when Cassandra had been unable or unwilling to be by his side. In hindsight, those frequent absences were significant. And he had grown to like the younger girl.

Admittedly her taste in dress was a little unusual, but she seemed willing to listen to whatever small suggestions he made. Above all, he felt flattered by her interest in his affairs: she always gave him her full attention. There was merit in the company of a girl who was not the most sought-after belle in society. And merit, a small whispering voice added, in a girl who was not prone to sexual flirtation.

Lady Katherine had come into the hall as the pair left. She looked questioningly at Cassandra still standing with her hand on the library door.

'Mama, I have to tell you that Sir Hugo and I have decided we do not suit.' The phrase ran glibly off her tongue.

'Do not suit!' her mother parroted. 'Whatever does that mean?'

'It means our betrothal is over.'

Lady Katherine sighed heavily. 'After what occurred last night, I imagine Sir Hugo had little choice.'

'It was a mutual decision.'

'Precipitated by your reckless conduct! Whatever were you thinking?'

Cassie ignored the reference to her encounter with Luke and tried to soothe her irate mother. 'It's for the best.

Really.'

Lady Katherine looked bewildered. 'But why in heaven's name, Cassandra? Everything seemed to be going so well between you.'

'"Seemed" is the right word. Sir Hugo and I were never really suited, though for a short time I persuaded myself otherwise.'

'And now you have a second broken engagement to your name. I hope you realise what that signifies in the eyes of society.'

'If you mean that now I have no earthly chance of finding a husband, yes, I do realise. But believe me, Mama, there are worse things in life.'

Lady Katherine groaned and twisted her hands. Her beloved daughter had committed social suicide and there was nothing she could do to rescue her.

'Don't be too upset – ' Cassandra warmed to the task of rallying her mother '– you might just catch Sir Hugo for another Latimer!'

Lady Katherine's expression was fiercely indignant and it was well for her daughter that a servant appeared at that moment with a note in her hand. The maid was unable to read, but was clearly agitated by having found the paper prominently displayed on her mistress's writing desk.

Irritated, Lady Katherine snatched up the note and dismissed the maidservant. She scanned the brief message and her face drained of all colour; she looked as though she were about to crumble to the floor. Cassie stepped swiftly forward.

'Mama, what is it?'

Chapter Twenty-Three

She took the note from her mother's trembling hand and read it quickly. 'I don't understand. He's gone to Paris? Dominic?'

'How could he?' her mother wailed. 'What more will befall us?'

'But what is this about Marianna?'

'It's evident, isn't it? They have eloped.'

'Forgive me, Mama, but that has to be a nonsense. Dominic eloping? He's never shown the slightest interest in females.'

'I am not at all sure that's so. He seems to have spent a great deal of time with this girl lately.'

Cassandra thought back over the last few weeks and had to agree: Dominic meeting Marianna at Almack's, laughing with her at the picnic, the regular rides in the park, and then last night at Annabel's ball, his fixed concentration on the girl. But her lover? That still appeared unlikely.

She said as much to her mother, but Lady Katherine refused to be comforted. 'If he is not her lover, then what is he doing going to Paris with her? It's clear to me they are eloping.'

'Mama, even if they wished to marry each other, why would they elope? Wouldn't it be more rational for Dominic simply to ask Marianna's guardian for permission to wed?'

'That's just it!' her mother produced triumphantly. 'He must know there would be little chance of obtaining permission to marry. The girl is only seventeen and, I understand, a great heiress. Dominic hardly figures as the most eligible suitor.' A sudden dreadful thought struck. 'Do you think he's eloping for her fortune?'

'How can that be? Dominic has lacked for nothing in his life.'

Her mother did not reply immediately, but began an agitated walk up and down the hall, her mind beset by this new enormity.

'I haven't said anything to you, Cassie' she began finally in a faltering voice, 'but I've become worried over some of his activities. I suspect he has begun to gamble more seriously than we know. What if he has plunged himself into debt, huge debt, and hasn't wanted to tell us?' She shook her head in despair and her tears began to gather.

'Not even Dominic would be foolish enough to think he could elope with an under-age girl and then make free with her inheritance!'

Her mother appeared deaf to these rousing words. She sank into the large leather chesterfield that stood against the wall and stared blindly into space. When her daughter bent down and tried to hug her, she began to rock backwards and forwards, keening quietly and seeming to disappear into a nightmare world of her own conjecture.

Cassandra was alarmed. Her mother's self-possession was renowned and had survived countless family troubles. But this new tragedy to strike Mount Street, coming so quickly after the events of the previous evening, had clearly overwhelmed her.

She came to a decision. 'Mama, I'm going to see Lady Foyle. She may know more than us.'

Galvanised by these words, her mother sat bolt upright. 'No! We cannot allow this news to be made public.'

'It won't be. Lady Foyle will be just as eager as we are to hush things up, and together we may be able to decide on a rescue plan.'

'Rescue? How can you rescue them? Dominic left the house before dawn. They could be anywhere by now.'

'We have the advantage of knowing where they're headed. If we could reach them within the next few hours, then nobody except ourselves need know a thing.'

Particularly Luke, she thought. For his sake, if for no one else's, she must do her utmost to rescue Marianna from this foolish journey.

'And who is to follow them?' her mother was saying querulously. 'Your father is hundreds of miles away in Cornwall and you have managed to alienate the fiancé who might have leant us his support.'

Before her mother could renew this still-raw grievance, Cassie rang for Lady Katherine's dresser.

'Her ladyship is feeling unwell, Mitford. She needs to rest. Could you ensure your mistress is made comfortable and then bring her some sweet tea?'

Once her mother had been safely despatched to her

room, Cassandra donned her bonnet and walked swiftly to Curzon Street. She had dismissed her mother's suggestion that Dominic had eloped because of money troubles, but the thought that he might have become seriously infatuated with Marianna could not be so easily lost. It was true that he had hitherto shown little interest in women, but Cassie could not deny that he had been dancing attendance on the young girl in recent weeks in a way that was quite foreign to him. What if Marianna returned his feelings? Where would that leave Luke? Her heart ached for him that he should be treated so shabbily by both the women he had asked to marry.

⤸

The moment Cassie was ushered into Lady Foyle's presence, she saw that the older woman, too, had received an unwelcome missive. Her face was unnaturally pale and she seemed to have difficulty rising from her seat. She came towards her fair young visitor and offered an unsteady hand. Once they were alone, she silently passed a single sheet of paper to Cassandra.

The note her niece had left proved much longer and far more informative than Dominic's. The errant pair, it appeared, were on their way to Dover and from there they hoped to take a boat across the Channel and make their way to Paris. Marianna was sorry to upset her aunt who had been so kind to her, but the situation in London had become intolerable and she had to escape. Dominic was to escort her on her journey to the French capital so her aunt must not worry!

'Miss Latimer, what are we to do?' Lady Foyle questioned as Cassandra finished reading the note. Her voice was broken and her hands moved restlessly in her lap. 'I had no idea, no idea.'

'No idea of what, Lady Foyle?'

'That Marianna was in love with your brother, of course.'

'She does not say that in her message,' Cassandra cautioned.

"Not in so many words, but why else would she have embarked on this scandalous journey? I should never have allowed them to ride together with only a groom as chaperone.'

'She says that her life here has become intolerable. Have you any idea what she might mean, ma'am?'

'I can only imagine that she has been carrying on this clandestine relationship for some time and has become frustrated with the secrecy involved. She knows well that her father would never agree to such a match, but if she had only confided in me...' Serena Foyle blinked back the tears. 'We have all been seventeen and convinced that our romance would last forever.'

Cassie scrutinised the letter again. It was hardly a message from someone about to elope with the love of her life: no impassioned declarations, no pages blotched by tears. On the other hand, the intolerable situation in London sounded ominous. Could that be, as Lady Foyle surmised, her love for Dominic, which she was unable to acknowledge?

She looked at the older woman, sunk deep in her chair, an expression of quiet despair on her face, the mirror image of her own mother, and cursed Dominic. Someone had to try to put things right, restore their peace of mind and ensure that Luke never discovered this new injury to his name. It would have to be her – there was no one else.

The decision made, she rose briskly from her chair. 'Please do not upset yourself, ma'am, the situation is not irretrievable. We know where they have gone and when they left. It should be possible to catch them before they can board a packet to Calais. Fortunately the weather has turned inclement and sailings are bound to be disrupted. We have a very real chance, you know, of finding them still waiting on the quay side.'

'We? But who can go? My health is not as good as it used to be, my dear. I cannot possibly contemplate such a journey. And Marianna's father is thousands of miles across the sea.'

At the thought of Ernesto and what he would say at this latest turn of events, her face lost even the little colour it still possessed and she plunged her head in her hands weeping copiously.

Cassandra thought it prudent to take her leave at this juncture. '*I* will go,' she said quietly. 'I will be away a day or so, I dare say, but I hope to have good news for you when I return.'

Her companion looked up wonderingly. 'You cannot possibly go yourself. My dear, think of it, you cannot travel alone, without an escort.'

'I'll take our coachman. Stebbings has been with the family all my life and is completely trustworthy.'

'A servant?'

Cassie was by now losing patience. 'If you can think

of someone else who could undertake this mission, then please tell me. Otherwise I will do what I'm able.'

The older woman's voice quavered. 'Lord Trelawny? I was wondering whether we might venture to call on Lord Trelawny's help. What do you think?'

But before her visitor could reply, the slight glimmer of hope had faded from Lady Foyle's face. 'But, no, I recollect now, he is on his way to Cornwall.'

Cassandra had reached the door and turned in surprise. 'Surely,' she murmured, 'he would be the last person you would wish to tell of this escapade.' She slipped out of the room, leaving behind her a puzzled woman.

⸺

Once back in Mount Street, she hastily threw a few overnight essentials into a small valise and gave orders for the travelling carriage to be brought round to the front of the house as soon as possible. While she waited, tracing and retracing her steps in the hall, her mother emerged unexpectedly from the drawing room. Cassie had imagined Lady Latimer to be laid down on her bed and had left a brief message of explanation with Mitford. She had hoped to avoid the confrontation that now looked likely.

'Why are you dressed for travelling?' was Lady Katherine's immediate question.

Cassie decided to meet trouble head on and said straitly, 'I'm going to Dover. Dominic and Marianna are headed to that port, prior to crossing to France. I think if I leave now I may be able to catch them before they embark.'

'To Dover? On your own? You cannot do such a thing!' Her mother's shocked face testified to the serious impropriety of her plan.

'I'm sorry if it distresses you, Mama, but I can and I must.'

'But why? What good will it do other than besmirch your name even further?'

'The weather has been stormy since they left and it's more than likely they will be delayed. I'm hopeful I'll be able to prevent them from leaving England.'

'And if you do not, is it your intention to continue this insane pursuit across the Continent?'

Cassie allowed herself a small smile at the image her mother had conjured, but said as soothingly as she could, 'If they have already sailed, then I will return immediately, you have my word.'

Still plainly very agitated, her mother tried another tack. 'But you will never get to Dover and back in a day.'

She indicated the valise at her feet. 'As you see, I'm prepared.'

Lady Katherine's face registered even greater shock at such brazen conduct and her daughter was forced to redouble her persuasion. 'If we must stay the night at Dover, it's surely better that I accompany Marianna.' She looked directly into her mother's troubled eyes. 'As you've already pointed out, I'm now beyond any consideration of marriage so what better role to assume than that of chaperone.'

'Why are you doing this, Cassandra?'

'I have just explained.'

'But not very convincingly. Your chance of success is slight. The packet boats sail in all kinds of atrocious weather, as you must know, and you will be stranded in

Dover – a young woman, putting up in an inn alone – and for what precisely?'

'I have at least to try to undo the harm that has been done.' She looked steadily at her mother. 'If Marianna continues with this journey, it will be because of my brother's thoughtlessness in aiding her. It will ruin her reputation and make it impossible for her to marry where she wishes.'

'But surely she wishes to marry Dominic?'

'I don't think so. Dominic is her escort. He may be in love with her, although I doubt it, but *she* is in love with Luke Trelawny.'

Lady Katherine paused. This certainly accorded with other gossip she had heard. It was more than likely, but why was Cassie becoming so involved? Out loud she repeated, 'Luke?'

'I believe they are to make a match of it. No doubt he is waiting until the year's mourning is over before an official announcement, but I think it clear they plan to be together. I imagine some silly quarrel must have sprung up between them and would have petered out to nothing if Dominic had not become embroiled.'

Her mother remained silent, still wondering at the fierceness of her daughter's concern.

'You must see that I owe it to Luke,' Cassie broke out. 'We have been an unlucky family for him: I broke his first engagement and now Dominic will be responsible for destroying the second. Unless, that is, I attempt to rescue Marianna from her own foolishness.'

'You owe nothing to Luke Trelawny,' her mother said quietly. 'Yes, you broke the engagement and no doubt it was very painful for him, but you have long expiated that sin. And after his behaviour last night, it is he who is in debt to you.'

'That is not so.'

'I think it is. He has cost you your betrothal; more than that, he has made quite sure you have little chance of any future marriage. His flagrant disregard of any acceptable code of conduct has more than balanced the books.'

'I have to help him, Mama.'

'He has ruined you, Cassie!'

'I have ruined myself. I tried to follow a path which wasn't mine. For a while I convinced myself that I was doing the right thing, but all the time I was being untrue to the person I really am.'

'You will have plenty of time now to be true to yourself,' her mother remarked tartly, 'and while you're doing that, you can enjoy watching your sister snare Sir Hugo for herself.'

Chapter Twenty-Four

It was past one o'clock before the carriage arrived at the front door and Cassandra was able to begin her journey to Dover. It would take at least seven hours to reach the town and she made herself as comfortable as she could, nestling into the velvet seat coverings and pulling a cashmere blanket over her legs to shield her from draughts. Outside on the box, his face disapproving, Stebbings set the horses in motion. He had promised Lady Latimer that he would not leave Miss Cassandra's side until they were back in Mount Street, and this he was grimly determined to do.

They were soon rumbling over Blackfriars Bridge, its elegant Portland stone glinting in the afternoon sunlight. Immediately south of the river, though, paved roads gave way to dirt tracks with cramped and ramshackle buildings huddled on either side. Vast numbers of the poor were crowded into these tenements and everywhere squalor and despair disclosed a very different London to the one Cassandra knew. Garbage was strewn at random and open tidal sewers dotted the landscape.

She felt a guilty relief when the carriage had left behind

these desperate areas and was trundling through the quieter suburbs where market gardening and pasturage for cows still interspersed the dark of London's brick.

⌒

It was a good two hours before they reached the Kent countryside. A panorama of fields and trees rolled past her window and Cassie had ample leisure to think. The more she considered the matter, the more she found it difficult to believe this was an elopement. Dominic's demeanour had never approached that of a lover and Marianna had treated him in the same carefree fashion.

It was clear that the girl was the force behind this crazy journey. Could she have quarrelled with Luke over some trifle – perchance he had not given her the attention she expected – and decided that running away was a means of teaching him a lesson? She was young enough and foolish enough.

After the recent spate of bad weather, the road they were travelling was potholed and bumpy, with immense muddy banks on either side, and in some places reducing almost to a track. The continual shaking and jolting of the carriage felt to Cassie as though she had been travelling for months rather than hours. Unable to sleep, she made plans for when they reached Dover.

As long as the delinquents were still in the town, she would find them. She must convince Marianna that any fears she had over Luke's indifference were groundless and that, if this flight were indeed a stupid gamble to regain his interest, the girl was in grave danger of losing him. Luke would never again allow himself to be mired in a scandal not of his making, that was certain, and Cassie must do what she could to bring an end to this reckless journey and protect him from any knowledge of it.

At this encouraging thought, she relaxed a little, and was able at last to fall into a fitful doze as the coach made its cumbersome way towards the Channel coast. She did not wake fully until she felt the horses moving sharply downhill. Leaning forward to peer through the window, she could see in the distance a strip of water streaking the horizon. They were descending a steep and winding hill leading into the town and gradually houses began to spring up on either side of the road and the gradient to even out.

She would bespeak a room at the Ship Inn, she decided. She knew it to be the best hostelry in Dover, her father having stayed there when he made the Grand Tour as a young man. Once settled there, Stebbings could make discreet enquiries of the smaller establishments. Hopefully, it would not take too long to run the miscreants to ground since Dover was not a large town.

The wind had hardly abated from the time they left London, but here on the coast it blew with added ferocity. As the carriage swung around the last corner and reached the promenade, she had her first clear view of the sea. A sheet of gunmetal water heaved and tossed alarmingly, foaming white flecks splintering the grey. Even from some distance Cassie could hear the thunder of surf crashing against the harbour wall, spray after spray of icy water breaching the top of the wharf and drenching anyone foolish enough to be walking on this stormy May evening.

Her heart warmed; surely no one would put to sea in

such weather? She lowered the carriage window and her hat was almost snatched from her head. The titian curls blew wildly in the wind as she attempted to give her coachman directions.

'Stebbings.' She had to shout to make herself heard. 'Please make for the Ship Inn. I hope to bespeak a room there.'

'That's where I was going,' he grumbled. 'Nowhere else suitable for you, Miss Cassandra, though heaven knows it's a bad day when a young lady has to venture alone to any inn.'

⌒

He left her shortly afterwards to find lodgings for himself in the cheaper part of town, but promised that once this was accomplished, he would begin immediately to make a round of the smaller hotels and guest houses that lined the promenade and the streets behind. It was probable that if the runaways were still in Dover, they would be discovered in one of these. And so it proved.

Within an hour of arriving in the town, Cassie was entering the tap room of the Pelican and encountering two pairs of startled eyes.

'Miss Latimer!'

Marianna had been sitting by the window, gloomily watching the tossing waters, but at Cassandra's entrance she sprung from her chair, then froze into immobility, a stricken expression on her face. Dominic, too, had jumped to his feet.

'Cass! What on earth are you doing here?' He spoke impetuously.

'Good evening, Dominic. I would think that question better belongs to me.'

Cassie glanced around her at the soiled furnishings of the dismal room, her eyebrows raised and a quizzical look on her face. 'So what *are* you both doing here?'

Marianna found her voice. 'I'm on my way to Paris,' she said tremulously, 'and Dominic is escorting me.'

'Escorting you?'

'There was no one else I could ask.' Marianna's shoulders drooped in despair, guessing correctly that the sudden arrival of Dominic's sister meant the end of her scheme.

Her escort scowled at her words. 'Thanks,' he said indignantly, 'and after all I've done –planning your escape, paying for the carriage, finding us somewhere to shelter!'

'I don't mean I'm not grateful to you, Dominic, just that you were my last resort.'

'Thanks again.' His face was red with annoyance.

It was evident that both parties to this escapade were so tightly wound they needed only a small excuse to explode. It would be wise to intervene, Cassie thought, while she was still likely to get a sensible answer.

'So you're not eloping?'

For an instant both of them looked astonished and then both burst into laughter. It broke the tension of the moment.

'Miss Latimer, how could you think such a thing?'

'Quite easily. You left a note for your aunt saying that you had to leave London because your life had become intolerable and that Dominic was travelling with you. What else was there to think but that you were escaping because you imagined – rightly – that you would both be deemed far too young to marry?'

'I should say so,' Dominic exclaimed. 'I'm certainly not in the petticoat stakes and never likely to be. I only came on this stupid journey because she mopped and mowed around me until I was driven frantic. I agreed just to keep her quiet.'

'I did not mop and mow! And you could have refused, but you liked the idea of journeying to France – admit it!'

'Not with you, that's for sure. We've been stuck in this inn nigh on six hours and watched boat after boat set sail. But could I persuade her on to any of them?' he appealed to his sister. 'No, of course not. We have to wait until the sea is dead calm, would you believe.'

'I, for one, am delighted that you decided the weather was too rough to cross the Channel,' Cassandra said. She turned towards the young girl who was now near to tears.

'Marianna,' she said gently, 'if it wasn't love for Dominic that drove you out of London, what was it?'

The girl looked frightened and said nothing.

'Come, my dear, there must be a very pressing reason for you to take such drastic action. And your aunt will have to know. So if you do not choose to tell me, at least prepare yourself to confide the whole story to Lady Foyle when we return.'

'Return? I cannot do that.' Marianna shrunk even further into her chair, her hands twisting the already crumpled muslin of her dress.

'You must. You cannot think to continue your journey now, and I am here to take you home.'

'But I must go on. I'm so sorry that you've been put to this trouble and I know Dominic will go back with you, but *I* have to continue.'

Cassandra rose and went to the young girl, taking her hands in hers and holding them in a warm clasp.

'I cannot allow you to do so, your reputation would be ruined. I've found you in time to prevent that disaster. Until we get back to London, I shall act as your chaperone. We can say that we've been travelling together from the outset and that will quash any rumours. I'm sure we can find a distant relative who lives nearby and who has suddenly become very sick.'

Cassie began to warm to her invention. 'You promised Lady Foyle that you would pay them a last visit. Yes, that's it. Naturally your aunt's health is not strong enough for such a long journey, so I offered to accompany you. We can forget the part Dominic has played. For the purposes of our story, he never left London.'

'That's fine, write me out of the script,' he complained bitterly.

His sister wheeled on him and said sharply, 'As someone whose conduct has been grossly irresponsible, you should be glad to be written out.'

She turned again to Marianna. 'I'm staying at the Ship and have ordered rooms for both of us. You must pack your valise now and return with me there. Dominic can remain at the Pelican and in that way we should be able to counter any possible gossip that might seep out. First thing in the morning Stebbings will bring the carriage round to the Ship and we will all three travel back to London together.'

The girl looked defiant. 'You don't understand. I have to get to Spain. Paris is only the first stage of my journey.'

'You're going to Spain?' Cassandra looked dumbfounded.

'I was to visit my relatives in Madrid later this summer, but now I intend to arrive a little earlier.'

'Does Lady Foyle know of this visit?'

'Of course, my father has discussed plans with her.'

'Then she is the person to arrange your travel and accompany you on the journey.'

'That's still weeks ahead. I cannot stay in London – I need to leave now.'

'Why is it so important for you to leave town immediately?' Cassie was deeply puzzled.

'Tell her,' Dominic advised. 'She knows nearly everything anyway.'

The girl looked scared, but in a small and halting voice, made her confession that she was badly indebted to Lord Amesbury and that he was intent on receiving payment in one form or another.

'Threatened her, Cass,' Dominic put in. 'Tried to force her to go to his house on the night of Annabel's ball. That's his notion of paying her debt.'

The tears began to course down Marianna's face as she remembered the terror she had felt at Lord Amesbury's threats. Cassie put her arms around the sobbing girl.

'He's a scoundrel, my dear, but he has no power over you,' she soothed. 'You're a minor and not responsible for gambling debts. There's nothing he can do to reclaim the money and he knows that well.'

Marianna stopped crying abruptly and gaped at her. 'You mean that all this time, I was in no danger.'

'None. But you have not acted well.'

The reproof in Cassandra's voice made the girl wince and she hung her head again. 'I know,' she managed to whisper.

'Lord Trelawny would be very disturbed if he knew of your conduct.'

Marianna seemed confused at the introduction of Luke's name, but said again, 'I know.'

'We will say nothing to him. He need never know what has occurred, but you must tell your aunt and beg her pardon, not just for such foolish behaviour, but for worrying her so much with this flight of yours.'

'Is Aunt Serena very angry?' the girl ventured.

'Not angry, but sick with worry. You have not been thinking clearly. If you had told Lady Foyle the true situation, she would doubtless have rung a peal over you and been displeased for a while, but she would have applauded your honesty and forgiven you very quickly. She would have paid Lord Amesbury what he is owed and that would have been an end to it.'

'Told you so, didn't I?' Dominic smirked. 'Now perhaps you'll give me credit for some sense.'

Marianna was just about to join swords again when Cassandra decided that she'd had enough. She was very tired from the journey and the thought of having to repeat it on the morrow with two squabbling children in tow was not a happy one. Nor was she anticipating with any pleasure her mother's and Lady Foyle's likely welcome to this wayward little party.

'You will accompany me back to the Ship, Marianna,' she said firmly. 'We will order a late supper and you are invited to eat with us Dominic, if you wish. Otherwise, we will see you outside the inn at nine o'clock tomorrow morning. If you are late, you will have to find your own way back to town.'

'No need to get on your high ropes,' he sniffed. He had never before known his elder sister to be so severe.

The image of Luke, never far from Cassie's thoughts, fuelled the anger she felt towards her brother and she lashed him with her tongue.

'Your behaviour has been as reprehensible as Marianna's – more so, for you are older than she and have been on the town longer. No doubt Mama will have something to say to you when we reach Mount Street.'

⌒

He found this to be only too true. Mama had more than something to say and Dominic received the dressing down of his life from his usually mild-mannered parent. He was barely through the front door when his mother had pounced, dragging him into the library and subjecting him to a lengthy and irate scolding.

Lady Katherine had decided that her son had enjoyed more than sufficient holiday in the capital. He was to start on the long journey back to Cornwall in two days' time and Stebbings would not be driving him. The coachman had already been forced to undertake an unnecessary and fatiguing journey beyond his normal duties and Dominic could make his own way to Boskenna Place by stage and then carrier. His mother derived a degree of pleasure in relaying this information; it went some little way to recompensing her for the worry and fright she'd suffered.

Lady Katherine followed him out into the hall where Cassie was waiting, pale but composed, ready to suffer her share of parental wrath. She had directly disobeyed her mother in going alone to Dover, but she could not be sorry for it. Marianna was returned safely to Lady Foyle's care and no one else was the wiser. Certainly not Luke. He was at Madron and blissfully unaware of the drama that had been enacted.

Her mother turned back to the library and beckoned her to follow. Although it was early May, a fire burned brightly in the grate in an effort to conquer the wind and rain which battered at the windows. The unseasonable weather matched the gloom of the occasion, but her mother's scolding appeared light.

'I am delighted that you are returned safely, Cassie, and that silly young girl is back with her aunt. But I cannot think it right that you involved yourself.'

'I couldn't let Marianna plunge herself into scandal.' Her voice was as quiet as her mother's and devoid of expression. 'Of all people, I know how dreadful it is to face down gossip and innuendo. And it was Dominic who would have been largely responsible. You would not have had that happen, I know.'

'Dominic is to return to Cornwall,' her mother said, not answering her directly. 'But what of you?'

'What do you mean?'

'You say that you travelled to Dover to protect the family's honour and to save Marianna from herself – that is understandable, given your own painful experience – but why else?'

'Isn't that enough?' Cassie challenged, hoping to steer the conversation in another direction.

'For most people, perhaps. But your emotions run deep, Cassandra. You told me that you did not wish Luke Trelawny to suffer another broken engagement. Why was that so important to you?'

A tell-tale blush suffused Cassie's cheeks and she said hastily, 'I believe him to deserve better. He is an honourable man and capable of true feeling.'

'Ah!' her mother sighed. 'As I thought. You are in love with him. What a perverse creature you are. Why could you not have loved him when you had the chance?'

The reproach went unanswered and Lady Katherine continued, 'You are in love with him and he is betrothed, you say, to this green girl?'

She shook her head in disbelief, but seeing her daughter's wounded face, moved swiftly across the room and clasped her hands. 'Cassie, what have you done? What will become of you?'

'Whatever do you mean, Mama?' The anguish in her mother's voice made her step back in surprise.

'I mean, my dear, that both the men who have figured so large in your life are now promised to others.'

She looked bewildered. 'Both men?'

'Both,' her mother repeated heavily. 'Sir Hugo has asked permission to pay his addresses to Annabel.'

Chapter Twenty-Five

Luke rode along the headland. On one side of the twisting pathway stretched a patchwork of small fields, ancient granite walls and, in the distance, gently rolling hills. On the other side and immediately below, the ocean thundered magnificently, the sun glistening on the rocks and the spray thrusting ever higher up the cliff face. It was a glorious morning; for a short while, as he relaxed into the rhythm of the trotting horse, his mind was free of care.

It had been an emotional homecoming. He had arrived amid a torrential downpour but Lady Trelawny had come running from the doorway as soon as she'd heard the noise of wheels on gravel. He'd hardly clambered down the carriage steps before she had flung her arms around his neck, trembling with a mixture of happiness and sorrow. His father's absence had hovered between them. Until that moment he'd not fully realised how frail she was and how desperate to see him.

Guilt at delaying his homecoming had cast a large shadow over his arrival. But this morning after five days at the Abbey and many hours together, life seemed a good deal brighter. He was home now and home for good. Lady Emma need worry no longer over the future of house and land. Already Luke had had several sessions with his father's bailiff and acquainted himself with many of the problems and a few of the pleasures of a country estate. This was surely one of its most agreeable: a solitary ride in the early morning sun, king and master of all he surveyed.

The seclusion was what he needed. His final farewell to Cassandra had been torture. So many things left unsaid, so many feelings unexpressed. He'd intended a brief farewell, a mere clasp of the hand and friendly smile, enough to tell her that she was free of him, free to make the life she wanted with Sir Hugo. But all his good intentions had vanished like dew in sunlight and the careful words he'd prepared had died unregretted on his lips.

She had looked magnificent, her beautiful form encased in a floating cloud of diaphanous gauze, her every movement sparkling in the light of diamonds. When the musicians had struck up for the waltz, he'd been unable to resist one last dance with her. It hadn't lasted long. Once his arms were round her, he was again a lost man. The intended farewell had been abandoned and in its place that long, lingering kiss. He'd wanted it to go on forever. Now, looking back, he wondered grimly how he'd ever torn himself away.

But he had, and he was home, and this morning was a gift from heaven. The physical ache of losing her must one day disappear – he had lived without her for six years and would do so again. His old defence of suppressing all feeling was now forfeit, but surely he would cease to think of her so often once he knew her married.

'Hey there! Luke? Is that you?'

A faint voice calling from a distance penetrated his thoughts and he turned his head to see another rider beating his way up the headland towards him. The figure was familiar and for a moment his heart skipped a beat. Surely the Latimers had not come home already?

'Luke, it *is* you. I thought so.' Dominic arrived in a pelter at his side. 'A bang-up morning, hey? Hope you don't mind my trespassing.'

Since the two families had always treated each other's lands as their own, this was by way of being a pleasantry. 'It's good to see you, Dominic, if surprising. Why so far from London?'

'I thought it was time I came home,' Dominic said awkwardly. 'I've been away a fair while and the old man was getting a bit Friday-faced. Started to demand that his son and heir return to the fold.'

'I see. I imagined you were fixed in London for the Season.'

'That was never the plan,' the boy rejoined quickly. 'I was only ever going to stay a few weeks. I'd had enough of town anyway – couldn't wait to get back home!'

Luke looked sceptically at his young companion, but said nothing, and they rode on together in silence.

Thinking that some further explanation was due, Dominic found himself talking again. 'To tell you the truth, there was a spot of bother and London got too hot for me.' He grinned engagingly.

'That sounds a little more likely.' Luke returned his

smile. 'What was it? Boxing the watch, gambling debts, a ladybird?'

Dominic flushed with annoyance. 'She was hardly one of the muslin company, if that's what you mean. Far too respectable, a chit of a girl, and I'm banished to Boskenna because of her.' His earlier carefree air left him as he remembered his grievances against Marianna.

'I never thought of you as being in the petticoat line,' Luke remarked.

'I'm not! Most definitely I'm not! All I did was to try and help someone and look what happened.'

'And dare I ask who it was that you tried to help?'

Dominic flushed again and realised he'd said too much, but it was too late to withdraw. 'Actually you know her pretty well,' he muttered. 'It's Marianna Marquez.'

'Marianna! What trouble has she got herself in for heaven's sake? I thought her aunt well able to take care of her.'

'There'd have to be a hundred aunts to keep *her* out of trouble. I can't tell you what bother she was in, but believe me, it was stupid. Still I'd better keep mum, lady's honour, and all that rot.'

'But why are *you* exiled from the pleasures of London?'

The younger man scowled at the thought of what he was missing. 'The silly chit took it into her head to leave town on the quiet. She wanted an escort and guess who was witless enough to agree.'

Luke's face was inscrutable. 'And where were you to escort her?'

'Supposedly Paris and from there she was to travel on to Spain, but we never got further than Dover.'

His companion looked at him enquiringly.

'You wouldn't believe her! Said that after her journey from Argentina, she couldn't cope with the sea unless it was dead calm. We must have seen half-a-dozen packet boats come and go and she couldn't bring herself to board any of them. I told the silly goose that the weather wasn't likely to improve and if she didn't want to be caught in Dover, she should just close her eyes and walk. But would she listen? Huh!'

'And did you get caught?'

'Oh, yes, and a right shenanigan that was. My sister turned up and gave us a real bear-garden jaw. Then she took Marianna back to her aunt and the long and the short of it was that I was ordered to pack my traps and leave London immediately.'

'Annabel?'

'Annabel?'

'Your sister who discovered you in Dover.'

'Of course not Annabel. Can you imagine?'

'Miss Latimer then?' Luke looked bewildered. 'Why would Miss Latimer come after you?'

'God knows. She's not usually interfering. She seemed very anxious about preventing a scandal.'

'But Miss Marquez is hardly her concern.'

'I suppose she thought *I* was her concern,' he said carelessly, 'although she seemed more worried about your reaction.'

'To Marianna's flight?'

'Yes, didn't make much sense to me. I couldn't work out why Cassie was so upset. Or why she thought *you'd* be upset if you knew Marianna had cut loose. There's been a lot of chatter in the clubs, but I never thought you had any real interest there.'

Dominic glanced across at the man riding beside him, but Luke made no answer. His mind was busy reviewing the hints he'd been at pains to drop over the last few weeks. He might not have lied outright, but he had led Cassandra to believe that he and Marianna might be engaged. She would see Marianna's flight as a threat to their betrothal. She had intervened, but was that for the girl's sake or for his? Whatever the case, it was based on a false premise.

'Did your sister travel all the way to Dover just to put an end to this journey?' He continued his train of thought aloud.

'Like I said. Brought Stebbings with her, too. He gave me a jobation as well. That's the trouble with servants who've known you all your life.'

'So Miss Latimer travelled a long distance, alone apart from her coachman, to find you both and bring Marianna back.'

Luke was slowly trying to make sense of what had happened. If Cassandra *had* braved that journey for him, it meant she had wanted to protect him, wanted to save him from the hurt of another betrayal. She must still care for him. Care for him with a deep and tender love, beyond the physical hunger he'd deliberately set out to nurture. He knew himself to be wholly undeserving, but could feel a warmth spread through his entire being.

Then conscious of Dominic eyeing him askance, he blocked such dangerous thoughts and returned to their conversation.

'I would say you were extremely lucky that your sister intervened when she did. You might well have found yourself in difficulties once you were the other side of the Channel without a friend to hand.'

'To tell you the truth, I'm glad now to be out of it. I was a bit blue devilled at first but not any more. I miss the fun of being in London, but not the family's constant carping. And now all this fuss over Annabel's wedding – that's beyond enough. The more I think about it, the better I'm pleased to be at Boskenna.'

Luke stared at him. 'Annabel is getting married? But surely...'

'Turn up for the books, eh? Sir Hugo decided she was a safer bet! He must want his head examined.'

'Are you saying that Cassie is no longer to marry him?' He felt the world shifting beneath his feet and inadvertently used her pet name.

'That's right. Bethrothal off. Then betrothal on – but a different sister.'

Surely Sir Hugo could not have taken such serious exception to his fiancée's rescue mission. After all, it had been an attempt to avoid scandal in the family. His conduct was inexplicable.

'Do you know why the engagement to Miss Latimer was called off?' he asked cautiously.

'They're puffing it off that they no longer feel suited to one another, whatever that means. Never thought they did suit, if you ask me. But no one ever does – ask me, I mean.'

'It seems to have taken them some time to come to that

conclusion.'

'Between you and me, Luke, and I know you won't spread this around, there's more to it than that. Cassie was crazy enough to kiss another man and Hugo saw her. That was enough to send him fleeing to the hills. Very straight, very proper, Sir Hugo.'

Luke felt an iron bar descend on his chest. Without a doubt he was that other man. Sir Hugo Thorne had seen him kiss Cassandra on the balcony and decided that she was not a fit wife for him. The popinjay! The self-righteous popinjay, to reject a woman like Cassie and turn instead to that screeching harridan of a sister.

And he was pretty sure that Annabel was responsible in some way for Cassandra's downfall; the girl was by nature underhand. Sir Hugo would soon realise his ghastly mistake, and there would be no going back on this one. He deserved every thing he got, Luke thought bitterly.

They rode on in silence, Dominic aware that somehow he'd upset his companion, but unsure just what he'd said that had been so disturbing. At the old mill post, Luke broke the unnatural calm to bid him goodbye.

'I have an appointment with my bailiff, Dominic,' he said with a faint smile. 'And regret I must leave you here. Enjoy the rest of your ride.'

'I will. Perhaps we can ride out tomorrow,' the boy said eagerly, hoping to put right whatever ill he'd unwittingly committed.

'Perhaps,' Luke said vaguely. 'But there is a great deal of work to be done in the estate office and I can't afford to play truant too often.'

'You can spare an hour or two, I'm sure,' Dominic coaxed.

'I would hope so, but I fear my affairs will very soon send me travelling again.'

And with that he wheeled his horse around and cantered off towards the Abbey, leaving Dominic puzzled and slightly alarmed at this sudden turn of events.

Chapter Twenty-Six

Luke did not fulfil his promise to go to the estate office, but instead left the stable lad to rub down his sweating horse while he strode towards his study. Flinging his gloves to one side, he wrenched off his boots and sat down in an easy chair to consider what he had just learned. If Dominic's news was correct, and he could see no reason why the boy would make up such a story, Cassandra was now a free woman.

How deeply would Sir Hugo's rejection bite? Luke had never been convinced that she loved the man, but in the end he'd accepted that she had the right to find happiness with him if she could. But now? Her whole life had been overturned and his kiss had been the catalyst. Marriage to Sir Hugo was no longer on offer and as a woman who had provoked two broken engagements, she was perilously close to social ruin.

How must she feel losing the man to that sister of hers? What was wrong with Thorne? How could he prefer Annabel, an ill-dressed, ill-tempered young woman? Cassie was just too much for him – that was the truth. She was too beautiful, too intelligent, too ardent. Thorne had been scared he could not live up to her or keep her satisfied. When he'd seen the way she had kissed another man, he'd realised the well of passion within her, a passion he could not begin to evoke.

Annabel was a far less daunting prospect, Luke could see. But if Sir Hugo could not live up to Cassandra, he knew a man who could. His love for her had made a chaos of his life. It had not let him go for an instant, even when he was denying its very existence. It had always been there and now finally it might have a chance to flourish.

He would post back to London, tell Cassie his true feelings, beg her forgiveness once more and ask her to marry him. Again. But this time it would work. His mother would understand his renewed absence when she knew why he was returning to London. She would be overjoyed at last to have the daughter-in-law of whom she'd always dreamed.

～

In truth, Lady Trelawny did not share her son's enthusiasm. She had never wholly forgiven Cassandra for the heartbreak she had caused. The catastrophic events six years ago had almost wrecked the deep friendship between their two families and here was Luke intending to ask the girl to marry him once more. Even worse, she had received a letter only last week from Katherine Latimer conveying the welcome news that her eldest daughter was to be married to a delightful and highly respected man. Emma would love Sir Hugo Thorne on sight, her friend had enthused. And now here was Luke telling her that this very betrothal, only a few weeks old, was ended. It seemed that Cassandra was still adept at breaking her word.

Lady Emma made no attempt, however, to dissuade her son – she could see that he was determined on his course. Six years of fending for himself in pioneer country had turned him into a decisive and forceful man and she recognised that it was useless to try to change his mind.

❧

Happily unaware of his mother's misgivings, Luke made the tedious journey back to the capital in the highest of spirits. He'd been foolish ever to imagine that he could excise Cassie from his heart and even more stupid to embark on a campaign to free himself from her power. Now that her betrothal to Sir Hugo was at an end, a future together was within their grasp, and he would make sure they seized it.

Rather than putting up at Brown's again, he decided he would go straight to the family's London home despite its dilapidated state. It was time to open the mansion in Grosvenor Square after all these years and make it habitable for Cassandra. Everything he did from now on would be with her in mind. For the first time in his life he was absolutely sure of what he wanted and what he had to do to get it.

❧

Nevertheless the condition of the house shocked him when he was shown around by a nervous housekeeper. The family had not occupied it since those dreadful events six years ago, his parents having lost any taste for London life. They could not bring themselves to return to a house which had seen such sadness.

'I'm sorry about the state of things, my lord,' Mrs Moffat apologised anxiously as she accompanied him on a dismal tour, 'but there's only me and Mr Moffat here and 'tis a large place to keep perfect.'

Perfect it was not. The furniture was shrouded in holland covers, layers of dust coated every visible surface and in the darkest corners of each room cobwebs hung undisturbed. Luke's spirits sunk a little as he contemplated the mournful sight; the contrast with the house's former glory was painful. So, too, were the images from the past: Cassandra excited and happy, displaying her latest purchases; kicking off her shoes and curling up on the chesterfield ready to chat; descending the staircase on her way to yet another ball, heartbreakingly beautiful. How young they had been then, how untried and untested.

He shook his head in an effort to dislodge such memories and strode to the window to pull back the long brocade curtains. Clouds of dust mounted towards the ceiling and the window panes beyond were grimy and streaked. But the sun was high in the sky, its beams catching at the carved architraves and the marble fireplace, and bringing the tired room to life.

He turned to the housekeeper. 'I realise what an impossible task you've had.' Mrs Moffat bobbed a curtsy at this reassurance. 'However,' he went on, 'could you bring the house back to something like its former condition – with extra help, of course.'

'It depends on how much more help there was,' the housekeeper offered cautiously.

'As much as you need. Hire however many people you think necessary. My only stipulation is that the house should be restored within a few days.'

The woman looked stunned at this demand, but the thought of employing an army of helpers to scrub, clean and launder a house that for years she had watched fall into disrepair, infused her with a new energy.

'A few days? At that rate, we'll be working morning and night. If I may ask, my lord, is there a particular reason for the haste?'

'There is. By the end of the week this house must be fit to welcome the most beautiful woman in the world!'

The housekeeper was alight with curiosity, but thought better of questioning her master further. Instead, she said with renewed determination, 'It will be, sir. I'll get Moffat on to the hiring straight away. Meantime I'll begin in the basement – we'll be using the family kitchen again and it's certain to need a deal of work before it's straight.'

Luke took a last look at the once beautiful salon and smiled. He was leaving behind an old tale of misery for a new and happier story. Mrs Moffat and her helpers would bring the house back to life and make it a home fit for the woman he loved. In time there would be renovation and refurbishment, but that was for the future. That could await Cassie's own choosing – once she became Lady Trelawny.

Chapter Twenty-Seven

As she came down the stairs at Mount Street, Cassandra heard laughter coming from the hall below. Annabel had returned from yet another shopping trip, but this time accompanied by Sir Hugo. Her transformation from the sulky and petulant girl of a few weeks ago to the smiling and agreeable young woman of today had been truly astonishing. Cassie rejoiced that both participants to this frankly odd marriage appeared happy.

Nevertheless there was a twinge of resentment: it rankled that Sir Hugo should have found it quite so easy to transfer his affections. But it proved what she had always thought, that he was in love with the dream of Cassandra and not with the woman herself. He had never truly known her. She smiled wryly – if her former lover had but witnessed half of her shameful conduct while Luke was in town! Those fevered interludes were ample proof that she was an unsuitable bride for such a model of rectitude as Sir Hugo. Annabel, for all her moods, was a pattern of conformity and unlikely ever to transgress.

But Cassie had always been what her father called "hot to handle" and though she had slept away these last six years, Luke's touch had instantly awoken her. His return had signalled a release of feelings she had denied for so long. From the night he had danced with her at Almack's, the passionate, unruly girl of old had risen into being and the cool, clear-headed Cassandra gradually sunk without trace. She ached for him. If she closed her eyes, she could see him plainly, their bodies a whisper away as he bid her goodbye: his grey eyes silver in the moonlight, the dark hair falling carelessly across his forehead, the feel of him, the smell of him, the sheer physical joy of having him close.

Cassie had always loved his energy, his sense of adventure, the way he took his pleasures so intensely. In comparison Sir Hugo's were muted. The two men to whom she had promised herself could not be more different. She almost laughed aloud as she remembered that swim long ago in the cove at Boskenna – the scattered clothes, the mad dash to the sea, the cleaving of their bodies in the cool water. Sir Hugo would have been scandalised.

Far better then that he had changed his mind and escaped a life of vexation. Thankfully only a few people had been aware of their betrothal, though the scandalmongers would have plenty to occupy them: had there ever been an engagement between Miss Latimer and Sir Hugo Thorne or had rumour simply fixed on the wrong sister? But Annabel would be married soon and any gossip would die with the wedding.

'Look what we've bought, Cassie!'

Her sister's tone was a little defiant, a little smug. Annabel had not yet managed to accustom herself entirely to the change in her circumstances and was unsure that she liked her sister to be so accepting of the new dispensation.

'Good afternoon, Annabel, Sir Hugo,' Cassandra said in a bright voice. 'I see you've both been very busy. Come into the drawing room and show me what bargains you've managed to secure.'

Sir Hugo beamed. Of all of them, he had felt most discomfort with the alterations to his marriage plans. He still could not quite believe how quickly he had changed his mind over such a momentous decision. His sister, Lady Russell, had scolded him roundly and told him he was a fool. If his feelings were so lightweight, she snorted, he should forget the whole business of getting married.

But he had not and had daily been surprised at how comfortable Annabel and he were going on together. She was never out of temper these days, he reflected, and she seemed genuinely interested in the details of his charity work. Even her choice of raiment seemed to have undergone modification. Today she was wearing a modest but becoming lilac muslin, trimmed with cream lace. Cassandra was similarly dressed in a simple muslin gown, yet still eclipsed her sister – and always would. Her ethereal beauty outshone every woman he knew, but ethereal could have its problems, he decided.

And he was not convinced that Luke Trelawny had finally disappeared from the scene. Sad to acknowledge but Cassandra was just a trifle unsteady. Lady Russell had probably been correct all along. Miss Latimer was not the right bride for him. No further proof was needed than the way Cassandra had abandoned all delicacy at her sister's come-out ball, kissing another man in public and in such a fashion. He felt himself grow hot at the thought of it.

She was smiling at him now, holding open the door for him to follow into the drawing room. On the whole, he thought he preferred her as a sister-in-law.

The front-door knocker sounded loudly just as Annabel had begun to unpack her first parcel. Cassie had little time to consider who could be calling in the middle of the afternoon before a footman was at her side with the message that Lord Trelawny wished to speak with her privately.

There was a sudden stunned silence among the little gathering until Cassandra recalled herself and said as naturally as possible, 'Please show Lord Trelawny into the library, Robert.'

She turned to her companions with a winning smile. 'I must leave you for a moment, but I won't be long,' she promised.

'Well!' breathed Annabel as her sister went out of the door.

'Well indeed!' echoed Sir Hugo.

Cassie was astonished by Luke's appearance at Mount Street. She had imagined him well and truly settled at his beloved Madron, acquainting his mother with the news of his betrothal and making preparations for Marianna to join him. Why he had returned to town was a complete mystery. His first words did little to enlighten her.

'How can you bear to see that charade?' he said, gesturing in the direction of the drawing room. He had arrived in celebratory mood, but the brief glimpse he'd had of Annabel's triumphant face had roused him to an angry defence of the woman he loved.

'If you mean my sister and Sir Hugo,' Cassandra replied coolly, 'I am delighted they have found happiness with each other.'

'Delighted? Delighted to be rejected for an ill-favoured, ill-tempered vixen?' Luke began to pace up and down the library floor. 'For God's sake, whatever is the matter with the fellow?' he exploded as he came to rest in front of her, his expression stormy. The thought was torturing him that he was responsible for the humiliation Cassie must now be suffering.

'As far as I am aware, nothing ails Sir Hugo. We simply found that we were not suited,' she replied composedly. 'It was you, after all, who took pleasure in pointing that out.'

'I take no pleasure in what has happened.'

She acknowledged this with a small bow of her head, but then looked directly into his eyes. 'Why are you here, Luke?'

'I met Dominic out riding and he told me the news. I came immediately.'

'But why?' she repeated.

'I have come to ask you to marry me,' he spilled out.

He had not meant to make such a stark declaration, but all his rehearsed speeches had melted away. Cassie stared at him, dumbstruck.

'Is this your idea of a bad joke?'

'Hardly.'

'Then you must have run mad. Or –' and she fixed him with a look of contempt '– you are still intent on distressing me and this is part of your plan.'

'It is neither. I am sincere.'

'You expect me to believe you?'

'My conduct has been unforgivable and I have confessed it. I set out to destroy whatever happiness you thought to snatch from your liaison with Thorne and I seem pretty much to have succeeded. You know that I regret the pain I've caused, but I cannot turn the clock back even if I would.'

She remained standing motionless, silent and bewildered.

'And I would not turn the clock back, because now you are free.' He advanced closer and took both of her hands in his before she could stop him. 'We have both made mistakes, Cassie. Can we not put them behind us?'

'I hope we may,' she replied in a dazed voice, 'but you need feel no obligation towards me.'

'It is not obligation that makes me offer my hand.' He was finding it difficult to contain his frustration. 'Dominic tells me that your engagement was broken after that fool in there saw you kissing another man. Who else could that be but me?'

'Dominic is a silly boy. He knows nothing.'

'But he was right.'

'The engagement was already in trouble.' Cassie sighed wearily. 'The manner in which you chose to say goodbye simply brought it to a swifter end.'

'It was in trouble because of me. Admit it! It was in trouble because of your feelings for me.'

She said nothing, her beautiful face pale and still. The emerald eyes were downcast and she could not answer him truthfully.

'You do have feelings for me, Cassie, I know.'

He pulled her roughly into his arms, his face buried in the red blaze of her hair, but she pushed him violently away and the green eyes were suddenly shooting fire.

'And what about your feelings for Marianna? How dare you ask me to marry you when you are privately betrothed to her! Is there no shame to which you will not stoop?'

'Betrothed to her? I assure you I am not, nor likely to be.'

'Yet you have made it abundantly clear over these past weeks that she will be your bride when the time is right. I believe the clubs have even been running wagers on it!'

'You know as well as I that men will bet on just about anything,' he returned defensively. This was proving more difficult than he had ever imagined. 'There *is* no betrothal, Cassie. I let you believe I favoured Marianna because I wanted to make you jealous.'

'Are you telling me that you have constantly lied about your relationship with Miss Marquez?' Her voice was tipped with steel.

'I haven't lied. I never once said I wished to marry her. I simply let you think I was attracted.'

'Then you lied by default.'

'You must understand.' His tone was desperate. 'I thought I'd banished you from my heart, but when I met you again that afternoon in Hyde Park, I knew that wasn't true. After all these years, you still took my breath away. You were so beautiful, so desirable. I wanted you for my own and that pompous fool, Thorne, was your suitor.'

'And that decided you to practice a loathsome deceit?'

'You jumped to the wrong conclusion and, yes, I used it against you. I regret doing so, but I have never felt anything but friendship for the girl.'

'And Marianna, what of her?' she asked crisply.

For the first time he looked shamefaced. 'It was a fantasy on her part, but it's over now.'

'She is seventeen, Luke, a vulnerable girl and you took advantage of her to continue a vendetta against me.'

He sighed inwardly. He had always known that this could be a sticking point. Cassandra's strong sense of justice had not diminished over the years.

'She is fine now.' He tried to sound confident. 'There has been no harm done. It was a girlish fancy on her part, without substance. I always made it clear to her that I had no interest other than as a friend.'

'A friend?' Cassie was looking shocked and the interview was not going the way he had envisaged. 'You stand there and tell me that she never once believed you loved her, that she always knew a serious relationship between you was a mirage?'

It was her turn to stride up and down the library, her mass of auburn curls breaking free from their simple band and tumbling around her face.

'You have not been a friend to her. You have been devious, cunning, even ruthless. Not only have you destroyed my peace of mind, but you have treated her abominably. And you dare to come here and ask me to ally myself with you!'

'I thought, hoped, that you had forgiven the mistakes I've made these past weeks,' he said with quiet dignity.

'When we said goodbye at your sister's ball, it seemed as though the slate had been wiped clean.'

'That was before I knew of this further deception. How can I ever trust you?'

Her anguished tone pierced his heart. Abandoning all pretence of dignity, he pleaded with her in a voice husky with longing. 'Cassie, my darling girl, I want you, I need you, please come to me.'

His arms reached out for her again, pulling her close, his fingers tracing the delicate white skin of her inner arms. She felt herself dissolving, longing for his touch. Any moment now she would abandon her paltry resistance. But the image of Marianna, happy and innocent, rose before her, and she pushed him away with a force that took him by surprise. He staggered back.

'I must ask you to go,' she said with as much composure as she could manage. 'And please do not return to this house. If we should ever meet in the future, I entreat you never to mention this matter again.'

'Cassandra, wait!'

In response she strode to the library door, her expression unyielding.

'Goodbye, Lord Trelawny. Robert will see you out.'

She was shaken and trembling and, though she managed to maintain her self-possession until the front door shut behind him, it cost her dear. She ought to return to the drawing room and pretend that nothing was amiss, but at this moment she could not face Sir Hugo and her sister. Instead she made for her room and cast herself face down on the bed in a paroxysm of sobbing.

It was several minutes before she could regain control of herself and dry her tears. She lay, staring blankly into space, engulfed by warring emotions: the passion she felt for Luke against his duplicity, the chance of happiness against the likelihood of crushing failure. Her mind circled ceaselessly. Luke must have returned to London within days of arriving at Madron. When he had heard of her broken engagement, he'd seen his chance and seized it, retracing the weary miles in order to ask her to marry.

It was possible that after all the deceptions he was now sincere in his protestations. But his infamy was even greater than she had imagined. He had pretended feelings for Marianna to further his own ends. He may have been honest with the young girl, but he'd still exploited her. There had never, after all, been any understanding between the two of them. The jealousy Cassie had felt at seeing them together came rushing back as an unstoppable torrent. All for nothing. All that pain for nothing. He had been trifling with her, playing her like a fish on a line. And Marianna, too. She could never trust him again.

Chapter Twenty-Eight

L uke made his way back to Grosvenor Square, enraged that she had refused to believe him, enraged that for the second time Cassie had turned him down. But most of all he was angry with himself for making such a mull of things. He had assumed that Cassandra must have learned the truth about his friendship with Marianna after she'd rescued the girl. He'd been sure that their journey back to London together would have put her in full possession of the facts, and she would know that whatever feelings Marianna had for him, they were unrequited. Not so, apparently. She had never doubted his pretence and it was only this afternoon that she'd learned his supposed love for the girl was a sham. She was willing to forgive him much, but not this one harmless deception.

But if he were honest, it had been far from harmless. If Cassie truly loved him, his intimacy with Marianna would have racked her with jealousy. *If* she loved him? But she did. She was as lost in love as he. When she had gone to Marianna's rescue, it had been for his sake as much as for the girl's. She'd thought his reputation at risk of compromise and refused to see him hurt, the subject once more of gossip and innuendo. She loved him, he could swear.

He hugged the thought to himself, allowing it to flood his body with new hope. Instantly, he was desperate to return to Mount Street, to hammer on the door, force his way in and simply scoop her up in his arms and tell her that they were wasting time, that they were made for each other and always had been, that he wanted her now and could not wait another minute to claim his own. But he was barred from the house, and trying to thrust his way in, no matter how much he longed to, would do nothing to endear him. He would need to be a great deal more subtle than that.

On reaching Grosvenor Square, he vaulted lightly up the front stairs to the open doorway. York tan gloves were thrown carelessly on to the battered cherrywood table and a caped greatcoat landed in the arms of the waiting footman. He strode purposefully into his study, calling for coffee to be brought. He had a good deal of thinking to do if he were to win back the woman he loved. e wasHe

He had to see her, try to make her understand that his dissembling over Marianna had been no more serious than the rest of his foolish actions. He must surprise her, create a situation where she was unable to escape easily and compel her to listen to all he wanted to say. He sat down to lay his plans carefully.

⌒

In the event he could think of nothing else but to intercept her at a time when she was without company and would not be expecting to see him. He knew from the past that she enjoyed riding alone with a single groom whenever she could and he was hopeful that she always hired a hack from the same stables. By dint of a few enquiries he had soon run to ground the mews she patronised, just around the corner from Mount Street. A cheeky stableboy, sufficiently greased in the palm, let slip the information that a mare had been booked for Miss Latimer the following day. Further largesse elicited the news that the Latimer groom had mentioned his mistress was wishful of enjoying a change of scenery on the morrow and likely to ride in the exclusive but largely unfinished Regents Park.

It suited Luke's purpose well since there was a good covering of trees running close to the bridle path and he would be able to wait for her unseen by all but the most observant passers-by. The weather favoured him, too. After recent days of high winds and squally showers, the sun returned the next morning and he rode out into the balmy air with an excited sense of anticipation.

He arrived at his chosen meeting place close on eleven o'clock and sheltered beneath a cluster of trees. Several groups of people passed him by: nursemaids wheeling out their charges to take the morning air, a dowager scolding her companion mercilessly as they made their slow way along the footpath, a lone horseman putting his new mount through its paces. But otherwise the park was remarkably quiet, ideal for the forthcoming encounter.

He hadn't long to wait until her trim figure hove into view, the groom keeping a respectful distance behind. She wore a fitted costume of forest green, decorated with golden epaulettes and half-braided sleeves, a tall-crowned hat with curled ostrich feathers completing the ensemble.

Whatever inner turmoil was ravaging Cassandra, the world would see only the fashionable woman they knew.

As she came abreast of Luke's shelter, he wheeled his mount on to the path in front of her and forced her to come to a halt. The groom moved up anxiously, but she waved him away with her hand. Whatever this ambush was about, it was evident she had no wish for the servant to overhear.

'A beautiful morning, Miss Latimer.' Luke doffed his curly brimmed beaver.

His riding coat sat tightly across powerful shoulders and the palest fawn breeches encased a pair of shapely legs. Gleaming top boots from Hoby and a freshly pressed neckcloth proclaimed him a true gentleman. He looked superb and Cassie had to exert every nerve to ignore the traitorous impulses of her body.

The two riders faced each other, their horses gently sidling to and fro until Cassandra's mare, growing restive at the lack of action, began to paw irritably at the ground, almost unseating her in its efforts to be gone. Instinctively Luke grabbed at her bridle and brought their two mounts together. His grey eyes were piercingly alive and she thought she saw a paleness beneath the tanned cheeks. It was as though this was the determining moment of his life.

Attempting to break the tension, she spoke with a boldness she did not feel. 'Good day to you, Lord Trelawny. I hope you are enjoying this fine morning. May I ask that you allow me to do so, too?'

Her cold politeness did not daunt him and he retained his hand on her bridle. 'This is crazy. We should not have to meet like this, Cassie.'

'The name is Miss Latimer, and you are quite correct, Lord Trelawny, we should not. If you would be so good as to release my horse, I will be on my way.'

'Cassandra, Miss Latimer, please hear me out. I apologise for accosting you in this fashion, but I have been unable to think of any other way to speak to you. I will take only a few minutes of your time, but I beg that you listen to me.'

The groom, seated on his mount a few yards distant, appeared increasingly anxious and Cassie sensed that he was getting ready to intervene. The last thing she wanted was any kind of brawl in a public place. Swiftly, she dismounted and threw the reins to her manservant.

'I shall be back in ten minutes,' she said. 'Please walk the horses until I return.'

'Yes, ma'am, if you're sure,' he replied uncertainly.

She nodded and strode towards the shelter of the trees. Luke dismounted and followed her.

'What is it you wish to say?' she demanded, turning to face him, her tone uncompromising.

All his prepared speeches were once again forgotten. He could think only of possessing the woman that he loved. 'Simply that we are made to be together. You must know it.'

'I know nothing of the sort.'

'You are not being honest, Cassie, either with yourself or with me. Surely we deserve that of each other.'

'I cannot believe you have the temerity to speak to me of honesty. How much honesty have you shown these past few weeks?'

He made no reply and she continued with barely a pause, 'I will answer for you. None. Since your return to England, you have waged a vendetta against me. You have been ingenious, leaving no avenue unvisited. Not content with destroying my plans to marry, you have shamelessly exploited a young girl's feelings in order to hurt me. I think you will agree that you have been thoroughly *dis*honest and succeeded admirably.'

Her voice was metallic and her eyes pools of emerald ice. She was desperate to harden herself against him, to build a protective shell even at this late hour.

'Take pleasure in what you have done, for there is nothing more. You have disrupted my life and made me as deeply unhappy as you could possibly wish.'

His dismay that she could think so badly of him forced him to defend himself. 'You must know that has not been my wish. All I want is to make you happy. I have said that I am truly sorry. I cannot do more.'

She looked stonily into the distance and exasperated by her obstinacy, he spoke what was uppermost in his mind. 'I accept I have caused suffering, but consider also that I have done some good.'

'What!'

'You say that you and Hugo Thorne found you were not suited. And why is that? Because you were suited to another man. If it were not for me, you would be contemplating a very unhappy marriage.'

She looked at him with scorn, but he would not be silenced. 'You may deny it, but you know that it's true. And whatever stupidities we may have committed, we belong together.'

'As you belonged together with Miss Marquez?' she asked waspishly.

'I have been honourable and straightforward in my dealings with her. You have to believe me. I would never deliberately set out to harm a young and inexperienced girl.'

The expression on her face told him that she was very far from believing him, and he burst out in frustration, 'You know what young girls are like. They can enmesh themselves in ridiculous dreams which are a million miles away from reality.'

'Indeed I do know what young girls are like. Who better? I was one once, remember, and thanks to another man *my* ridiculous dream almost crushed my heart. I survived – just – and now you have come close to crushing it a second time. But I will not allow you to succeed.'

Her face was pale and, though she remained standing tall and proud before him, he knew she was in a state of agitation. Her breath came short and irregular and the smooth curve of her breasts rose and fell with emotion. He longed to reach out to her, pull her close to him and let their bodies end the argument.

'I want to win your heart, not crush it,' he said urgently. 'Despite all that has happened, maybe because of all that's happened, I know I can make you happy. We have tested each other to the limit and have survived. Our love will endure.. Give me a chance, Cassandra,' he urged. 'Take a chance.'

'I cannot.' In an instant, she seemed visibly to shrink within herself. 'I have already suffered too much and all I want now is to be left in peace. Leave me that at least.'

Her sadness fingered him with its hurt. The fight had gone out of her and he was responsible. He had destroyed the fire and the spirit that he had so loved.

'But –' he tried to rally once more.

'No "but". The game is played out, Luke. This is its end.'

She walked slowly away and he watched, immobile, as the groom helped her remount and together continue along the bridleway. He was as certain as he could be that she still loved him, but in the end he had been powerless to keep her by his side. He knew that nothing he ever said would make any difference. The game between them was indeed played out.

He flung himself into the saddle and struck out across the park, his mind tormented by the destructive passions that had brought him to this pass. It mattered not where he was heading – there was nowhere to go. He had striven to convince Cassie of his love; he'd been so sure that he would be able to win her over. But all his energy and resolution had not been enough. She would not contemplate a future with him.

Blind to his surroundings, it was some while before Luke heard the voices hailing him. A carriage drew up alongside and he slowly emerged from a brown study.

'Good morning, Lord Trelawny, how delightful to see you back in town, and so soon. Has Cornwall already lost its appeal?'

It was Lady Foyle with her friend and neighbour, Miss Anstruther, and sitting squashed between them, Marianna, startled by his presence but smiling shyly. He made no answer and Lady Foyle went on, 'We thought we would explore Mr Nash's new project, but there is a sad absence of company in the park.'

'I imagine most of the *ton* will wait until the Regent's vision is more nearly realised,' he replied, trying for an easy tone.

'As we seem to have the place to ourselves, I wonder if you would be good enough to walk with us for a while.'

'Of course, Lady Foyle,' he replied gallantly, though wishing himself a million miles away.

He handed the two elder ladies down from the carriage and they began to walk slowly ahead, still animatedly discussing the topic of the empty park. He turned to help Marianna, but she had already scrambled down the steps. Offering her his arm, they followed in the footsteps of her aunt and companion. Neither spoke for some while, but when he glanced down at her, he found her eyes anxiously scanning his face.

'I'm surprised to see you here,' she said. 'I thought you had left for home and would never return to London.'

'I thought so too,' he replied evenly, 'but unforeseen circumstances brought me back.'

She did not feel bold enough to enquire what those circumstances might be, but she was struck by the fixed look on his face. She had never before seen him looking so grim or so dispirited.

'Is there something wrong?' she asked at length, and when he did not reply, repeated more urgently, 'What is the matter, Luke?'

He had no wish to unburden himself to a girl barely more

than a child, but her sweet face was looking up at him in genuine concern and his heart was sore. Without meaning to, he found himself describing the recent encounter with Cassandra. He was succinct, skimming over his campaign to prove his former sweetheart unworthy and deliberately avoiding any mention of the role Marianna had unwittingly played. She must have guessed something of the truth but gave no sign.

'I'm a fool, ' he finished. 'But I must not repine. I must learn to accept Miss Latimer's decision.'

Marianna squeezed his arm in sympathy. 'How can you?' she asked impulsively. 'You love her. I've always known that. I think that perhaps I knew it before you did. And I'm quite sure that she returns your love. The engagement with Sir Hugo never looked likely to last, or so Aunt Serena said.'

'Lady Foyle is most perceptive,' he muttered a little sourly. 'But it's clear that Cassie prefers a single life to being with me.'

'I'm sure that isn't so,' the girl protested. Nobody could!' She blushed bright pink in confusion.

He ignored this telltale comment and said gently, 'Your good wishes do you credit, my dear, but I fear I've made a complete mess of things. There's no chance now that Miss Latimer will change her mind.'

'Then we must change it for her.' Her tone was defiant and Luke stared at her, his dark brows raised in astonishment.

'*You* must change it for her,' she amended quickly.

'I wish that were possible, but it's out of the question.'

An enigmatic "hmm" was her only response.

While they had been deep in conversation, the sky had clouded over and a blustery wind begun to blow. Serena Foyle signalled to her coachman just as the first drops of rain began to fall. The ladies were swiftly handed into the carriage and Luke bade them a brief farewell.

Looking back over her shoulder, Marianna saw him riding away in the opposite direction, a solitary figure amid a rain-drenched landscape. She was sorry to leave him so evidently unhappy, but she needed time alone. She needed time to think, to contrive a solution to his difficulties, for she was quite certain there was a way through the maze.

Chapter Twenty-Nine

Cassandra, too, spent a good deal of time alone in the following days, seeking sanctuary from the prying eyes and listening ears of the household. She wanted more than anything to quit London. The triviality of the Season had never sat well with her and any pleasure she'd had in it was now dust. But she could not go home to Cornwall. Luke was unlikely to stay long at the Grosvenor Square mansion and she could not bear to run the risk of meeting him.

She felt listless and unbearably cross. Her mother put it down to Annabel's forthcoming nuptials: the excitement of purchasing bride clothes, planning the ceremony, organising the honeymoon, had taken over Mount Street. It must be a difficult situation for her beautiful elder daughter to bear, Lady Katherine surmised, even though she had brought this fate on herself.

But Cassie was immune to the upheavals permeating the rest of the household. If pressed, she would have acknwoledged a mild happiness that Annabel was no longer proving so intractable, but beyond that she had little interest in the wedding preparations. She was too sick at heart.

Luke had been right when he'd said that she loved him. She desired him intensely, but this ache, this longing, was more than simple lust. Lust she knew. It was what had destroyed her first betrothal to him. This was love. She loved him, all of him. She loved him, but she had no faith in him; that was the nub of it. However much he protested, she could never trust him again, and without trust there could be no lasting bond.

Her mind endlessly played out the conflict, trapping her in a disordered world. It was with only half an ear that she listened to Sir Hugo as he detailed his elaborate plans for the family to celebrate his new engagement. This was to include a splendid dinner at his town mansion, followed by an evening at the Drury Lane theatre where he had managed to obtain precious tickets to see Edmund Kean performing in a much-acclaimed *Hamlet*.

Sir Hugo still felt awkward at the very rapid transfer of his affections and was hoping that a dazzling social occasion would smooth any feathers that were still ruffled. He need not have worried. Cassie felt only gratitude that she had been spared a loveless marriage, and her mother was relieved that one of her daughters, at least, had found an eligible husband.

The evening's dinner and theatre visit was the Season's last social event for the family. In two days they would leave London for Thorne Park so that Annabel could be introduced to her new home for the first time. From there they would travel on to Cornwall to make final preparations for the wedding. Unexpectedly, her sister had rejected a smart London ceremony in favour of being married from

Boskenna. It augured well for her new life, Cassandra thought, that the city had lost some of its magic allure.

❦

Sir Hugo's town house stood imposingly at the corner of Brook Street and their arrival that night was greeted by liveried footmen at its entrance, holding aloft lighted torches. Once inside two more footmen lined the hall and relieved the ladies of their cloaks, then bowed them into a drawing room glittering in the light of a dozen chandeliers that ran the length of the ceiling. Heavy velour furnishings in the deepest red, ornamented with gold piping, completed the room's opulence. Cassandra felt overpowered by so much luxury, but Annabel, relishing these evident trappings of wealth, did a small dance of congratulation in her head. Sir Hugo himself handed round glasses of champagne and made ready for a considered but lengthy toast to his future bride.

The dinner that followed was as lavish as the surroundings, one laden course after another. Tureens of soup and a series of entrées were removed for platters of baked turbot and salmon, followed in turn by dishes of roast sirloin and goose with sides of French beans, peas and asparagus. Once his guests had eaten their fill of these delights, Sir Hugo's well-trained staff whisked away the starched table covering and replaced it with new linen. An assortment of pastries made their appearance alongside a chafing dish of pancakes, creams, jellies, ices and small bowls of preserved fruits.

The room was airless and Cassie ate sparingly while trying hard to maintain her part in the empty trivialities of table talk. It was with relief that she heard the carriage being announced that would take them to the main attraction of the evening.

～

At the theatre Sir Hugo had ensured they had seats in one of the most comfortable boxes available, with an excellent view of the stage. Even so Cassandra quickly opted for a chair towards the rear, hoping in the darkness to be left to her thoughts. But until the lights went down, she must force herself to show enjoyment. She looked around the auditorium at the array of colours and costumes that shimmered beneath the theatre's blazing lights. The buzz of conversation was almost deafening, the noise hanging overhead in the heavy atmosphere.

Glancing to her left, she thought she glimpsed Marianna Marquez in an adjoining box and was about to remark on it to her mother, who sat alongside, when Sir Hugo turned to them, holding his finger to his lips.

'The curtain is going up!'

Contrary to her expectation, Cassie became immersed in the play. Whether it was Kean's electrifying performance or simply that her overwrought mind had found some kind of relief, she didn't know, but the next hour passed on wings and before she realised it an interval was being called.

Their small party filtered slowly out of the box and into the wide carpeted space which encircled the rear of the auditorium. Many other patrons were already taking a turn and attempting to find a little fresh air. It had steadily become more oppressive as the play proceeded and a thunderstorm appeared likely.

Cassie saw Marianna out of the corner of her eye walking nearby with Lady Foyle, both fanning themselves vigorously. Quite how it happened, she was unsure, but in a trice it seemed her mother was conversing animatedly with Lady Foyle while she found herself walking arm in arm with the niece. After Luke's admission that Marianna had been an unwitting pawn in his game, she felt an unease in the girl's company. Yet she wished to talk to her, to hear that the young woman had not suffered irreparably from his intrigue.

They were walking slowly together along the wide corridor, their steps keeping time, when she ventured to break the silence. 'This has been a most enjoyable evening, Marianna. And such a pleasant surprise to see you again – this time in more agreeable circumstances.'

'Indeed, yes,' the girl rejoined quietly. 'Our last meeting was not at all a happy one.'

'And how have you been since your return from Dover?' The question was imprecise, but Cassie could not bring herself to be more specific.

'I've been well, thank you, Miss Latimer.'

The girl's uncertain tone did not match her words and Cassandra thought her troubled. The ghost of Luke rose between them. But she was saved from having to probe further when Marianna continued, 'I've wanted to thank you properly for rescuing me from my foolishness. I know I should have called on you immediately I returned to town, but I felt too ashamed after the trouble I caused for Dominic.'

'You need not worry about Dominic. He got himself into trouble, and it's far better that he is in Cornwall learning from my father than racketing around town. And you've no need either to thank me,' Cassandra added.

'Oh, but I have. I can't thank you enough. You saved me from scandal when you could have simply turned away.'

They had once more reached Sir Hugo's box and Marianna paused her steps. Her planned encounter with Cassandra had so far gone smoothly, but there was a good deal more to be accomplished before she could walk away. She touched Cassie on the arm in a gently restraining gesture and said slowly, 'I don't fully understand why you came after us, but I think that it was partly for Luke's sake.'

Cassandra made no response. It seemed to Marianna that now his name was out in the open the beautiful woman beside her had become strangely paralysed. She appeared unable to move or to speak, and was looking blindly ahead at the theatre box where the door stood ajar, and seemed to want nothing more than to seek refuge in its shadowy depths.

Sensing that her quarry was about to escape, Marianna said impulsively, 'There was never anything more than friendship between us, you know. I was infatuated, that's all, a naïve romance – nothing more. Poor Luke, he had much to bear with me, but he always behaved impeccably.'

'I'm glad to know that.' Cassie's voice stuttered into life. 'But after all that has happened to you in London, are you still happy to be here?'

'Why do you ask?'

'Forgive me, but on the few occasions I've glimpsed you

lately, you've looked a little pale, a little anxious. Though that's probably my imagination running away with me.'

'No!' Marianna said quickly, delighted that her plan was at last unfolding successfully. 'It's not your imagination. I wasn't telling the truth just now when I said I was happy. Things have not been well with me lately, but it has nothing to do with Luke.' She hoped she was proving a convincing liar.

'What then?'

'May I confide in you Miss Latimer – Cassandra?'

Cassie nodded assent, but privately took herself to task. She was certain she did not want to hear this.

'Since I returned from that stupid flight, I've felt trapped.' Marianna was speaking so quietly that Cassie had to bend towards the younger girl to catch her words.

'Aunt Serena watches me all the time. I know I can't hope to be trusted completely now, but she spies on my every movement. I have absolutely no freedom.'

Cassandra looked shocked. 'Surely you must be mistaken. Lady Foyle has always seemed to be the most indulgent of guardians.'

'She may have been once, but that escapade changed everything. She is nervous of my father, you know, and desperate to make sure that nothing else goes awry during my visit here.'

'But spying?'

'She observes me constantly. *And* she opens all my messages and makes sure that I receive only visitors she is aware of.'

Glancing across at Lady Foyle, still deep in conversation

with her mother, Cassie could not help looking sceptical. Desperate to convince her, the girl threw out what she hoped was a clinching line. 'She says she will even accompany me to Spain when I leave in a few weeks' time.'

'But surely that's an excellent idea. You will need a chaperone on your journey and who could be a better companion than your aunt?'

'Not at all. She will be watching me closely and, when we arrive, will tell tales to my relatives, so that after her return to London they will continue to keep me fast. I will enjoy no liberty whatsoever.'

'But your father, can he not intervene on your behalf?'

'My father is thousands of miles away and the family has always said that he is far too lenient with me. When my mother died, they pressured him to send me back to Spain to be raised as a "proper" young lady. He resisted and kept me with him. This will be their revenge – they will keep me locked up, I know,' she finished triumphantly.

'Don't you think you may be exaggerating?' Cassandra suggested gently.

'A little perhaps, but my life in Spain will not be happy. If only I could prevent Aunt Serena from travelling with me and poisoning minds against me, I might persuade my relatives to believe my story. Maybe, then, I could enjoy living in Madrid.'

The interval bell rang sharply and it was time to return to their seats. Cassie took the young girl's hands in a farewell clasp, but felt powerless to help her. The rest of the play seemed to pass in a blur. In some measure she felt responsible for Marianna's plight. If she had not intervened in that earlier journey... but she could never have guessed that Serena Foyle would treat her niece so badly.

After their return from Dover, Lady Foyle had certainly scolded Marianna soundly, that was to be expected, but she'd seemed too relieved to have her back safely to dwell long on the girl's reckless conduct. It was true that lately Marianna was never without her aunt at her side – a proof of their closeness, Cassandra had thought. Surely the situation could not be as bad as the girl had painted?

Yet she had been looking anxious and ailing ever since her return to London and it seemed clear now that it was not Luke's conduct that was to blame. Cassie had it on the girl's own authority that he had not deceived her and had always behaved towards her as a gentleman. She felt cheered by this revelation. It meant she could think better of him even though she could not trust him.

Meanwhile Marianna had resumed her seat beside Lady Foyle, well pleased with her evening's work. Her aunt looked questioningly at her, but she simply smiled a sunny response. Better Aunt Serena knew nothing of her intentions. It was time to proceed to the next stage of her plan; only one or two obstacles to clear and it would be complete.

A roll of thunder just then reverberated through the building. It was a fitting signal, she thought, for the denouement to come.

⌒

A few days later Cassandra was sitting alone in the drawing room at Mount Street. Her mother and Annabel were busy paying afternoon calls prior to the family's departure, but she had asked to stay at home. In the bedroom above, her maidservant was packing her London wardrobe and, though earlier she had tried to decide on which gowns to take with her to Thorne Park and which to send directly to Cornwall, she had eventually left it to Rosa to choose, saying she had a headache. She seemed to be using that excuse frequently of late, but she hardly cared if she were believed or not.

She wasn't agreeable company for anyone, not even herself. Since coming downstairs she had tried reading one of the marble-backed books from the circulating library, so beloved of Annabel, but its silly plot sickened her. She had picked up her long-discarded needlework, but it made her eyes ache. She thought she might write to an old friend in Cornwall – she had been meaning to for an age – but what could she say that would come anywhere near the truth of her life?

For probably the fourth time that hour she wandered over to the drawing room window, but this time saw with surprise a liveried servant mounting the front steps. In a moment Robert had knocked and entered the room bearing a crisp, white note on a silver salver. As she took the paper from the tray, she glanced at the signature at its foot – the letter was from Marianna Marquez. How strange. With some curiosity she began to read the unexpected missive.

Dear Miss Latimer, Marianna wrote, *I did not want to leave London without saying goodbye or thanking you once more for all your efforts on my behalf. You have been a good friend to me and I hope you will forgive my decision to leave. I find I cannot bear to remain in London a moment longer. My aunt has behaved very* properly and on my behalf has settled the debts I incurred. For that I am grateful. But as I told you the other evening she now keeps me so confined that life has become insupportable.

I am desperate to travel to Spain on my own for the reasons I mentioned and have decided to set out again for Paris and ask my father's friends for help to finish the journey to Madrid. This time, though, I will leave England on my own. I still feel very badly that I caused so much trouble for your brother. By the time you read this, I shall be on my way. Please forgive me for not coming to see you at this time, but remember me instead with affection.

Yours ever, Marianna

Chapter Thirty

Cassie stared at the sheet of paper for minutes on end, hardly able to comprehend the words she'd read. Since her conversation with Marianna at the theatre, a worry had been niggling at the back of her mind that the girl might do something foolish, but she'd come to the conclusion that she was fretting unnecessarily. It was more than likely that Marianna had been involved in a minor altercation with her aunt that evening and was magnifying the difficulties between them.

But now this! It hardly seemed credible that the girl had fled again, and this time completely alone. Without even Dominic's protection, she was exposed to every hazard facing an attractive and wealthy young woman on a long and solitary journey. Cassandra felt a shiver of fear.

This time, too, there was no indication of when the girl had left London, nor the port she was making for. It was unlikely she would choose to travel to Dover again for fear of being discovered, but there were any number of small ports dotted along the Channel coast and searching for her would be near impossible. The last rescue had been diffi-cult enough when Cassie had known where the runaways were headed and when she'd had the faithful Stebbings to drive her.

It was a desperate situation, yet she could not let the girl disappear into a world of unknown danger: she must make some attempt to save her from this folly. But she would need help and who could she turn to? Certainly not Lady Foyle. She would be even angrier with her niece than before. No, Marianna must be found and brought back before her aunt got wind of her disappearance.

Sir Hugo would assist if she asked him, but he was caught up in a whirl of wedding preparations and would be shocked to the core by the girl's conduct. The image of Luke swam into her vision and was dismissed.

But not for long. His name persisted in her thoughts. A few days ago he had vowed that he had no interest in Marianna, but it was undeniable that he'd been close to her, accompanying her on the long journey from Buenos Aires, escorting her about town in her aunt's stead. And Marianna trusted him. Even if she were no longer in the first throes of infatuation, she must still count him as a friend. If anyone could run her to ground and influence her to return, it would be Luke. He would know what to do, what and who to ask, and he would be able to ride across country if necessary, travelling far more swiftly than any carriage.

Cassie made a brave decision. She must put aside her own feelings and seek him out immediately. Casting social propriety aside, she threw on a silk pelisse and walked swiftly to the end of Mount Street. It was lucky an empty hansom cab was passing the end of the road and she hailed it. She had no idea of the fare, but the jarvey seemed content with the few coins she had in her reticule.

Only thirty minutes had passed from Marianna's message being delivered until Cassie stood on the top step of the Grosvenor Square mansion and pulled at the bell. The footman's stare brought home to her the imprudence of calling on a single gentleman alone, without even a maidservant as company. Discomfited by his obvious astonishment, she assumed a haughty air and commanded him to find his master immediately. The curt tone had its effect and in a moment he had shown her into the drawing room and disappeared to find Lord Trelawny.

Cassie walked nervously up and down the room she knew so well. Signs of neglect were everywhere for the house had remained unloved for too long. The blue brocade drapes had faded in the sun and the deeper-blue velvet chairs exhibited bare patches here and there, but it was sparkling clean and a large Venetian glass vase full of sweet-smelling roses from the garden gave the room a welcoming fragrance.

The minutes ticked by and she began to fear that Luke was not at home, or that he had decided to punish her further with a protracted wait in a room which held such bad memories. Her face flushed with the shame of remembrance and she was almost ready to flee when his tall figure strode into the room. His elegance might proclaim him every inch a gentleman, but he was also a man who could be trusted to take action.

Warm grey eyes searched hers intently, though Luke's face betrayed none of the surprise he felt. 'Miss Latimer, how kind of you to call,' he said smoothly, as the door shut behind the footman.

Once on their own, he moved swiftly towards her, taking her hands in his and studying her troubled face with concern.

'Cassie, what is it? What's happened?'

Her eyes filled with unbidden tears. She had been right to come – already she felt a burden being lifted. Mutely she proffered Marianna's letter.

He scanned the sheet of paper quickly, but apart from a puzzled expression, he showed no other reaction. Doesn't he understand what has happened? she thought. Surely he cannot be so unfeeling that he intends to ignore the letter.

'If you have any kindness for the child,' she broke out in an agitated voice, 'please help me to find her and bring her back.'

He read through the missive again, this time more slowly. Then puzzlement gave way to a wry smile.

'I realise that I should not be here asking for your aid after all that has passed between us,' she began again, her voice brittle. 'But will you not help?'

'Why ask *me*, Cassandra?' he asked quietly.

'You know Marianna well, you have the power to influence her and...' her voice was hardly audible '... you are the only person I can trust in this difficult matter.'

Again he took her hands in a firm clasp. 'The word "trust" fills me with hope.'

'Luke!' She snatched away her hands. 'This is urgent. I don't know when Marianna left or which port she's making for. She may have half a day's start.'

He reached out and stroked her cheek with one finger. 'Stay calm, my darling girl, all is well.'

'I don't understand. And I am *not* your darling girl! You forget yourself.'

'And you forgot yourself in coming here to seek my aid. I imagine that's exactly what Marianna hoped for.'

She was stunned into silence, thoroughly bewildered by his words.

'Come with me,' he said, and she allowed him to lead her by the hand into the adjoining garden room with its tall windows looking out on to a wide expanse of lawn. Beneath the shade of the trees a table was set with white linen and the pretty flowered cups that Cassandra remembered so well. Marianna and her aunt, looking happy and relaxed, sat chatting and sipping their tea.

Cassie whirled around. 'I don't understand,' she repeated.

'A hoax, I fear, but one perpetrated with the very best of intentions.'

'You mean that the letter is false. But why? Why would she wish to upset me so?'

'I'm sure she didn't mean to disturb you so badly. She is very young and not always mindful of the consequences of her actions. But I think I know why she decided on this ploy. After you and I parted the other day in Regents Park, I met Marianna out driving with her aunt. I was thoroughly downcast and confided to her something of our conversation. I told her that you had lost all faith in me. She must have set out to prove to you that was untrue, that you still trusted me despite my crass behaviour.'

'But why would she do such a thing?'

'Because she knows I love you. She's always known, even before I realised the truth myself. And she guesses that you feel the same about me. She wants us both to be happy – together.'

Cassandra pushed the thought away and instead returned to Marianna's deception. 'I really believed she was in danger. The letter frightened me greatly and, as it turns out, quite unnecessarily. I don't know what to say.'

'Forgive her, Cassie, she's brought us together.' He moved closer to her and she felt his breath on her cheek.

When she remained silent, he said with force, 'Well, hasn't she? My darling, say she has!' And with one swift movement he pulled her into his arms and held her to his heart.

She struggled to disengage herself. Things were moving far too rapidly. She needed time to think and her mind was in a daze. 'I'm relieved that Marianna is safe,' she said carefully. 'Of course I am, though I cannot think her actions anything but thoughtless. Her plan to bring us together was, at the very least, ill-advised.'

'But you are here,' he pointed out, the shadow of a smile lightening his face.

'I came to seek your help, not to say I trust you.'

'But isn't that exactly what you're saying? Why didn't you go elsewhere, why come to me?'

'Because you are a capable man and you know Marianna well,' she answered awkwardly.

'They are superficial reasons. You came to me because you know in the deepest recesses of your heart that I am the one person in the world who is here for you – and always will be.'

He was right, Cassie realised. Until her foolish disloyalty had severed them, he had been her refuge and a rock that anchored her to the world. But did she believe that still? She wanted to, desperately, but she was still unsure.

'And Marianna, what of her?' She was eager to change the subject.

'Does she seem to have suffered unduly?'

As she stood watching Marianna through the window, Cassie heard the girl's laugh ring out across the lawn. A wasp had evidently interrupted the tea party and Marianna was dancing this way and that to escape its attentions. Luke looked down at the woman he loved. 'Marianna and I are the best of friends, but that is all. I hope you can see that.'

Even if she could, Luke remained the cold man who had plotted so adroitly against her. Knowing what he had done, could she ever really trust him, ever really forgive him?

'Find it in your heart to forgive me,' he pleaded, knowing her thoughts. 'I was shocked when I saw you again, shocked at the way you made me feel. I was wounded and I wanted to escape the hurt which came crashing back at me. I lashed out with this stupid intrigue to prove to myself that you were not worth the pain.'

But he had failed, Cassandra told herself. He might have plotted, but he'd not been able to continue. She thought back to the picnic and the way he'd looked at her by the lakeside, unable to bear her misery. His campaign against her had hardly started before he'd abandoned it. Surely it was possible to forgive him.

He was looking fixedly at her, watching her every fleeting expression. Then for the third time in his life, he said, 'Marry me.'

'You don't have to ask me.' Cassandra sounded defiant. 'I know you feel you've disgraced me and destroyed my chances in life. But you haven't. If I stay single, I shall have no regrets.' It was a brazen lie but one she needed to utter.

'But *I* will. I will have regrets for the rest of my life. I love you, Cassie. I've never stopped loving you. And that love is not going away – and neither am I!'

And once more he seized her in a crushing embrace.

'I don't know what to say,' she mumbled. Her mind remained dazed, but her body was coming to life.

'Then say nothing.' He gently nuzzled her face and buried his hands in the disordered mass of red curls.

She began to murmur, but he stifled her protest. 'There *is* nothing more to say. Everything is decided.' And tipping her face, he brought his mouth down hard on hers.

She sighed her surrender. Luke was right, everything *was* decided.

Chapter Thirty-One

Cornwall, 1817

It was a perfect August evening when they met on a headland stippled with brilliant yellow furze, and strolled slowly down the rocky path towards their cove. The languorous air of what had been a hot summer day bathed them in its warmth. A gentle breeze was blowing now, signalling the turning of the tide, but it barely lifted the leaves of the tall hedgerows either side of the lane. The scent of dog roses and meadowsweet was everywhere, enveloping them in a heady perfume. In the distance, the surf rolled itself lazily against the rocks, the noise echoing back towards them and gradually growing more thunderous as they made their way downhill towards the beach.

'I thought you might not escape this evening.' Luke smiled down at the carefree girl beside him.

Cassandra wore the lightest of muslin dresses, almost a shift, her long limbs moving easily in the simple garment. Her hair flowed free, the auburn curls moving in the breeze, aflame in the last rays of the sun. Her smile was luminous.

She looked no older than the girl he had fallen in love with so long ago.

'Mama is still fretting.' Cassie grinned. 'She has written and rewritten every one of her lists, but she's convinced herself that something is bound to go awry.'

'So why aren't you there, fanning her fevered brow?'

'I'll have you know that I've worked very hard at being daughterly all day. But when Mama began to wrinkle her brow and tap her pencil again, it was clearly time to slip away.'

'So you're not here for the pleasure of my company after all?' he teased.

'What do you think has kept me going all day?' She reached up and kissed his cheek.

'That's much better, a little appreciation is in order!'

Hand in hand, they walked in companionable silence towards the sea and the setting sun. When he spoke again, Luke's tone was pensive. 'I can hardly believe that tomorrow – finally – we become man and wife. This day has seemed an age in coming.'

'We had to observe the year's mourning, Luke, or we would have offended too many people. And the wedding *is* here at last.'

'Not soon enough for me,' he protested, hugging her close to him. 'These last twelve months since your sister's strange marriage have seemed interminable.'

'Not so strange, by all accounts. She and Hugo are making a success of married life, and I think she is truly happy. She has become a different girl.'

'Now she's no longer in her sister's shadow?'

Cassie wrinkled her forehead. 'Is that why Annabel was so difficult, do you think?'

'I'm pretty sure of it. It must be tough having *a nonpareil* for a sister. But she is amazingly improved, I agree. These days even I find her company bearable, though I still think it's a strange pairing. For all her newfound good nature, Annabel is the queen of triviality and Hugo is such a...' Luke struggled to find a word that would not upset his beloved '...a serious person.'

'Admit it, you were longing to say a stuffed shirt. Hugo is a good man and works very hard on his charitable projects.'

'That's what I meant.' Luke laughed, unrepentant. 'But how he ever thought you would make him a suitable wife!'

'An illusion, I fear. His relationship with Annabel is far more down to earth and that's why it works so well. He really didn't know me.'

'He was dazzled by the exterior – and what an exterior!' Luke stroked her arm softly and then slipped his own around her waist, pulling her into him as they walked.

'Be careful, someone may come by.'

'They won't. Dusk is falling – and do I care if I'm seen embracing the woman I love? No, I don't think I do.'

'You should. You are the lord of Madron. You're supposed to set an example to your tenants.'

'I am setting an example – to every red-blooded man in all of Cornwall, by marrying the most beautiful, the most exciting, the most enchanting woman in the world!'

At that moment, they were rounding the last bend in the lane and the noise of the ocean, which had gradually been growing louder, burst fully on their ears. Waves crashed headlong into the jutting rocks on either side of the cove, but between the two spurs of outlying granite, a crescent of white sand lay pristine and inviting.

They ran down the last of the path, holding hands and laughing as they almost lost their footing on the downhill slope. The soft sand swallowed their footsteps and prompted them to kick off their shoes. He watched smilingly as she performed an impromptu pirouette, a homage to the heart-stopping beauty all around them: the green headland and the grey rocks, the indigo sea with its white frills of foam and the evening sky now streaked with pinks and purples, a harbinger of good weather.

'It looks as though we will have a beautiful day,' Cassie said quietly, intensely aware of the solitary beach and Luke so close to her.

'Almost as beautiful as this evening.'

His voice was rough with desire, and with a tug of his fingers he pulled the ribbon of her bodice undone and began slowly to roll the dress from her shoulders.

'Luke, this is a public place!'

'Do you see any public here? We are as alone as we possibly could be. You didn't used to be so cautious, Cassie.'

She blushed at the memory of their youthful indiscretion, but allowed him to continue undressing her. Soon he had divested himself of his own clothes and together they stood gazing at each other in pleasure.

Luke took her hand then, breaking the spell, and together they ran to the sea's edge. For a moment the water's impact took their breath away, but then they plunged headlong into the surf. Luke struck out immediately, powering through the waves towards the darkening horizon and shouting to her to hurry and join him. The cold fingers of the sea crept insidiously over and around her body, and it was a while before the water began to warm her bare skin and slowly bewitch her with its movement. Luke was already far out and she called to him not to go further. She needed to share her delight.

He turned back instantly and was soon treading water at her side. Both of them were laughing with the sheer joy of the moment.

Her red tresses encircled him with their ring of fire, challenging the watery environment and setting him alight. His legs slowly entwined around hers and he held her close to him, supporting her body against his, kissing her face, her arms, her breasts in rapid succession. She clung to him exchanging one rapturous kiss after another, but when he felt her shiver, he released his hold.

'We should get out of the water before you catch a bad chill – I'll race you back to the beach.'

'You do realise,' she giggled, as they tumbled up the sands to reach their pile of clothes, 'that we haven't a towel between us.'

'Why do you need a towel, when you have me?' The look in his eyes was disturbing and she felt her breath catch.

Before she had time to protest, he had spread his jacket on the sand and pulled her down to join him.

'This should keep you warm,' he said softly, his voice barely audible above the sound of the breaking surf.

It was dark now but for a handful of stars tossed into

the night sky and the light of the moon edging the scene with its silver: the empty beach, the constant surf and two lovers, their bodies entwined, lost to the world. For long minutes they stayed curled in the tightest of embraces, Luke's severely crumpled jacket swaddling them in its folds, while above the night sky offered its benevolent cover.

Then hee rolle raised himself on one elbow and began to stroke her hair, allowing her tangled curls to slide through his fingers strand by strand. 'Think of all the evenings we have to come,' he murmured. 'I can't believe I've been so lucky, after the mess I've made of my life – and yours.'

'We've both made a mess of life.' Cassie looked up at him tenderly and brushed a lock of hair from his face. 'Do you remember a night like this all those years ago? We came here then to escape mayhem in the house.'

He gave a twisted smile. 'How could I ever forget? It's burned into my memory. If I'd been less of a prig that night, the whole course of our lives would have been different.'

'You were shy,' she excused him. 'We both were. We didn't know what to do with our feelings.'

'Not now though,' he teased, nibbling at her ear.

'No, thank goodness.' Cassie sighed. 'I thought our betrothal meant nothing more to you than a way of bringing our families together. I can't imagine how I got it so wrong.'

Luke gave a groan. 'And I can't imagine how I could have been so stupid as to allow you to believe that.' He tightened his grip, holding her close to his heart. 'What an age it's taken us, Cassie, but we've come through.'

Her face was alight with feeling. 'We have. And it's been

worth the wait.'

'And the pain?' he asked, his voice filled with remorse. 'Has it been worth the pain?'

'That, too. Love is sweeter, don't you think, for being hard-won?'

Her fingers traced the outline of his face, pale and glimmering against the dark of the night. 'I know this will last, Luke. What we have now.' Her voice was not quite steady. 'It will last forever. Nothing can separate us.'

'*Nothing*, darling Cassie,' he whispered, and took her into his arms again.

If you enjoyed reading *Masquerade*, do please leave a review on your favourite site. Authors rely on good reviews – even just a few words – and readers depend on them to find interesting books to read.

Other books in the Allingham Regency Classic Series:

Duchess of Destiny (2017)
Dance of Deception (2017)
Romancing the Rake (2019)

About The Author

Merryn Allingham was born into an army family and spent her childhood moving around the UK and abroad. Unsurprisingly it gave her itchy feet, and in her twenties she escaped an unloved secretarial career to work as cabin crew and see the world.

The arrival of marriage, children and cats meant a more settled life in the south of England, where she's lived ever since. It also gave her the opportunity to go back to 'school' and eventually teach at university. Merryn loves the nineteenth century and grew up reading Georgette Heyer, so when she began writing herself the novels had to be Regency romances.

For more information on Merryn and her books visit http://www.merrynallingham.com/

You'll find regular news and updates on Merryn's Facebook page https://www.facebook.com/MerrynWrites/ and you can keep in touch with her on Twitter @MerrynWrites

Printed in Great Britain
by Amazon